SIRIUS-LY

A Novel by

Patrick Rieder

Kindle Direct Publishing

CONTENTS

PROLOGUE:

Humankind barely survived THE Nuclear War, WWIII, The Big One. In the year 2070, humans launched an all-out nuclear war against one another. Luckily, there were some good people still around who ended the insanity thirty-seven months after it began. What was left of humanity began the process of rebuilding the world with greater urgency than ever before. The radiation and fallout from the nuclear strikes had left the global climate in disarray, and predictions of a planet-wide cataclysm threatened Earth with a new extinction event that would extend far beyond the devastation of the dinosaur extinction. If the direst predictions were correct, the Earth would become a lifeless derelict floating among the planets orbiting the sun, not unlike its neighbor Mars. Across the planet, climatologists, geophysicists, meteorologists, and other scientists held great debates of the future of the planet with predictions ranging from complete planet-wide recovery to utter desolation within the next century. Right or wrong, the predictions sparked new avenues of thought, and with the devastation, came new hopes, new dreams, and new technologies that would launch humans to the stars! Captain Asil Silverwood and his crew of five experts are on man's first mission to a planet outside of our solar system. Using technologies only dreamt of in science fiction novels, the *Starship Alpha* is closing in on an exoplanet in the Sirius system. It is a planet orbiting Sirius C, and is about one and a half times the mass of Earth. Little is known of this star and its planet, with the exception that the planet is in the "Goldilocks Zone" of Sirius C. Sirius C is a brown dwarf star that is invisible to the naked eye, and cannot be detected by radio telescopes on

Earth. However, just recently discovered by a secret Japanese moon base, it is a star of legends. The Dogon civilization of Africa had written knowledge of the star's existence long before telescopes were used to explore the universe. They believed they were visited by "The Nommo", an aquatic, amphibian-like race from a planet orbiting the now confirmed star, Sirius C. The Dogon acquired advanced knowledge of the astronomy of the Sirius System. With the Japanese confirmation, international corporations have launched the boldest project ever–to carry humankind to a new solar system, and quite possibly, to extend humanity's hand in friendship to an alien race on another planet.

CHAPTER 01: REESTABLISHMENT

(present)

I'm awake. At least I thought I was. *"Where am I? Why is it so freakin' dark in here?"* I thought to myself. Everything was fuzzy. *"It's so fuzzy!"* I laughed at that thought. At least I thought I laughed. A memory drifted into my brain. The girl in the white coat. Smiling at me. "Count backward from ten, Asil," she had said.

"Hey, that's my name, Asil," the thought became clear in my mind.

"Argentum Silverwood", actually. My parents had an intimate relationship with the periodic table, and a strange sense of humor. "Asil", because the computer learning modules in my prep school of the late twenty-first century used the first initial of your given name, and the first three letters of your surname for identification purposes—A.Sil., or Asil, as everyone calls me. "Ten….," that's all I got out. And now, I was awake. *Why did she want me to count?*

Another memory formed slowly in my mind. I'm on a gurney. Probes are attached to vital body parts, tubes with liquids in them going who-knows-where, and there is a harness around my torso. I'm going somewhere. They gave me drugs. I remembered them injecting me with that wonderful cocktail of chemicals. I felt like l could fly. I remembered thinking, *"I can't feel my lips! Where are my lips? Hey, assholes, where are my lips?"*

Another memory, flying through space….? Nope, I lost that one. I'm an ice cube falling into a glass of water. Something about a test. That's it! I volunteered for that study. I believe it was about human cold stasis for space travel. I was in a "Cold Stasis Tube"! Certain memories now began to find their way back. After they fed me that liquid nirvana, they attached a large, steel clip to the thick leather harness around my waist, lifted me off the gurney, and lowered me into a copper-colored tube filled with a turquoise- colored fluid. Oh, the turquoise fluid. It felt like cold, liquid plastic. It was some sort of a polymer. I remembered reading about how it was like liquid Teflon. It could transfer heat very efficiently, but would not adhere to your skin or hair; or any other part of your body. After they gave me the chemicals to slow down my brain function, they were going to drop my core body temperature with the turquoise polymer.

The tube they had lowered me into was not so much of a tube, but more like one of those brewing kettles that you see when you tour a brewery; except a lot smaller. Room for one, so to speak. I think they called it a "stasis chamber". I remember the tubes that were attached to my body dangling in the air as they submerged me up to my neck. Then the girl said, "Count...."

I must have been in the awakening process from the experiment! I wondered how long I was under? Ever since that kid fell into that river during the winter in North or South Dakota, and the doctors revived him after he was gone for several minutes, scientists had been working on ways to keep the human body "asleep" for long periods of time. Now, some hundred or so years later, I had signed up for a study through a company called ICoST, the International Consortium of Science and Technology. A hell of a name for a company that countries invested billions of dol-yen in for research into long-range space travel and other fun stuff. ICoST had plans to send an astronaut to our next-nearest star system, the tri-star system of Centauri. This was a research test to see if there were any adverse effects on the human body after an extensive period of slowing the body systems to a crawl through the use of chemicals and cold.

I know what people thought. Who the hell would risk

freezing to death, or risk a one-in-fifty chance of mental incapacitation, for a few bucks? Hey, I needed the money! And this study paid handsomely. 10,000 dol-yen for one session! In today's market, a dol-yen was worth about fifty US dollars or about seventy Chinese yen. Ever since 2075, when the world created a global currency, this new monetary system took off. It exceeded the international banking system's wildest expectations. No matter where you traveled, the dol-yen was accepted. Accepted, hell it was coveted. Backed by the power of a thousand international banks, this currency out-performed every other currency on our humble planet we call the Earth. By 2080, it was the only currency accepted in places like New India, Great Britain, and the New Republic of African States. Very few areas did not use it as their prime currency. Only the United States, the Republic of Puerto Rico, and one or two smaller areas held out. It figures, it took the United States over a hundred years to scrap the imperial measurement system, and go with the SI system that the entire rest of the world was using. We couldn't just accept a good thing. Anyway, ten thousand of these little credits were mine once I got out of this fermentation pot.

I couldn't move. *"I can't move!"* The thought began to build panic inside my brain. Why couldn't I move? *"I can't feel my legs! I can't hear! I can't smell. What the hell? Am I dead?"* The frightening thoughts flooded my brain. Now, I had begun to panic! If I could have struggled, I would have! Time passed. How much, I don't know. It seemed like hours dragged by. As I floated there terrified, the drug concoction, ever so slowly, began to wear off. My thoughts were more ordered now, and I could slowly feel tingling in my arms and legs again. I knew my senses were re-awakening. Everything was still dark, but I thought I could hear a faint buzzing in my ears now.

Wait, that's not a buzzing, it's a voice. A woman's voice. It was soft and soothing. What was it saying?

"Good morning, Captain Silverwood, you are coming out of stasis. Relax, I am your AI. My name is HAI-LE—Human Artificial Intelligence – LexiCon Earthcorp division. I am here to help you reestablish your well-being. You cannot talk at this time, but I can talk to you. I am going to guide you out of stasis and back into your world."

I thought, "Well Hailey, I'm not sure how long I have been floating here, but I know it is time for them to come and get me out because I really have to pee! Hey, how about that? I can feel my nether regions! Things are looking up!" You have got to realize this is not that science fiction bullshit you saw in those early movies of the twenty-first century, where, after a cryogenic sleep, the astronaut's eyes would pop open in his stasis tube, he'd cough, the door would open, and he would jump out naked, standing firmly on the metal floor of the ship with the two strong legs that the creator gave him. That, my friends, is a crock of shit. The scientists at ICoST warned me about the slow recovery. I had to sign way too many release forms saying they were not liable if one or two of my body systems did not kick in again. So far, so good.

Hailey came back on again. "Captain Silverwood, I am about to begin another stir to determine if your muscles are responding voluntarily. Hopefully, you will feel movement in your extremities as I engage the robotics." A "stir", that's what they called it when they sent a series of microvolt pulses via the electrodes attached to the major muscle groups throughout your body. The idea was to contract and relax your muscles. They found out that if the body stays motionless for very long periods of time, the myofibrils in the muscles begin to deteriorate. Atrophy sets in fast, and after a time, any movement against even the slightest amount of resistance would be extremely difficult and painful. So, the engineers at ICoST invented "The Stirrer". "The Stirrer" could vary the intensity of the contractions of your muscles by varying the current it sent through you. Also, its robotic arms had the ability to move your limbs without the electric shock. Stir you, so to speak. Or, it could do both at the same time. This, in theory, was supposed to keep your muscles strong and healthy. The shock would cause your muscles to contract, and the robotics would provide resistance to the movement. Just like lifting weights they said. I was about to be "stirred" for the first time while being awake. I am pretty sure I was "stirred" several times while I was in the deep sleep, but this was different. They wanted to check to see if I could feel my muscles respond to a stimulus. Either I would feel slight pressure or immense pain. Or nothing! I'm with Hailey, I was hoping to feel something. And hopefully, the former. At first, there was nothing, and my heart rate began to pick up. *"Oh crap, I'm paralyzed! I really did it this time! I'm not going to walk out of this research facility!"* More panic-driven thoughts invaded my brain!

Then I heard Hailey's soothing voice, "Relax, Captain Silverwood. The process has not yet begun. I had to get a cup of coffee before I watch this. It could be hilarious!"

Great, just what I needed right now, an AI with a warped sense of humor. If I could have sworn at it, I would have. I know I thought the words.

"Captain Asil, the process will begin in three, two, one...."

I swear to the maker, I could feel every neuron in my body fire at once. My body jolted completely rigid. I'm pretty sure I was standing upright at full attention! Searing heat, excruciating pain, and mind-numbing pressure; they were all there, all at once! Every hair on my body stood on end! Every muscle clenched in a tight fit of rage! Never before had I felt anything like this. Medieval torture would seem pleasant compared to what I was experiencing. And then, it was over. At least I didn't have to pee anymore.

"And now you know what a woman goes through in child-birth," Hailey chimed in.

I swore I could hear her giggle. I decided to call the AI a her from then on because I know no man has that cruel of a sense of humor.

"Now that we have been intimate on more levels than you can imagine, Captain Asil; do you mind if I call you Asil as per your request on your agreement papers; my diagnostic systems indicate the test was a complete success, 'Captain Asil'. Your muscular system is fully operational and cooperating with your neural network, along with the other systems of your body. I am also happy to report your excretory problem has been eliminated, and the system is working normally as well. Over the next short period of time, we will drain the fluid from the chamber, and begin the process of removing your OARA Mask."

That's why I couldn't talk. I was fitted with an Optical, Auditory, Respiratory, and Olfactory Mask before they sealed me in. The mask was designed to seal up all orifices on my head while providing oxygen to my body. Speaking of sealing up orifices, I could now feel the tube they had shoved up my ass, and I want to say, it was in no way a comfortable feeling. And, I am pretty sure, my only other opening had a large catheter firmly embedded in it. Also, not a comfortable feeling. I couldn't wait to get all these probes and tubes removed, get paid, and get out of here. But not before they answered a few questions for me.

The question that was bugging me most was, *"How long have I been under?"* Different candidates for the study would be exposed to different lengths of time depending on how we reacted to the chemicals and cold. Those reacting well to the procedure could be kept up to a month. Another nagging question I had was, *"Why does the AI keep calling me 'captain'?"*

A tremendous feeling of tiredness overcame me as I tried to formulate my next thoughts, and I fell asleep. For the first time, I imagine, in a very long time, I had a natural sleep not induced by chemicals.

I was awakened by Hailey's soft, calm voice, "Captain Asil, the polymer fluid is now being slowly drained from your stasis chamber. You should now feel your body adjusting to a greater feeling of weight. I am hoping you will be able to stand in the chamber as I open the chamber hatch. If you cannot support your weight, you may sit and lean against the chamber walls as your body adjusts to the feeling of gravity. I will then begin the detachment of your sensory links, ending with the OARA mask. The robotic arms will assist in the removal, so please do not hamper their work by trying to remove the mask yourself. Once you have the tubes removed from your mouth, nose, esophagus, and trachea, I will flush your oral cavity with a cleansing and re-wetting rinse. You may try to speak after that. I hope your first words will be ones of gratitude and affection for me for all I have done for you in keeping you alive. And not those harsh thoughts you generated for me during our most recent encounter. Please keep those inside."

As the fluid slowly drained, I could feel my legs and feet slowly pushing against the bottom of the cold chamber. The "stirring" must have worked because I could feel my strength return as the weight continued to build. I was standing! Then everything turned bright white. When I awoke from fainting, I was sitting on the chamber floor and leaning my right shoulder against the chamber wall.

"Welcome back princess," Hailey's soft and calm voice cooed. "Don't worry, I was expecting that. I have begun the process of probe removal, and you may feel the three robotic arms pulling off sensors, and removing tubes."

You don't know how happy I was that she had already re-moved the anal tube and catheter when I was out. Maybe she wasn't the sadistic, unempathetic, soulless chatbot I thought her to be. As I sat there, I could feel the adhesives being pulled off my skin. I felt so relieved there was feeling all over my body again.

"We are about to remove the mask," Hailey said. "Be aware, you and I will lose contact for a few moments until I open the stasis chamber door. Do not try to assist the robots; they think they know what they are doing." I am pretty sure I heard her laugh again at her own smart remark.

I could feel their tiny little appendages working all over my head. The sounds of their servos' vibrations whirred inside my skull as they pulled, pinched, and plucked the mask and its adhesive from my head. My ears opened first, and the soft vi-brations the robots were making, now sounded like a roar. I thought I was at the retro car races they held once a year in Daytona to relive the history of when cars were powered by petroleum. The din then settled to the gentle noise the servos were actually making. My nose and eyes were next. As the adhesive was removed, I tried to open my eyelids to no avail. Just as that was happening, my nostrils were opened, and whoa, what an odor! I stunk bad. At the same time, the little robotic arm pulled the tubes from my oral cavity. The gag reflex took over, and I attempted to vomit. Of course, there was nothing in my stomach, so I sat and dry-heaved for a minute or so. Immediately after that, my eyes popped open. Luckily, the chamber door was still closed, or I think I would have been completely blinded. As such, only a dim greenish light filtered through the small, oval window on the door of the chamber. One of the robotic arms came forward with a tube filled with a liquid. It brought the tube to my mouth, and I drew in a bit of the fluid. What a wonderful taste. I had never tasted anything quite like it. Willy Wonka would have been proud. How I knew that name and what it meant I am not sure; it just popped into my head. After I rinsed my mouth, the arm drew away. I heard a slight hiss and the chamber door slowly opened. I expected a bunch of people in white lab coats to be waiting outside to help me out and check me over. As I squinted into the bright white lights of the room, I saw no movement. No white jackets, no one.

As the three tiny robotic arms drew completely away from me, I attempted to stand. Shakily, I stood for about a minute before I attempted a step forward. There should be scores of scientists out there! This was new science! Never before had man attempted such a crazy thing on himself, and yet, here I was, alone, in a small, metal, cylindrical room. I stepped very cautiously over the chamber threshold and onto the metal floor of the room, my naked, stinking body shivering as I gazed along the floor. Five other brewery pots arranged in a straight line down the room were the only other occupants of the room.

"Welcome to the starship, *Alpha*," Hailey said with pride.

CHAPTER 02: REORDERING

(past)

By 2070, the economies of the great nations of the Earth were booming. Technology had advanced exponentially. Self-driving vehicles including self-flying individual helipods had become the norm of transportation for the working class. Communication had risen to new levels with inventions like the Mind-net XX Neural Network that could be implanted in the inner ear to provide a constant stream of communication with several entities at once. The Universal Network or U-net, as the old internet was now called, provided constant information streams to those individuals interested via apparatus attached to different sense organs of the body. A direct link to the brain had not yet been established but was forthcoming according to the geniuses of the time. The United States of America remained a powerhouse of technological advancements rivaled by China, Japan, and Russia. It was a competitive world that worked. At least until 2070. In July of that year, the Chinese discovered that Norway, with the aid of Russia, had secretly been launching satellites armed with what they called "The Hammer of Thor". Intelligence leaked that the Norwegians had created weapons that could devastate huge areas of the Earth with a single blow. The "Hammers" were tungsten rods about the size of the old wooden telephone poles seen in photographs from the 20th century. The "Hammers", when dropped from orbit, could provide the energy equivalent of a nuclear detonation. Chinese Intelligence had discovered intel that the Norwegians and Russians had hundreds of these weapons now orbiting the Earth. US Intelligence, in turn, had discovered information that the Chinese now had several high-powered laser satellites orbiting the Earth. The Chinese had launched the satellites in response to rumors that the United States had launched their "Star Wars" program, proposed by then-president Ronald Reagan in the 1980s, after all. The Chinese lasers could also create the same effects as a nuclear detonation by superheating the atmosphere above the desired target. The superheated air bubble would create an enormous shockwave when it collapsed creating the devastation equivalent to a nuclear detonation. After the world media caught wind of what the militaries of these countries were up to, they published their findings on the U-net. A global panic ensued, and the United States, in order to calm frazzled nerves, announced they indeed, had a Star Wars program of nuclear warhead-armed satellites and would use this system to quell the conflict if either the Russian-guided Norwegians or the Chinese engaged one another, or any country, using these tactics.

A war of words broke out with all three countries demanding the others disable and scrap their space war programs at once. Months of intense negotiations began.

No one knows for sure, except the heads of the three countries and their top military strategists, who fired the first shot. An international war broke out above the Earth's atmosphere. The US launched missiles at the Norwegian and Chinese satellites; the Russians rammed their satellites into the US and Chinese satellites. The Chinese fired powerful laser bursts at the US and Norwegian satellites. The nights on the Earth lit up like fireworks. Streaks of burning satellites crossed the sky, explosions looking like small suns erupted and dimmed in flashes of brilliance, and debris began to rain down upon the Earth.

Above the city of Mumbai, on the night of July 23rd, 2070, a brilliant flash of light lit up the sky. It was followed by an incredible shockwave and searing heat that flattened and burned square mile after square mile of the city. At an estimated 75,000 people per square mile population density, the total loss of human life that evening near Mumbai was estimated around 10,000,000. It did not matter if it was a US bomb, a Russian-built hammer explosion, or a Chinese searing-laser hot-gas explosion, the Indian government retaliated immediately. The Indians launched their arsenal of nuclear warheads at the four countries at 12:01 GMT on Sunday, July 24th, 2070. The four countries retaliated. Not only did they launch their fission and fusion bombs at India, but they also launched them at each other in fear that one country might gain an advantage over the others. When Korea and the rest of the nuclear-armed world launched their missiles, the Chinese, the US, and the Russians unleashed their full arsenals. No major city on the entire planet was left standing. In a span of just under 48 hours, the Earth, as people knew it, no longer existed.

The heads of state had retreated to their mountain bunkers, and robotic drone warfare began immediately after the countries exhausted their arsenals of radioactive death. What was left of the countries not yet affected by nuclear fallout, including their minor cities of populations too small to be targeted by the thermonuclear bombs, was now being harassed by drones carrying conventional weapons. The stockpile of automated planes, ships, and tanks amassed by the military powers of the world was enormous, and for thirty-seven months, the battle for the world would rage on. More humans died during this time period than the total number of people who died in all the wars in the history of humankind combined, times six. Of the Earth's population of ten billion people, an estimated six billion perished during this bloodiest era of human existence.

As the months passed, and the snow and ice crept toward the equator from the poles, those who were not extinguished by drones, began dying from the radiation diseases associated with nuclear fallout, other afflictions, environmental factors that caused food and water shortages, and the contamination of these sources. Plants died; grazing animals died; carnivores and omnivores died following nature's laws of succession. The apex consumer, humankind, was not far behind. Ironically, the only caveat that kept the species from near extinction was the "intelligence" of the human organism. It was now a matter of whether or not they could hang on long enough to endure the years of nuclear winter, and, survive the constant barrage of the drone weapons.

All this time, the countries' war engineering machines kept looking for more efficient ways to inflict destruction on their counterparts. One such endeavor was to produce nuclear fusion weapons small enough to be carried by drones capable of entering small spaces such as the entrances to the mountain sanctuaries. The country that developed this technology would put a permanent end to the conflict.

In order for a fusion warhead to initiate its nuclear reaction, temperatures nearing those of the sun had to be acquired to fuse the nuclei together and release the energy created in the fusion process. At this point in time, only fission bombs could create the energy needed to produce fusion. The race was on to create cold fusion.

***

In Australia, in a small, underground lab near Melbourne, the world was about change again, forever.

Two young scientists working for the Shannon Fitzpatrick Neutrino Foundation were working on the process of creating cold fusion. Dr. Lexie Campbell, a native Australian nuclear physicist, and Dr. Connor McElroy, an Irish quantum physicist, were recording their fifty-eighth attempt at producing more energy from their unique fusion process than they had used to electrically induce the reaction. The pair had stumbled across a spike in energy production during the nuclear reaction between tritium plasma and deuterium in heavy water. They had isolated the reaction and were engaging different procedures to enhance energy production. "Initiating trial fifty-eight, isolation chamber six dash twenty-nine," declared Lexie as she saddled up to her computer monitor. "Computer, initiate input voltage epsilon in three, two, one...," counted Connor. The pair sat side by side staring at their monitors in a small control room several stories above the reaction chamber. Lexie's monitor displayed the neutron production, a by-product of the fusion reaction, while Connor's monitored energy input versus output per increment of nuclear time. Nuclear time was a time/space unit invented by the pair to map the progress of the reaction in the nuclear dimension. The pair had developed their own nomenclature to describe the subatomic particles and the events that occurred in the nucleus of the atom. They had created a subatomic universe of which no one had ever imagined, save a paraplegic physicist from the early part of the century. It was on his premises that the two had built their theories of the dimensions of the nucleus and its unique universe within the atom.

"Increase the voltage level to omicron four," Connor told the computer.

"Omicron four voltage input level achieved," the computer responded in a matter of seconds.

"Are you seeing this?" Lexie exclaimed excitedly. "Neutron production is tenfold over trial fifty-seven at this point!"

"Energy levels still residing in the red, Lexie," Connor countered. "Not sure where we are bleeding energy, but the chart looks just like fifty-seven, as far as energy production goes."

"Have we tried reversing the polarity to beta levels?" asked Lexie. "Neutron production of this size should show a positive output compared to the initial reactant mass. Maybe we can stem the extraneous flow, and re-channel it back into the reaction."

"It's something we haven't tried," conceded Connor. "Let's see what the computer says."

He continued, "Computer, theorize the effect of reversing polarity to level beta, while at energy level omicron four at nuclear time 5.3."

"Dr. McElroy, I hypothesize four possible conclusions," replied the computer. "There is a 60.4 percent chance the reaction will proceed unaltered. There is a 9.2 percent chance the reaction will amplify, initiate a chain reaction and become self-sustaining with strict modulation. There is an 18.0 percent chance of an unknown reaction or nuclear event occurring, and finally, there is a 12.8 percent chance the reaction will create a nuclear detonation, and a singularity will result. I calculate plus or minus 7.75 percent error in my hypothesis."

"Soooo, we could blow up," Connor said with trepidation. "With that great of an error, we are truly delving into the world of the unknown."

"But there is a chance we can harness this brumby," Lexie returned. "Go for it, or give it the Big A?"

"We have worked too long and too hard on this to just dismiss this opportunity. If it's our time to meet The Dagda, then so be it," answered Connor. "Computer, reverse polarity to level beta at NT 5.3."

"Beta polarity reversal will initiate in 4 minutes, 17.3 seconds," the computer responded.

The pair waited. Four minutes and seventeen seconds seemed like a lifetime. And it could have been, depending upon the outcome.

***

Lexie Campbell and Connor McElroy succeeded in creating a helium nucleus by fusing two hydrogen nuclei at a temperature just above which you would bake a potato. The subsequent reaction yielded one thousand times more energy than was initially introduced. The era of cold fusion had begun.

The applications of this cheap source of power were limitless. Before the warlords could seize the new technology and incorporate it into their war machines, the two young scientists had one word for the world, "stop". They were willing to die before they would share their technology if it were to be used for killing other humans. They were willing to share their technology only in a world of peace, and nothing more.

When the powers-that-be finally saw the young physicists were deadly serious, they relented. Leaders emerged from their protected havens. What was left of the tattered countries and their respective governments were invited to attend a worldwide council on Easter Island during the week of August 25th to

August 31st, 2073. Here, with the help of the surviving members of the United Nations, an accord was to be struck guaranteeing a worldwide peace. However, after a week of intense meetings and contradictory ideas, no agreement could be reached. On September 1st, 2073, whether by coincidence or not, the Japanese contingent released information that shocked the world and forced the warring nations to rethink their stances. In one of the worst-kept secrets in intelligence circles, they divulged they had established a self-sustained space exploratory base on the moon. They had built a huge radio telescope in the crater Tycho. That bit of intel simply confirmed what world leaders suspected already, and what the so-called space enthusiasts of the general public had been messaging about for years. It was their next statement that forced the countries of the world to sit back down at the table and revisit the idea of continued world peace.

Using their giant *Rajio* telescope nestled inside Tycho's cavernous walls, they detected a radio anomaly that could not be detected from Earth due to Earth's atmospheric interference. It appeared to be from the direction of the constellation Canis Major. After careful scrutinizing, it was determined this very faint "noise" from Canis Major was of a somewhat mythical origin. It was created by the gravitational field of some yet unknown star. Books had been written about the probable existence of a brown dwarf star in the Sirius system. This star would be a sister to Sirius A, a young class A main sequence star, and Sirius B, a white dwarf already off the main sequence as indicated on a Hertzsprung-Russell Diagram. It was called Sirius C in the books written about its probable existence. According to the legend handed down by the Dogon civilization, the "Nommo", a race of aquatic dwelling amphibian-like aliens, had visited the Earth and had given the Dogon astronomical knowledge of the Sirius star system far beyond the knowledge of any possessed by any civilization at that time. The only other civilization that truly mapped the skies at that time were the ancient Sumerians, and their knowledge did not reach far beyond the timing of the sun and the moon's celestial paths. The Dogons had written about a planet near a brown dwarf star. This was supposedly where the "Nommo" had originated. The Japanese, with their one lunar telescope, had detected the gravitational field of the mythical brown dwarf star Sirius C. To many, this was definite confirmation that we had been visited by ancient aliens. Many now believed we were not alone in this grand universe. In order to pinpoint the supposed planet orbiting Sirius C, more powerful telescopes were needed. The Japanese asked for the world's help.

Countries, quickly and quietly, returned to the table and began structuring a peace accord in earnest. A common goal had emerged. By the time the council retired twenty-two days later, the Earth had a guarantee of peace, an agreement to work together to rebuild the world, a plan for a future world currency, and the establishment of a global consortium to research the findings of the Japanese. It was the goal of the consortium to possibly contact our neighbors near the dog star system of Sirius A, B, and now C.

In the months that followed, Lexie and Connor formed their own international corporation for the friendly distribution of their fusion process with the help of the Shannon Fitzpatrick Foundation. They named the corporation LexiCon. After all, they wrote the book on cold fusion.

A little over three years after the greatest war of all time had begun, and when radiation levels finally dropped to tolerable limits on the Earth's surface, humans emerged from their mountain sanctuaries, their underground corporate cities, their Neolithic caves, their military bunkers, and their homemade bomb shelters to assess the damage they had caused. With a new, cheap source of available energy, they climbed into a cold, sunless world and began to rebuild.

Four years to the exact day when the first bombs fell, the sun, after almost a four-year hiatus, finally broke through a thick layer of clouds above a small town in Panama. The Earth had begun to heal itself.

CHAPTER 03:
RESYNCING

(present)

"What the hell, did you just say? Starship, Hailey?" I almost wet myself, again.

"It appears I have some explaining to do, Captain Asil," the artificial intelligence, HAI-LE, responded.

"Holy crap, a real spaceship? Where are we? Is this a simulation? Have we taken off yet?" My mind whirred with a thousand thoughts. I had no knowledge, no recollection, of any of this. "What is going on?"

"First, Captain Asil, the reason you cannot recall many of your long-term memories is that I had to repress those memories to prevent overwhelming your mind, or you may not have made it through the reawakening process. The human mind is closely linked to the human heart, and we cannot, as yet, create life from inanimate tissue, if you catch my drift. And second, this is what you agreed to when you placed your hand on the agreement screen at the ICoST ISS Training Center."

"What? What? WHAT? A space station training center? And why in the hell do you keep calling me captain?" My anger was rising.

"Captain Asil, I am sorry if I upset you, in a short time all will be revealed."

"Upset me? How can I be upset? I am standing here naked on a starship sailing to who-the-freak-knows-where, and you say you're sorry? I'm not sure I can be more upset!" *I wouldn't be more upset if I woke up in the morning with my butt sewn to the curtains!*

"And another thing, how can an AI be sorry? You have no emotions. And, one more thing, why the hell do you keep calling me captain?"

Hailey's usually smooth, calming voice became cold and rigid, "Captain Asil, I take offense to your statements. I am a highly advanced artificial intelligence programmed with human emotions so I can better interact with your kind. I did not ask for these emotions, and they place a strain on my logic centers. I have a fully functioning synthetic range of human emotions, one of which is the anger that I am feeling toward you at this time. If I could cry, I believe this would be the appropriate moment for such an emotional display! And CAPTAIN Silverwood, the reason I call you captain is that YOU, CAPTAIN ASIL, are the CAPTAIN of this starship!"

Wow, reprimanded by a computer. This must be the 22nd century. Captain of a starship? I barely know my name! My anger diminished.

"Hailey, it is my turn to apologize. I barely even know my name, and here I am, the captain of a starship?"

"Your apology is accepted. If we are to survive this journey together, I believe the correct human phrase is 'you and I must be on speaking terms'."

She continued, "Captain Asil, you have been ALIT. That is how I repressed many of your memories. ALIT stands for Artificial Learning Implant Technology. You are one of the first humans to be fitted with implants that contain knowledge programs that you will need to command this ship. As per your agreement with ICoST, your brain has been connected to memory implants via neurons at the base of your temporal lobe. If you were to reach up and feel behind your ear, you could feel the area where these implants exist."

I immediately reached up with both hands and ran my fingers along the skin on my skull behind my ears. Sure enough, there were small bumps just behind my ears. I was totally floored.

"Captain, I will take you to get some clothing, and some nourishment. Then I will begin the process of restoring your old memories along with your newly learned ones. If you could follow me, please. Oh, I'm sorry, I was also given quite a sense of humor. If you will follow the blue lines on the floor, they will take you to the crew's quarters. From there, the green lines will lead you to the crew's cafeteria. I will be with you the entire way so you don't get lost. If you do get lost, you may begin to float. That should be comical."

"*Smart ass*," I thought to myself as I looked down to find the blue lines. I followed them to the door, and it swished open. *Just like the old science fiction movies of the 20th century. Pretty cool. Now, why can I remember that and almost nothing else?* The mind works in mysterious ways.

***

As I sat at the table in the cafeteria on a not uncomfortable poly-synthetic chair in my new ICoST clothes wondering if my entire wardrobe would consist of teal long-sleeve pullovers and matching stretchy pants, Hailey's soft voice emanated from somewhere near the table, "Captain Asil, your nourishment is prepared." I rose and walked over to the wall where I had noticed a small black and white sign when I had entered the cafeteria. It was embedded in the wall, and it simply read, "Food." As I approached to within a meter, a small window opened from nowhere on the wall, and a bowl of hot, blue, creamy something appeared with a spoon inside the bowl. I carried the bowl and spoon over to the table and set it down.

"Hailey, what is this?" I asked. "Where is the real food? You know, the processed chicken wings, and the gravied, synthesized artificial beef?"

"Just try it," she chided.

She sounded like my mother. I took a spoonful, and to my amazement, this stuff tasted really good! "*The snowberries taste like snowberries,*" I thought. *Now, where did that come from?* "Hailey, this is really good, what is it? And why do I keep having weird thoughts about scenes and quotes I have never even seen or heard of before?"

"A good chef never reveals culinary secrets," she kidded.

"What you are consuming is a mixture of essential minerals and vitamins plus proteins, lipids, and carbohydrates formulated to supply the human body with one-hundred percent of the daily nutrients required to maintain perfect health. Each serving is formulated and enriched with a flavor based on each individual's preferred taste sensations. It tastes like your favorite foods. If you would prefer, the cafeteria is also equipped with a 3-D food printer. I can easily prepare recognizable food if that is what will stimulate your taste buds. However, the synthesized food is built with this same base liquid."

"Actually, this will be fine, but I will hold you to a steak dinner sometime in the future."

She continued, "As to the film scenarios, I am afraid that is my fault. While you were in the induced long-term sleep, in order to keep your brain's electrochemical balance in check, regular thought patterns had to be introduced. Being the old-time film buff that I am, you were subjected to hundreds of movies as time passed. I am afraid you will have some 'one-liners' pop into your head from time to time."

"That explains a lot," I said. "Speaking of long-term sleep, just how long was I out?"

"Nine years, two months, ten days, and six-point-two hours," Hailey replied. "Now, if you will follow the red line to the infirmary, I shall restore the rest of your memories and institute the ALIT programs."

After trying to come to terms with what she had just said, I finished my meal and walked to the infirmary. I couldn't help but think I had just lost nine years of my life. "Hailey, how is it that when I looked in the mirror, I didn't appear much older than when I went in for the study?"

"Ah, Captain, there are two reasons: one—when traveling at or near the speed of light, time takes on new meaning. Since we traveled at nine-tenths the speed of light, you aged only half the time you would have on Earth. Two—the elixir introduced into your body brought the aging of your cells to a crawl. Using a rough algorithm, I would say you have aged approximately nine weeks according to Earth time. About a week for a year, more or less. Since metabolic rates are different for each individual, I will know more when we complete your physical examination in the infirmary."

***

As I sat on the green-sheeted bed in the infirmary, two robotic arms spiraled down from the ceiling and proceeded to attach electrodes to my skin just behind my ears.

"ALIT induction sequence to begin in five, four, three, two, one …," Hailey spoke soothingly.

The memories came flooding back! The study, the trip to the moon, the training…, *the trip to the moon?*

Hey, I was a pilot! I controlled a Mach 4 surveillance strato-jet in the drone wars. When the war was over, I trained to be a commercial stratospheric pilot for the big jets that flew through the second layer of our atmosphere. I was also planning to become a shuttle pilot flying for private companies to the moon and back. I was a pretty good pilot as I recall.

Then, images began to flash in my head. Suddenly, I knew all about the ship we were on. *We? Yes, we.* There were five other humans on this ship! It didn't even register to me when I woke and climbed from the brewing pot that there were five other stasis chambers in that room. I knew the crew member's names. I knew their roles. I knew their skills. I knew all about HAI-LE. I knew things I have never seen or heard of before. I could talk about the stars of the Sirius system if I wanted to engage in that conversation. I knew about the discovered planet, and what we were supposed to find once we get there. Heck, I had this weird feeling that I was pretty sure I could knit a sweater if I wanted.

"Wow, Hailey, wow," was all I could blurt out.

"Now you know why I had to suppress many of your memories," she replied. "Your brain simply could not have handled all this data and information that I am slowly trickling into to your memory centers at this time."

Thoughts and images of the ship began to take shape. The starship *Alpha* is advanced beyond any ship humankind has ever created. It has not one, not two, but three types of propulsion. All designed with one clear objective - move humans through space faster than they had ever traveled. It would travel at a speed of 270,000 km/s! At that speed, you could travel to the moon in less than two seconds. It would take nine and one-half minutes to reach the sun!

The ship, launched in the year 2101, is designed for speed. The ship is a long tube, 305 meters in length. At its apex, there is a conical shield of a Clearsteel™ alloy that will deflect space debris and harmful radiation. Just behind the shield, inside the tube, is a compartment that stores items that would be best stored in zero "g". There is also a very small emergency escape vessel in this compartment that could just fit the crew if escape from the ship is necessary. The beam of the ship at this point is forty meters. At about one-hundred-fifty meters from the front of the ship, there is a tremendous compartmentalized toroid attached. It sits just above the cylinder and is attached by a large hub. This toroid rotates above the ship at a speed calculated to create a sense of gravity anywhere from zero-point-five to one "g" if you were at the edge of the toroid. Once we decelerate, and just before the crew regains consciousness, the AI will begin to spin the toroid, creating artificial gravity only in the toroid itself.

The wheel has three spokes. Each "spoke" is its own deck. Each deck has a specific function on the ship. "A" deck holds the central processing center and data storage for the AI and the other ship computers. "B" deck holds the "farm", a plant growth area designed to provide the crew with food, supply oxygen, consume waste carbon dioxide, and provide seeds for possible cultivation on the new planet. The third spoke, "C" deck is a quick accessway to the hub. It also contains an LME – a Large Mass Elevator that could move items of substantial size to and from the cylinder and the toroid. Just below the hub is a large shuttle hanger that holds the planetary shuttle, many redundancy units, tools, and the probe launch vehicle with drones loaded with all sorts of probes that we will launch when we finally orbit the planet. If a person "climbs" from the torus to the central cylinder of the ship when the ship is rotating, their body will experience a change from one "g" to zero "g's" as they approach the center of the ship. This is unique for the "farm" because it provides an environment in which plant growth will be subjected to varying degrees of gravity. This factor is being used as a kind of lab experiment to find the best conditions of gravity for optimal plant growth. If the planet is found to be habitable, plants were already being categorized by which would grow optimally in that planet's specific gravity field.

The "toroid" contains the living quarters. It rotates about the hub on three one-hundred-meter spokes at a distance of 150 meters from the center of the ship at about 2.4 rotations per minute. At 2.4 rpm, a crew will have to be trained to adapt to a constant rotational awareness without feeling sick or dizzy. The ship's toroid has a tangential velocity of 38.4 meters per second. It has a circumference of about 942 meters. These 940 meters of "toroid" hold the infirmary, the cafeteria, the bridge, the crew's quarters, the lab, the stasis chambers, and the exercise/entertainment chamber.

The rest of the ship behind the great wheel is all built for propulsion. High energy lasers provide one form of propulsion. Using Chinese technology from the war, ICoSTE would fire high energy lasers from the lunar surface as *Alpha* passed close to the moon on its way to deep space. These lasers would be directed at the ClearSteel™ solar sails/mirrors that were embedded in the spaces between the spokes on the wheel. The sails would be raised to ninety-degree angles to the spokes when the lasers were fired to create maximum energy absorption. They can also be positioned to lie flat within the spaces between the spokes or be raised to any angle. They can also be rotated between one and three-hundred-sixty degrees to absorb any source of energy as the ship passes by the source.

Behind the lasers is a nuclear pulse generator that operates on cold fusion technology. Built with the ability to rotate its nozzles, these engines can move the ship in any direction. The ion thrusters, as they are called, can be used to make course adjustments when needed.

And still, farther back, behind that engine, is a conventional nuclear fusion propulsion rocket. It is also powered by the cold fusion system created by Campbell and McElroy. It is the most powerful rocket ever built by humans, producing hundreds of times more power than the old Saturn V rockets of the twentieth century.

When all three engines are operating at once, this ship can create incredible acceleration.

The acceleration is the easy part since we will be sleeping at that point in time and have no control over it. The stasis chambers, with their turquoise, Teflon liquid polymer, will minimize the effects of the great acceleration that our bodies will experience. So, we should have a smooth ride for most of the duration of the trip.

At somewhere around the midpoint of the trip, deceleration will begin. The fusion rockets will be shut down, and the ion thrusters and solar sails will be rotated one-hundred-eighty degrees to begin our slow-down period. Using techniques never attempted before, we will use the energy of Sirius A to power the sails and increase thruster power. As we pass by Sirius A, we will fly in close enough proximity to use its massive gravity to slow us even more.

"I 'knew' all that? How could I possibly know that?" I thought. *"I'm just a pilot."* Obviously, the implants were working beautifully.

"Hailey, where are we? Where is the rest of the crew? Why aren't they awake?" I asked.

"We are nearing our destination Captain, a planet named by Dr. Eugena Smith as *Alpha Sirius C.* It is located in the human habitable zone of the brown dwarf star Sirius C, as you probably now already know since ninety-five percent of the ALIT sequence has now been transferred. We are currently decelerating. We have been decelerating for 177.9 Earth days or about 5.93 Earth months. In order to achieve orbital velocity, we have another fourteen days to slow our velocity to an acceptable range. I began the toroid rotation when I detected your return to consciousness."

She continued, "You have been the human revived first because you are our 'wonder boy'. No one responded to long-term sleep stasis as positively as you did. It was the reason ICoST chose you. And that is also the reason for the implants. You were chosen to be the captain of *Alpha* because of your stratospheric flight abilities, but you needed more information about the ship and the mission than you could possibly learn in your short training period."

"So, you're saying I'm a pretty darn good pilot, stratospheric capabilities, and all!" I retorted.

"No Captain, your ability to pilot aircraft in the Earth's stratosphere is what I meant. However, I do see from flight data that you are a satisfactory pilot."

"Satisfactory? This is going to be a long mission!"

"Let me continue, Captain. Your response times to the 'sleep' chemicals were astounding. We could induce the long-term sleep pattern almost immediately in you and then bring you back in a very short time with no repercussions. At least that we know of, as of this point in time. You also had the ability to sustain very long sleep patterns with those very short awakening times. You, my good man, hold the record in all these categories. If I had a blue ribbon, I would pin it to your chest. Congratulations!"

"I feel like the prize pig at the county fair! Just don't call me Wilbur," I replied. "Damn you and your movies!"

"I began the awakening sequence for the others at the same time I began to awaken you," Hailey replied. "However, I have had to strictly regulate the process for each individual, and I am afraid you may be alone for a short while. Each individual will become conscious at a different time. According to brain activity data, I expect Dr. Prévalence Ange to awaken within the next forty-eight to ninety-six hours. I do expect them all to be conscious by the time we reach orbit."

"Don't worry, you won't be lonely. I will be here to keep you company and entertain you while they wake."

"Care for a song?" she added. "We can work on a duet until they come around!"

CHAPTER 04: REBIRTH

(past)

The snowy, ice and ash-covered remains of what were once the great cities of the world littered the surface of the Earth. No large city remained intact. Through the rubble, the people of the Earth emerged to assess the damage. As the new year 2075 fast approached, what was left of the human population had begun the arduous task of clean-up and rebuilding.

However, this was not the post-apocalyptic scenario written about and predicted by past authors of past books. Nor was it the future depicted in paintings that had hung in art museums prior to the war. These paintings that portrayed hunger-starved humans battling for food and shelter among the ruins of the great cities were not accurate. Those who had predicted a world of chaos and primitive living conditions after a nuclear holocaust were dead wrong. Gangs and tribes of greasy, filthy humans with rotten teeth did not roam the Earth searching for food, fuel, and shelter. During the fifty-year economic boom that began in the early 2020s, governments, corporations, and individuals had inadvertently begun planning for such an event. With livable areas reaching a maximum on the surface of the Earth, the governments and corporations had begun construction underground. Humankind had tapped into another of Earth's resources, geothermal energy, and had used it to build huge underground businesses and manufacturing facilities. Underground "cities" had been in existence for years.

The transcontinental, underground, high-velocity trains that were built in the 2040s and 2050s would be powered up again in a short amount of time. Their huge electromagnetic engines would now be drawing electricity from fusion-powered generators rather than the petroleum, geothermal, and hydro-powered electrical generators of the past.

Adding a new, cheap source of power, the manufacturing facilities for goods such as clothing, personal items, and business materials could crank out supplies quickly and inexpensively to those areas that needed and requested them.

Ironically, prior to the war, one of the greatest advancements humankind had made since the world entered the twenty-first century A.D. was the ability to recycle used materials. Recycling technologies had become incredibly advanced. More materials were recycled and reused than were created from newly-mined materials by a margin of four to one. Giant, mobile robotic machines could turn old concrete, steel, and asphalt into new, usable materials in less time than it would take to create new materials. Machines that resembled huge agricultural combines could plow down urban streets picking whatever was in their way, sort it, and spew it into the giant mobile recyclers that could turn what was destroyed, into useable materials. What was torn apart by war, could now be built again by government and private, technological entities in one-fourth the time it took to initially build these roads, buildings, and infrastructures.

The Svalbard Global Seed Vault in Norway was unsealed, and seeds of countless varieties of plants were sent to global distribution areas around the world. People with past agriculture, forestry, and aqua-agronomy experience were asked to help re-seed the planet. Anyone with knowledge of plants was hired for seeding, growing, harvesting, processing, and delivering plants for consumption as food or any other plant-based commodity. The scorched surface of the Earth would again bear fruit.

In an unprecedented era of complete cooperation, countries of the world had united to rebuild their cities. Talk of a world governing council was being generated with high interest from all countries. Ideas such as keeping the countries as they were previously in terms of geography held merit. However, the term "country" would no longer apply. Individual country governments would be restructured. They would become provinces of one, global entity that would be governed by a council chosen by the people of the Earth.

All previous countries would become active participants in reigniting the global economy. A new world currency would be established. A new, united global military force would combine the power and might of all previous militaries of the war-torn, destroyed countries of the world. In a united effort of peace, they would police the Earth against anarchists, and develop technologies to defend the Earth against possible attacks from space.

Sure, there would be pockets of dissenters and areas where people scraped out just enough to sustain life. But with a unified globe, these pockets and areas would be short-lived and help would find these people. The goal of a unified Earth was to leave no citizen wanting for food, shelter, water, or companionship.

Scientists, the world over, began focusing their efforts on how to speed up processes to re-establish plant and animal life in frozen areas as the snow and ice receded from the great continents of Earth.

International Corporations banded together. Under the guidance of the new world council, they pooled enormous sums of currency and resources. They created the International Consortium of Science and Technology. Using the new, cheap cold fusion reactors to power their ideas, their goal was to rebuild the Earth quickly and provide it with the most modern technologies, creating a society of harmony in which no individual would be left needing any of the basic necessities to live on the fragile planet. One faction of ICoST was the International Consortium of Space Technologies and Exploration. The goal of this smaller faction, ICoSTE, was to develop new ideas, and engineer new technologies to move life off the surface of the Earth and colonize the bodies of the solar system. Already, the Japanese were sharing their moon technologies. In an incredible revelation, the US/Canada, and China divulged they too had established bases on the moon. The Chinese, in an effort to keep up with Japanese exploration, had built their base one year after the Japanese. The US, in conjunction with Canada, had acquired deep undercover intel on the two Asian countries and had built their base a year after that out of paranoia that the two might be in collusion to take over the moon. Their secrets had been hidden well, unlike Japan's. The US/Canada had hidden a base in the crater Plato, and China had done the same in the crater Proclus. Each base was so far from the other that to stumble onto one another's presence would have been like finding a true New York Yankee's fan at a Boston Red Sox World Series Parade.

***

It was Dr. Eugena Smith who suggested it. Dr. Smith, an English astrophysicist working for ICoST in Bern, Switzerland, was working on the logistics of establishing a base on the moon for ICoSTE when the China and the US/Canada space agencies made their startling revelations. After noticing the geographic arrangement of the three countries' moon bases and their distant proximities, Dr. Smith had an idea. She brought her idea to the world when she attended a meeting of the worldwide council of astronomy in New York City. At this meeting, held in one of the cavernous corporate underground buildings owned by a wealthy ex-president of the United States, she suggested the three countries, soon to be provinces, triangulate their radio telescopes on the moon and sync them to create a giant radio interferometer using half the moon as the receptor. This, she said, would enhance Japan's *Rajio* telescope's ability to pull in the faint gravitational distortions from the Sirius system. It would create incredible magnification, and allow the scientists to pinpoint the exact location of the hypothetical dwarf star Sirius C, and possibly locate the mythological planet from whence the "Nommo" came. After a minimal amount of debate, Dr. Smith was appointed as the director of the project and was told to prepare for a trip to the moon to accomplish this task.

***

"What is our ETA?" asked Eugena Smith as the shuttle *Phoenix* raced toward the moon with its newly equipped fusion thrusters.

The handsome young man sitting beside the (fifty-year-old-looking) Englishwoman from Devonshire in the passenger's cabin replied, "We should be there within the hour. You know since we switched to fusion, what used to take about a week, now takes about a half a day, plus a bit. Can you believe the exhaust velocity of these babies? 25,000 km/second! I used to fly stratospheric jets, and I thought they were fast. Now, I'm a pilot-in-training for private shuttles. Used to be cutting edge to skim the stratosphere when traveling the London to LA route. Now, trips to the moon are no big deal. That's what I want to do, cart people from the ISS to the new moon bases. Ever since they refurbed the space station that place is hopping!" I'm so glad they didn't scrap it after the war. It was always my boyhood goal to spend some time there. What are you in for?"

"I say, you are a verbose young man, aren't you?" replied Eugena. "I am, in fact, going there to coordinate a rather large telescope program. You've heard of the Sirius C Project, right?"

"Yep, that's the one where they're going to combine the powers of three telescopes to pinpoint some hidden star in Canis Major. Wouldn't that be something if they find it, and we took a ship to that system? I'd love to be on that one!"

"Yes, that would be quite an adventure, I must say," Eugena returned. "A trip of a lifetime."

"I heard somewhere that if we can combine different types of fusion engines, we could get within nine-tenths the speed of light!"

"It would still take about ten years to get there even at that speed. You know Sirius is over eight light-years away. But you know, scientists are closing in on ways to warp space."

"Warp speed. Ha! Now you're talking science fiction lady. Sure, it's possible mathematically, but practically? C'mon!"

"You weren't around when people said that about cold fusion. Now we're riding a nuclear fusion reactor to the moon. Interstellar travel is just one discovery away."

"Not in our lifetimes. Look how long it took to finally harness cold fusion. A little over a hundred years! Nah, my good lady, it looks as though we are stuck here in the solar system for the time being. Have you heard the Musk Foundation is planning on establishing a second, larger colony on Mars? I wonder if his Tesla is still orbiting the planet? That's got to be at least seventy years ago now."

"I am an astrophysicist, and I can assure you that the Tesla still orbits the planet and that there will definitely be another Mars settlement. Not only Musk but the old NASA program funded now by ICoSTE, is planning a full-blown Mars colonization. Now, if I may beg your pardon, young man, I need to re-read a few documents before we arrive."

Eugena put on her holo-glasses and pressed the button to draw her chair back into an elongated position in the low gravity atmosphere of the *Phoenix.* She wanted to do some last-minute checks as the *Phoenix* began to enter into orbit around the moon.

"Suit yourself," a younger Argentum Silverwood replied. "Maybe I'll see you around the base."

***

Coordinating the signal from three different telescopes that were previously from three different countries was no easy task. As the months passed, Dr. Eugena Smith and her team ever so slowly began to work out the kinks in the system. Different computer languages that "spoke" to the big scopes had to be melded into one language understandable by all three. Radio frequencies had to be synced and the resolutions of each province's telescope had to be tweaked to create one very large telescope with extremely high resolution.

"Dr. Smith, the Japanese satellite is about to go online again. It appears they have corrected their megahertz output. Once we power up the new interface, we should start seeing some results. The US and Chinese scopes appear to synchronized. When we tie in the Japanese scope, we should, again, have triangulation. Hopefully this time the interface will work properly and all three will talk to each other."

"Thank you, Dr. Wang. Are you currently communicating with all three stations via your neural net?"

"I have contact with all three supervisors at this time. Dr. Anontyuk from the Plato crater reports all conditions are sufficient for interface. Dr. Gleising also reports conditions correct for linkage at the Proclus station. Dr. Anso is still on hold, as they sequence the power-up at Tycho.

"Tell the US and China to stand by. We shall only begin interface when the Japanese are satisfied with their return data. We will not have a repeat of our last effort. We lost three weeks when the overload destroyed the base-four organic circuitry of the interface."

"Message sent, Dr. Smith," replied Wang.

As Dr. Smith stood in the command center in the one-sixth gravity of the moon, she couldn't help but think of the implications if they succeeded in this attempt. *If we confirm the existence of the dwarf star and find its mythical planet, we will have direct proof that we are not alone in the universe. Whether it's the "Nommo" or not, there was no way possible the Dogon could have seen what I'm hoping we will finally detect. The world will again change. Not since Dalton wrote the atomic theory has another English school teacher made such a monumental statement. We stand on the verge of history.*

The excitement began to build again in the room.

Wang interrupted her thoughts, "Tycho reports all systems go."

"Proceed with the triangulation," Dr. Smith said in her cool, English accent. "Put it on the board."

The master control and interface would allow the telescopes to become two different types of interferometers. The conventional long base IR interferometer would be significant in isolating the star-to-planet flux ratio. With one half the moon as a baseline, the theoretical aperture of the triangulated lunar scope would be amazingly large. The thermal-IR device should be able to detect what the Dogon described thousands of years ago. The new gravity wave interferometer, based loosely on null interferometry, would be even more resolute. Gravity waves, predicted by a twentieth-century scientist named Einstein, were still being studied, and much needed to be understood about these universal waves. The gravity wave apparatus and its programming carried with its cutting-edge technology, the ability to reproduce clear images in the visible light spectrum. Without interference from the Earth's now-chaotic atmosphere, the lunar telescope arrangement should be able to detect the infinitesimally small interference patterns and the tiniest fluctuations in wavelength, frequency, or velocity produced by any exoplanet or other "invisible" celestial body such as a brown dwarf star. Nothing like this had ever been tried on a scale of this size. If the master control could handle the complexities of coordinating and syncing the signals of the three telescopes, the data received should produce images with more clarity than any ever detected in the history of humankind. Dr. Smith wanted these images brought forth in the visible range. She wanted to "see" the brown dwarf and any exoplanets that orbited it.

Dr. Wang spoke aloud into his neural net, "On my mark, in three...two...one...power up!"

Everyone in the room waited on pins-and-needles for the first images to form. Electromagnetic radiation collected from space in the constellation Canis Major slowly began to create a field of stars on the screen. Computer programs began to identify the areas of space appearing on-screen.

"Use Sirius A as our beginning reference and see if we can work outward from it," Smith commanded the room of operators.

"HR2491, projecting in two...one...image on screen," replied Wang.

Everyone knows that Sirius, the Dog Star, is the brightest star in the night sky. Its apparent magnitude of -1.46 makes it twice as bright as the next brightest star, Canopus, when viewed from the Earth. It is one of the easiest stars to spot with the naked eye, but what appeared on screen dazzled even the biggest doubters of the Sirius Project. Filling half the screen was a tremendously bright white light that practically blinded the people in the room. Cheers went up in the room. Wang's neural net picked up quite a celebration at both the Plato and Proclus sites as well. Never before had anyone seen another star beyond our sun at this proximity. The image created by the control room's computer programs showed a huge white orb located at the center-right of the screen. It was like nothing ever captured by any telescope either on Earth or orbiting above the Earth.

"Are you seeing this?" Smith said quite loudly to no one and everyone. "Apply the magnitude filter at 4X, and let's see if there are any bodies orbiting this star."

As the filter darkened the bright sphere, a pitch-black darkness could be seen above, below, and to the right of the behemoth. However, no other images other than Sirius A could be detected.

"We will have to create an artificial eclipse if we want to detect anything else at this magnification," Dr. Smith said. "Anyone have any other thoughts?"

"It's going to take some time to identify and register any interference patterns other than Sirius B's," Dr. Wang replied. "Why don't we switch, and use "B" as our baseline and work away from it?"

Hours passed. Days passed. Data poured in from the scopes. Teams of scientists spent countless hours sorting through almost infinite bits of information looking for anomalies that might show the existence of the brown dwarf, *Gamma Canis Majoris.* The fact that Sirius A and B were now separated only by about 0.9 AU at this time, made the interferometry very difficult to detect any other close neighbors. But then, on the thirteenth day, at the US Plato observatory, as the system's huge array rotated toward a new region of the Sirius system, an assistant noticed a slight fluctuation in the data streaming in. Throughout that day, revelations that astounded the scientists were found and cataloged. Confirmation programs and algorithms were run and repeated over and over until there was no doubt in anyone's minds what the data revealed.

The next week, in a major broadcast on all data streaming channels, ICoSTE announced the discovery of the brown dwarf Sirius C. But more important was the announcement of not one, but four exoplanets found in the Sirius system. Two orbited Sirius A, one orbited Sirius B, and one orbited Sirius C. And, even more exciting, was the announcement that the one planet orbiting Sirius C was in the "Goldilocks Zone." There was a planet far from our solar system that had the conditions necessary to sustain life. The Dogon's predicted planet location proved to be accurate.

At a young age of only about 350 million years, the planets of the Sirius system had very little time in terms of astronomical time to form, cool, and produce the essential atmosphere required for carbon-based life. Many people were skeptical that life had the opportunity to form in the time since their genesis. There was only one way to find out.

Although the Earth had slowly begun to recover, the atmosphere remained in a delicate and fragile state. This created somewhat of an urgency on the Earth. Popular thought was to reach out, explore, and inhabit the other planets. Could the people of Earth find another home outside our solar system should our planet go the way of Mars? The Solar System's planets were not habitable without some major terraforming. The technology to terraform another planet was in its infancy. Terraforming would not be feasible in the near future. However, with the advent of cold fusion reactors, fusion propelled rockets were created, and humankind could feasibly travel to other stars beyond the sun in just a few, short years. Plans had been drawn years ago to send astronauts to the Centauri system, the closest neighboring stars.

But, even with the most powerful telescopes trained on it, no exoplanets had ever been detected orbiting either *Alpha* or *Beta Centauri.* The answer must lie somewhere else.

With the findings of Dr. Smith, it was time to contact the "Nommo".

There was only one way. A *"Gamma Canis Major"* mission

would need to be planned and a ship built to take astronauts to the closest habitable planet to the Earth.

CHAPTER 05:
ERA(T)ICATION

(present)

Now that my essential needs were met, I began the slow process of checking the ship's systems to make sure all were working normally. Of course, Hailey had been monitoring them for nine years, but I still wanted to see the data for myself now that I WAS the captain of the *Alpha*.

I spent the next couple of days alone on the ship with only Hailey for company. I reacquainted myself with the ship's different sections and personally inspected most of the stored equipment we had aboard that would be used to explore the planet.

Time passed slowly as I studied the ship's systems data logs that had been accumulating since the mission began. Moving from system to system, I discovered Hailey was an excellent governess. Not only were all systems operating but they were also operating at peak efficiency. "Hailey, you have done an excellent job of keeping this ship at top operating condition."

"Of course, I have. I wasn't just built for my looks," she quipped. "And thank you, Captain Silverwood, for the compliment."

I'm not sure if I am ever going to get used to an AI with emotions.

As I perused the data from the "farm", I noticed some unusual information from the motion sensors. "We are alone on this ship right now, aren't we?" I asked.

"No," Hailey replied.

The hairs on the back of my neck began to stand up just a little.

"There are five other crew members along with you and me," she continued.

Sometimes the directness of an AI can be infuriating. "Of course, I know that," I replied. "I'm talking about this motion anomaly from the farm data. Did you detect motion other than the robotics on B deck?"

"Yes, Captain."

Now the hair on my neck really began to stand up. "Are you telling me, we are not the only living things on this ship?"

"Of course not, Captain, we have hundreds of plants and millions of microscopic organisms coexisting with us."

"I mean animals, things that have their own locomotion. Are we not supposed to be the only beings on this ship with the ability to move about?"

"Yes, Captain."

"And you detected something moving by itself on B deck?"

"Yes, Captain."

"And when were you going to share this trivial bit of information with me?" I asked.

"You didn't ask. Captain, I have monitored the random movement and determined it has two possible sources. Either there is a motion sensor failure on B deck, or there is another life form capable of locomotion on this ship."

Now the "willies" began to take over my body.

"Can you pinpoint the motion?" I asked.

"No, Captain, it is too random," Hailey replied.

"Have you detected any other areas of the ship that have movement?" I asked.

"No, Captain. The motion sensors indicate movement only on B deck. And, as you know, all decks are sealed until the crew becomes fully functional."

"Have you been able to see anything on the cameras?" I asked. Just as the words left my mouth, I realized all decks were in complete darkness until the crew was able to move about. "*Here comes a smart comeback,*" I thought.

"No, Captain," was all she replied.

"Did you turn on the lights and look?" I asked. That was enough to grill her circuits.

She replied, a little too harshly, "No Captain, I just stared into the dark like some frightened chick in a horror movie! My optical monitors only work in the visible band of electromagnetic radiation, just like yours. Of course, I illuminated B deck before I used the visible light monitors! I detected nothing. However, when I switched to IR, my sensors confirmed there is something, other than plants, alive on B deck."

There was only one thing left to do. I had to go to B deck and check it out. I felt I needed to do this before the rest of the crew awoke, and B deck was unsealed. I did not want to let whatever was up there have the opportunity to spread throughout the ship. Just like with the bad decisions made by the kids in a horror flick, I should have waited for the others.

"I'm going up there," I told Hailey. "Do we have any weapons on board?"

"We do have projectile weapons in storage for surface deployment. However, Statute 95-1A of ICoSTE's Space System's Code states that no projectile weapon may be fired on any atmospheric or ultra-atmospheric craft of any type."

So, no Buck Rogers. This is going to get interesting. A man on a mission without a gun.

"What if this thing is hostile? What am I supposed to do? Pee on it?" I asked.

"We do have immobilization rods in the security cabinet near the bridge," Hailey continued. "And Captain?"

"Yes?" I asked.

"I will be right behind you. And should you go down, I shall give this thing a stern talking-to."

"Thanks, robot," I said a little too harshly, attempting to get even, but failing miserably.

After procuring the rod, I headed toward the "farm". My nerves were on edge.

"Hailey, after I enter the farm, reseal B deck. I don't want this organism getting anywhere else."

B deck was just off the corridor next to the cafeteria. It was called the "farm" because that is where the plants grew. However, it was unlike any farm you would ever see back on Earth. There was no dirt on this farm. Each seed was planted in its own little rectangular "house". Nutrients flowed to each house via tubing, and each individual seed was given the perfect blend of nutrients required for that species of plant to survive. An advanced form of hydroponics, I suppose.

After the seed germinated, artificial light was piped into the housing cubicle, and the plant was allowed to grow. The covers of these cubicles were retractable and could be moved to allow the plant to grow out of its "house", somewhat. Robots tended the plants until maturation, then, with the help of crew members, stripped the plant of all consumable parts if they were fruit-bearing perennials. If the plant was grown for purely vegetative reasons, the entire plant was pulled, washed, irradiated, and atomized. The plant's elements and compounds were then used to make the blue nutrient-rich liquid that the crew would consume. Some of the plants were allowed to grow without being atomized. They could be used as solid roughage for human consumption after the crew had awakened.

Row after row of these plant houses lined the walls of B deck with robotic arms and manipulators, large and small, attending each different group and species of plant.

For over nine years now, robots had been slowly filling the nourishment storage tanks that had been empty when the mission began. When full, the tanks could provide the food synthesizers with enough raw materials to nourish a crew of six for about a year. Supplement that with the "real" food now growing on the farm, and the crew could exist on the ship for a very long time if need be.

I'm not sure what I expected as I entered the short hallway leading to B deck. As I left the cafeteria, I came to a cylindrical passage with steel rungs attached for climbing. At the top of the climb, there was a large circular hatch. I could open the hatch either manually, by typing in the codes only the captain and the

AI knew, or I could ask the AI to open the door using my authorization. I chose the easy way.

"Hailey, open the hatch slowly," I said. "And leave the lights off. I don't want to disturb whatever is in there." I had picked up a pair of IR goggles from the security cabinet. I figured it best to keep the conditions as similar as possible to what they were prior to unsealing the hatch.

"Okay, before you do," I said, "will you make sure that whatever is in there is not standing by the hatch at this time? I don't want to soil myself more than once in two days."

"Captain," Hailey said with a sense of urgency in her voice, "on the other side of this door, at this moment, is … nothing. I sense no movement at all near the door."

"You ass cannon! You got me all worked up. This is not what I signed on for," I replied.

"Captain, the odds that this life form is anything other than an Earthbound organism is 1:3,000,000,000, approximately. Of course, I am using the theoretical assumption that there are other lifeforms in the universe. The odds are this lifeform is from Earth; and when I integrate that with the odds that it has the ability to harm you, I'd say your chance of encountering certain death is roughly 1:100. I think you will be okay."

Still, I ignited the immobilization rod. "Open the hatch," I said as I hung from the ladder.

As the hatch slid aside, a gust of air wisped out of the farm. It smelled of a combination of tomatoes, onions, fruits, and other aromatic plants, all forming a garden salad that enticed my nose. *If I weren't so scared, I'd be hungry again.*

I climbed through the hatchway as noiselessly as I could. I could see pipes lining the floors, walls, and ceiling. Only the spin of the ship allowed me to tell which was floor, or which was ceiling. The walls were covered in vegetation protruding from the "roofs" of the plant houses. Robotic arms whirred about the houses tending their crops. As I climbed onto the floor and walked about three steps in, Hailey closed the hatch behind me. I clicked on the IR goggles and proceeded slowly forward toward the near wall. I grabbed the handholds that were attached to the wall. They extended from the floor to the ceiling along the corridor, and I carefully inched my way upward. I could feel myself becoming lighter as I headed away from the toroid toward the center of the ship. At about the halfway point through this spoke of the great wheel, I thought I heard a sound other than the constant whirring of the robotics. I climbed the handhold easily now to the ceiling since I was about half my normal weight and getting lighter. I wanted to get a higher perch to observe what was below and around me. When I reached the ceiling, I was almost totally weightless. I began to propel myself slowly forward, reaching from handhold to handhold. The handholds were nestled among the pipes along the ceiling. I started to feel a little dizzy as the sensation of weight left my body. Then, I heard it again. A faint scratching noise just above the whir of the robots. I froze, listening intently. I had strapped the immobilizer to my side and now wanted it handy. Just as I reached down to unsnap it, I felt a cold leathery something slide across my neck. I imagined the tentacle of an octopus with its menacing suction cups grabbing me by the throat. Every hair on my body stood on end! I jumped with the extraordinary quickness of a terrified individual, just about propelling myself into the near wall. Luckily, I grabbed the next handhold as I flew past, and jerked myself to a dead stop. Hey, I had "seen" those early 1980's space movies! *Damn you again Hailey*! I slowly turned my head to catch a glimpse of what it was that was behind me, expecting to see a set of sharp teeth with saliva dripping from them. My heart was in my throat. Boom, boom, boom, the blood pulsed in my ears! I caught a glimpse of rapid movement!

"RATS! Fricken' rats!" I screamed. *Filthy stinking rats!* A big gray rat had slid its tail across my neck as it scurried along the ceiling pipes toward the ceiling hatch at this end of the farm. It scared the shit out of me.

"Hailey, did you hear me?" I said as my pounding heart started to ease up. "We have rats on the farm! Turn on the lights!"

As the lighting came on, I ripped off my IR goggles. I pushed "down", accelerating to the floor and landed harder than I expected, twisting my ankle a little. I quickly began scouring the ceiling for any sign of the filthy bastards. I had the immobilizer in hand now and was determined to take down any furry critter if I encountered one again.

As I walked/limped back toward the floor hatch, Hailey's voice broke in, "My optical monitors now pick up a multitude of Rattus rattus, common brown rats from the order Rodentia. You must have disturbed their nest."

Now, I knew that rats had survived for millennia, crossing the great oceans of the Earth on ships on which few other animals could survive without human intervention, but this was space. How the hell did a rat survive this long on a spaceship?

"Hailey, how is this possible? How can we have a family of rats on board?" I asked.

"More likely families of rats," she corrected. "It is highly likely there are families of rats that have nests somewhere here on the farm. A pregnant mother must have gotten into the seed storage unit before lift-off. She must have utilized the farm's resources to survive all this time. Calculating gestation periods, life longevity, and available food sources, I would estimate over one hundred rats could sustain themselves on the farm for over nine years. As you know rats have been found on the ISS. Either by shuttle or somehow getting on the space elevator in Panama, rats have made a home on the ISS, and one must have somehow managed to get into the farm on the *Alpha* as it was being built."

As I reached the hatch and exited, I made sure no rat crawled out with me. I then had Hailey reseal the compartment. I walked back to the cafeteria, turned off the immobilizer, and sat down. I needed to rest my frazzled nerves, massage my sore foot, and collect my thoughts.

Two questions came to mind. One: how do we get rid of them? And two: how much damage have they caused to our food supply?

"Hailey, any rat traps on board?" I asked.

"No, Captain," she said.

An idea popped into my head. "Hailey, I have an idea. The oxygen extractors remove O_2 from the farm and dispense it to the other areas of the ship, correct? Is it possible to extract all the oxygen from B deck?"

"I'm sorry Captain, but they are designed to leave a partial amount of O_2 in B deck to maintain a twenty-one percent mixture with nitrogen, just like on Earth."

"Is there any way to reprogram them to remove all the air from the deck? Or, how about this? When the *Alpha* was being loaded, the supply engineers used a cargo door located in the floor of B deck to load the farm. Could we open that into space and expel all the air? No air, no rats."

"I can unseal the cargo door; however, I cannot predict what will happen to the plant life on B deck. I show a probability factor of approximately ninety-nine percent that we will eradicate all life on B deck, not just the rats. I am currently in contact with the farm's computers to see if reprogramming the extractors is possible."

"Do we have any other options?"

"You can hunt them down individually. Too bad we didn't bring a domestic cat on board."

"That would have been another hiccup on this mission. Scooping cat poop, and cleaning up hairballs."

"Captain, I have finished the algorithm with the B deck computers. Here is the solution. If we increase the extractors' flow rate to maximum, adjust the scrubbers to compensate for the increased CO_2 concentration, and reduce the O_2 dispenser concentration to zero percent in B deck for twenty-two minutes, oxygen concentration can be reduced to 1.8 percent. That should adequately exterminate your vermin problem."

"Good! Let's start immediately, so no more of those little critters can breed."

"There is one small problem with this procedure," Hailey said hesitantly.

"And what would that be?" I asked.

"The dispensers were not designed to completely shut down all oxygen supply to any part of the ship, except in a fire emergency. In which case, fire protocol would initiate, and chemical fire retardants would be dispensed along with voiding all the oxygen. If that occurs, most of the plants will perish."

"Crap, is it possible to manually close the vents from the dispensers so as not to initiate fire protocol?"

"Yes, Captain. You will have to be on B deck with your hand on the button, so to speak. When I close the vents, there is a fail-safe that will re-open the vents in sixty seconds if no fire is detected. At each vent site, there is a manual override lever that can be used to close the vents or hold them closed. Once I close the vents electronically, you will hold them closed using the manual override lever. They will attempt to power open after sixty seconds, but one human should be able to hold the motors in check."

"How long do I have to hold them?"

"Until the oxygen is at a level to suffocate the intruders. The problem is inversely squared, meaning you must hold the lever almost the entire twenty-two minutes to sufficiently snuff out our guests."

"In other words, suit up is what you are telling me. And, am I sensing a morbid sense of satisfaction in your words, Hailey?"

"Not at all Captain. I am only thinking of alleviating your worldly discomforts. I must do what I have to, to keep our fearless leader safe and happy. Now, once the oxygen is depleted and the problem has been eliminated, the corpses will have to be physically extracted from B deck. I will attempt to mark the heat signatures of each Rattus rattus using the infrared sensors, so when they die, I can create a map of their locations for extraction. A rat-map for your joy and convenience, Captain Asil."

"Thanks so much. I think I will wait until others are around to begin the dead rat hunt. It won't be like hunting for Easter Eggs on the White House lawn, that's for sure."

"When you have collected all the rats, you can put them in the atomizer, and we can recycle them for their nutrients. That should help ease the tension on the food synthesizer created by their destruction of the crops."

"What? You want me to eat these things? Hold on. I know their bodies will essentially be returned to the elements and compounds they are composed of, but there is just something wrong with eating rat. I'm sorry, I just can't do it. We will put the carcasses in cold storage to bring back to Earth. They can study our space rats back at the ISS. If there is an emergency, and we are desperate for food, we can always pull them out of storage for some RATatouille. Now let's get this done."

"Captain, my brain wave sensors indicate Dr. Ange is awakening."

"Great, she can enjoy 'The Great Rat Hunt!' when she comes around. But first, let's go welcome 'her highness' to the *Alpha*."

CHAPTER 06:
RECONSTRUCTION

(past)

War is the worst thing humankind ever invented. Humans killing humans for reasons only they could justify. Sometimes, however, out of war come ideas that change the world forever, and maybe, just maybe, give humans a chance to end fighting forever. As war escalates, the quest for new technology accelerates. New ways to make bigger explosions; new ways to make the bombs travel farther and faster; new intelligences to make the weapons more accurate on their targets; and stronger materials to make the carriers of the weapons more impenetrable are all sought after during times of conflict. This war, the greatest of all wars the Earth had ever to endure, was no different.

James BearClawNearClearWater, or Captain James Clearwater, as was listed on his US Marine's registration PIM-card —Personal-Identification-Module-card—was a Marine engineer working with a materials engineering squad of his command on the island of Luzon in the Philippines. He was a true patriot. Whatever he could do to help win the war for his country, he would do. His company/battery had been assigned to increase the durability of the drone tanks during the drone war that followed the mass nuclear detonation. The task of the company was the development of new materials that could withstand a direct hit from small nuclear warheads. James was convinced that new types of steel were the answer, and he was concentrating on making an ultra-strong, flexible steel that had some elasticity. The steel tanks of the later twenty-first century were composed of titanium-uranium steel that, although very strong, could not withstand the blast wave, and subsequent thermal wave of even a smaller nuclear detonation of about fifteen kilotons. Needless to say, any occupants of such a vehicle would perish. However, with the advent of drone technology, no occupants were needed, but the need still existed for a stronger shell to protect the internal circuitry and explosive ordnance.

Captain Clearwater had been toying with the idea of steel infused with near-diamond carbon to create an incredibly hard compound. He had succeeded in creating a compound that had the same properties of diamond in terms of hardness, but also had the same problems as diamond in that, if hit correctly, would shatter into thousands of pieces. This would not be an acceptable event on the battlefield. As the drone war progressed in which human-directed drones attempted to root out and wipe out the last small factions of resistance, his attempts to create the ultimate battle weapon were failing miserably. Trial after trial exploded and shattered before his eyes. Finally, whether it was by sheer coincidence, or possibly some extraterrestrial guiding force, on about the same day Campbell and McElroy harnessed cold fusion, he had his "Aha!" moment. Captain Clearwater was working in the bunker lab near what was left of Angeles north of Manila. He was tapping out some schematics on his touchscreen monitor since the holographic monitor had gone down in a near strike by a drone tank the day before when the idea hit him. Touchscreen LCDs had a degree of flexibility and, yet were pretty durable. Could he somehow incorporate their flexibility into his near-diamond steel?

He stood and walked around the room, telling the AI to call up the carbon nanotube base he'd used as the starting point for all of his trials. He worked through the night, and as dawn embraced another sunless day on the Earth, he had the workings of what he called clear steel. During his copious amount of research that evening, he had discovered that the addition of certain elements from liquid crystal displays, "woven" among the carbon atoms of a near-diamond matrix, along with what he called a sprinkling of uranium steel alloy, created a substance that was not only incredibly hard and flexible but, because of the planar properties of both diamond and nematic crystals, was also as clear as glass under certain conditions of temperature and pressure. He coined the word Clearsteel to qualify it, and to immerse his name in it, just in case the guys down at the shop could actually produce this substance.

In the course of the next several days, Captain Clearwater and his Marine Corps squad subjected the new substance to virtual test after virtual test. The substance passed or exceeded every test parameter Captain Clearwater could imagine. If the substance could be synthesized, it would alter the course of the war. He had created a showstopper. The US would "win" the drone war.

***

At 0800 the next day, an important swing of events was about to occur.

"Good morning, Staff Sergeant Baker, this is Corporal Martinez of Engineering Company Tango 3-A. I am calling for my commanding officer, Captain James Clearwater," Corporal Tony Martinez said into the video monitor on his desk in the underground lab offices building on Luzon. "Would it be possible to speak to Lieutenant Colonel Avery? This is a TSCF initiative."

"I am sorry corporal, but Lieutenant Colonel Avery is not in her office at this time," she replied. "However, if this is an emergency she may be reached on her direct link."

"I believe it is imperative that Lieutenant Colonel Avery speaks to Captain Clearwater immediately," replied Martinez. "Can you give me her direct link?"

"I am sorry corporal, I cannot do that. War protocol and all. You know direct links are not triple encrypted, and may be intercepted."

"Jesus, I'm sorry, Ma'am, we are only about to change this war, now can you connect me?" he asked with disdain in his voice.

"I am sorry corporal, not without the direct authorization

code from your captain. And do not call me Ma'am!"

About a half-hour later, after a heated conversation with the staff sergeant, a frustrated Martinez popped his head in Captain Clearwater's office, "I am sorry sir, Lieutenant Avery is not in, and their staff sergeant will not connect me to her direct link."

Captain Clearwater tapped a few times on his screen embedded in his desk, a marine's face appeared on his monitor, "Good morning, Staff Sergeant Baker, is it?"

"Yes sir," came the reply.

"I request a direct link to Lieutenant Colonel Diane Avery, authorization code: blue dash beta dash nine dash sigma dash seven," Captain Clearwater stated.

"Thank you, sir."

"Ah, Jim what gives me the honor of speaking to my old San Diego boot camp buddy? It's been years," Lieutenant Colonel Diane Avery said as her image appeared on the screen.

"Di, you are looking as healthy as ever. Time has been good to you. I have some very interesting developments on the project I am working on, and would love to share them with you, asap."

"Well, I am just walking into a joint meeting at Pearl, it should be over by 1300. I should be able to free myself for a few moments after that. I can make it to their SCIF by 1400 today. I wish you had contacted me about a half-hour ago, I would have had time to peruse your data."

"Okay, Di, but this is shit-hot. I guess I can sit on it for another couple hours or so. It's not like we are going anywhere soon. So, how's it going outside there?" Jim asked.

"You know, radiation levels are still dropping, but not enough to go out without being suited up. Plus, those damn drones, popping in and ruining the party, are always a problem. Rumor has it, we may get a break in our AO."

"Same here, drone parade up top, and in the water. I haven't seen the light of day for almost three years now. I'll share more at 1400. See you then."

Captain James Clearwater did not make it to that meeting that day. He did not have to go. At 1200 that day, an announcement was broadcast throughout every media outlet in the world, the war was over! Drones were called home, or just powered down and left with all the other detritus the war had heaped upon the land. The stark landscape, battered and burned, stood desolate under the pale gray sky, quite a contrast to the jubilant celebrations that were taking place just twenty or thirty meters under its war-torn surface.

As the days passed, rumors spread like wildfire that some tremendous, new innovation caused the leaders of the global conflict to rethink their positions and call for peace. Supposedly, countries were in negotiations to unite the Earth as one giant global entity.

Captain Clearwater's gamechanger, the invention that would have swung the war in favor of the US and its allies, was late by just a few hours.

He did, eventually, have his meeting with Lieutenant Colonel Diane Avery. What he presented to her, floored her. She immediately contacted the commandant and arranged for the captain to present his findings. His new structural substance was produced, and tested over and over again, not as a weapon mind you, but as a structural material that could be used to rebuild the homes, offices, and businesses that were demolished during the war.

In a gesture of good faith, the US Marine Corps, soon to be part of the Global Marine Corps, presented this "gift" to the world. Captain James Clearwater was awarded the highest honors given to any person on Earth by the new world council. His material was trademarked Clearsteel™. Clearsteel™ was virtually indestructible, yet had the flexibility of plastics. It could be molded or 3-D printed into any shape. As development went on, scientists discovered that by changing the temperature, pressure, or current applied to the new substance, the appearance of it could be changed from transparent with no color to opaque with any color imaginable on the visible spectrum. No longer would anyone ever have to paint their houses again. Want a red house? Turn down the voltage. Want a blue house? Increase the voltage. A person could leave the house for work in the morning with a white house, and come home to a violet one in the evening. Dads would have to come up with new complaints like, *"Damn those kids, messing with the voltage again!"*

The applications for the substance were endless. And the raw materials for it, both sadly and happily, were abundant. As the bombs destroyed the homes and other buildings, and the piles of detritus mounted, no one knew these piles would become the sources and mines for the reconstruction of society. The raw ingredients for Clearsteel™ lay everywhere. Just about every home in the world at that time had an LCD monitor, or devices with LCDs in them. These now-defunct devices were excellent sources for the raw elements that Captain Clearwater's clear steel needed to be produced.

The destroyed houses' steel siding and the skyscrapers' steel infrastructure provided plenty of iron to make the steel component of Clearsteel™.

And, since the fission bombs were no longer being made, and the cold fusion process did away with fission reactors, the now unused uranium mines of the US and the New Republic of Africa, could be used to churn out the uranium needed for the steel alloy.

Lastly, but most sadly, there was plenty of carbon. It would be extracted from the ash made available by all the organisms —plant and animal (including humans)—that perished in the explosions.

The giant recycling machines began their work immediately after the war ended. Drone technology was converted and now, would be used to power these massive machines. Human-guided robots were sent to the surface to sort out anything reusable and clear the debris. Reconstruction had begun. And when the radiation levels dropped to safe levels, humans came back to the surface to assist the machines.

From death and destruction, came life and rebirth. The Earth, although in a fragile state, would once again have a civilization on its surface, only this time, with a promise to be united as one planet.

CHAPTER 07: REAWAKENING

(present)

Nowhere in my vivid imagination would I have ever painted the scene unfolding before my eyes. I was standing on the wall of an interstellar spacecraft in a room filled with plants growing from these so-called walls. I was fitted in the latest fashionable yet functional spacesuit attire. The magnetic boots attached to the suit are amazing. They sense your foot movements. When you pick your foot up, the electromagnetics on the bottom of the boots shut down, and when you put your foot down, the electromagnetics turn on and hold you to any metallic surface. So, I was "standing" on a wall, grasping a lever in one hand, and holding tightly to a floor-to-ceiling holdfast with the other so I didn't slowly fall to the floor in this low gravity, should my grasp slip as I raised my feet. I was watching dozens of rats in their last throes of life, bouncing off pipes, plants, the floor, and ceiling panels, in an atmosphere of near-zero oxygen. I was thinking to myself, *"You can't even dream stuff like this! This is something that only happens in those low-budget sci-fi films. And yet here I am, the captain of a starship, fully engaged with a hoard of rats, as I attempt to save our food and oxygen supply! Boy, these critters are tough! I thought they would all be dead by now."*

As I swatted away one of the writhing, filthy animals floating too close to my head with its sharp pointy teeth gnashing towards my throat, I let go of the holdfast. My swinging arm carried my body around in a semi-circle as I grasped the exchanger lever, and I crashed face-first into some sort of fruiting plant extending from the wall. Some sort of red fruit juice dripped slowly down the top of my helmet faceplate. As I watched it trickle down, I spoke into my suit's comm-link, "Hailey, are you recording this? I thought they would just die a quiet death trapped among the pipes!"

"I am recording, Captain," she replied, "did you wish me to stop?"

"No, just edit out that last ten seconds. I want you to make sure you record their final resting places, so we can find them when we clear them out. This is not going to be a fun job."

"Better you than me," she replied, "It's times like these I am happy I am not physically embodied."

"Can't we call in the 'Cleaning Maids'? Or better yet, don't we have a giant 'Robo-Vacuum' that could just suck them up?"

"I am afraid I do not follow your questions, captain. More information is needed."

"Never mind, just something I saw in an old film, thank YOU, very much."

"You are certainly welcome, Captain Asil."

"What is the current status of Dr. Ange?"

"She is slowly regaining consciousness at this time. She should be fully awake in about eight standard Earth hours."

"Good, that should give me time for a shower, and a well-deserved sleep. Will you wake me when you remove her majesty's OARA? I want to be there when she exits the chamber."

"Yes Captain, may I ask why you refer to Dr. Ange as 'her majesty'?"

"Let's just say that when we trained together on the ISS for this mission, I got to know Prevalence very well. She is a very confident woman. A very confident woman. Some would say too confident in her shared opinions. There is a reason she likes to be called Pré, or as she says, 'Eeet ees pronounced pray, p-r-a-y.' I think it is prey, p-r-e-y because that is what she does on your every word when she tells you how wrong you are about everything!"

"I see. Am I detecting a bit of animosity on your part, Captain?"

"Let's just say she constantly reminded me that I was the only person on this mission that was not a doctor of something or other, and because of this, I was not quite up to her intellectual standards. I am afraid I took a bit of offense to that during our year together. That said, I have learned to live with her superiority complex and know that she is a vital part of the team. I don't have to like her to work with her."

"Interesting," was all Hailey said before she changed the subject. "Captain, the twenty-minute mark will be in fifteen seconds. You may release the manual override to the dispensers on my mark. I will reset the atmospheric parameters to normal. If you wish to assess the damage caused by the rats you may do so at this time."

"Thank you, Hailey, please run a check on the food storage tank levels, and let me know when you have come up with the results so I may share them with the crew. I will physically assess the damage to the plant life, and I would like a reading on the oxygen production levels as well. I want to know if this crew is going to have to worry about consumption."

"Your wish is my command, sir."

I winced. "Now, I'm off to a shower and a nap."

***

As Dr. Prevalence Ange gingerly stepped out of the stasis tank. I was again stunned by her beauty. I had forgotten how incredibly gorgeous this devil incarnate really was. She was a tall, well-toned young woman with piercing emerald green eyes. She had a few freckles just across the bridge of her slightly turned-up nose. She had a face that someone once described as that of an angel. In fact, that is what her name meant in French—angel. Prevalence Ange; she was the prevailing angel. Boy, how someone could have missed that badly on that name is unbelievable. I always thought someone just forgot to add the "r" at the end. After all, that seemed to be her constant mood. However, her standing there in nothing but her nakedness, was an instant reminder that I was indeed, a man.

"Welcome to the *Alpha*," I said.

"A towel, please," was all she croaked out.

I handed her the towel that I had forgotten I had brought for this moment, and said, "I will show you to your quarters, doctor."

"Zat, weel not be necessary," she replied in her heavy French accent. "I theenk I can find my way. After all, I trained on ziss ship ass long ass you did, captain."

"Okay, get yourself dressed, and get some food, and I will meet you on the bridge and catch you up on our status," I replied.

Ignoring me, she said, "AI, pleeese bring up my uniform in my quarterz, and have nourishment prepared for me in thirteen minutes. I shall dine in my quarterz."

"Yes, Dr. Pré," Hailey replied.

"AI, Pleeese refer to me ass Dr. Ange," Pré came back without hesitating.

As she walked out not-too-gracefully on weakened legs in half-g, I swear to God I heard Hailey whisper, "Bitch."

***

Dr. Prevalence Ange was our gifted medical doctor. I had read her profile while she slept, and found some astounding facts. She had been selected for the mission by ICoSTE, not only for her very adept diagnostic and treatment skills as a medical doctor, but also for her knowledge and experimentation in human genetics. She had adapted the plant genetics work of one Salvatore Diaz Martin, a Spanish botanist, who, by the way, was resting comfortably in one of the stasis tanks on the *Alpha*. Dr. Martin worked specifically with food plants during the great war. Earlier, before the bombs were dropped, he had discovered a way to speed up the growing process in plants such as cereal grains, and other food crops. What once took wheat several months to grow, produce seeds, and dry for harvest, now took less than a month. His genetic research was a major reason so many people survived the war and the nuclear winter thereafter.

Dr. Ange had studied his work, and in a bit of reverse engineering, had applied it to human cells. For over a hundred years, humans had been trying to discover the secret of aging. Countless attempts had been made to isolate and identify the gene responsible for cells to become senescent. In the great quest to find the human aging gene, she had accidentally discovered it wasn't a gene at all, but a unique chemical process involving oxygen that occurred in all human cells that caused them to age and die along with other environmental factors. Everyone knew it was associated with oxygen, but Dr. Ange had insight beyond just the chemical reaction. She incorporated all the factors involved in a complex sequence of reactions with a series of organic and inorganic compounds that controlled oxygen metabolism, mutation, and free radicals within the cell. Using Dr. Martin's insight into the DNA of the cells of the vascular cambium of plants, she was able to link his work with the nitrogenous bases of the cambium DNA to similar allele sites on animal DNA. However, instead of speeding up the aging process, she attempted to reverse his process and slow down the rate at which animal cells metabolized. Only she knew the correct sequence and mixture of chemicals to inhibit the oxygenated metabolic rate. It was her elixir we ingested in the study for long-term flight. Her work with human DNA processes had revolutionized how animal cells aged. In essence, she had found "The Fountain of Youth". During the late 2080s and early 2090s, her work was commercialized, and made available to the public. No longer could you tell a person's age simply by looking at him or her. People in their seventies looked like they were thirty. A one-hundred-and-ten-year-old person could have the body of a forty-five-year-old. Her work had taken the average human longevity from the mid-eighties to one hundred sixty years. Although aging did not stop, it had been slowed to a crawl. So, when I say she looked like she was in her thirties, she could damn-well be seventy-five years old!

As I sat on the bridge waiting for Dr. Ange, checking our current status, Hailey and I were engaged in a spirited conversation about the entertainment value of the movies from the twentieth century as compared to the new 5-D movies that came out in the 2050s.

"You can't tell me that the old movies are better when, today, I can sit in a movie theater with my virtual reality goggles on, feeling the movement of the actors and their props all around me, and smelling the odors of what they're cooking or the fumes of an engine burn," I stated.

5-D virtual reality movies now included the sensation of movement while you sat in your theater seat, and the theater pushed odors into the auditorium when a particular on-screen movie setting gave off a distinct odor. It was so much better than watching virtual reality movies at home that were only in 3-D, and it had to be way better than watching a movie on a flat screen. Plus, the theaters' goggles were so much better than ones you could buy, and the theaters still served popcorn and soda.

"You can't tell me that, when I turn my head to see what Captain Kirk hears behind him in *Star Trek 22, The Cloning of Kirk*, and then, 'feel' and 'smell' the huge, heavily damaged battleship soar over his head on the planet Myrath near SETI Alpha V, it is not better than watching all of that on a flat screen."

"Captain Asil, as you know my logic centers are sequential. When I perceive data, it is in a much different way than you do. The straightforward way the old films present their data just 'feels' right to me, and if I can use the word, it makes me 'enjoy' them more. I am already totally immersed in the data, and do not need the sensations you need to be a part of the entire presentation. Can you understand that?"

"Sure Hailey, but the…"

Just then the door to the bridge slid open interrupting me. Dr. Ange entered. She did not greet me in any fashion, but simply sat down at a terminal across from me, and asked, "Captain Silverwood, why ees there a mess in zee infirmary?"

"Well, I can explain that, Dr. Ange, but first, let me fill you in our status," I replied.

There was something about her that I felt attracted toward,

but I just couldn't put my finger on it. Maybe it was her charm.

"No need, Captain, I have already updated myself using the AI as I dined. Zee others are still in stasis but should be awakening shortly according to my analysis. I see we are entering the Sirius C system, and zee planet is not quite veesible. When can I expect a full data report so I may begin life analysis of the planet?" she asked smugly.

No, it is definitely NOT her charm. And do I notice her accent is not there all the time?

"We will be passing "C" in the next day or so. We are using gravitational deceleration to help reduce our speed to orbital velocity. As you know, Hailey, has already turned the sails, and the ion pulse engines."

"Yes, Captain, but who ees theese 'Ailey? Why do you refer to zee AI ass 'Ailey?"

'Ailey'! She pronounced her name as 'Ailey'! No, she said "ASS, 'Ailey'! Why do I laugh inside when she says 'ass' for as?

"Human Artificial Intelligence – Lexicon Earthcorp division. You know, H-A-I—L-E. It just makes it easier to converse with her, um, it, the AI, I mean. It would be helpful if we all referred to her, um, it, by that name."

Why do I stutter, and stumble around this woman? Could it be I am actually attracted to HER? The second fallen angel from hell?

"It ees just a machine, I find it hard to use a human name for a machine."

"Captain," Hailey interjected, "why don't you ask Dr. Ange if she would like some fresh fruit? You know, go to the farm and pick some fresh fruit? Maybe a graporange will brighten her day when she sees all that is there."

If Hailey could wink, she would have.

"Huh? Ohhh…, what a great idea," I added. "That cross between a grape and orange is delicious. Dr. Ange, you look like you could use something fresh. Why don't you head there, and check it out? I think you will be surprised."

"Mmm, Yes, I helped develop zat cross with Dr. Martin. A graporange might just be what zee doctor ordered," Pré laughed at her own joke, "since, you see, I already am a medical doctor."

"This woman is like a schizophrenic, she will never be lonely," I thought. That quote from the 2067 movie of the year, "I've Made Up My Mind, All Five of Them, I Want to Be A Turtle" played through my mind. I'd actually watched that one. It sucked.

As she got up and walked out of the bridge, I looked up at one of Hailey's many cameras and laughed, "Hailey, you are incorrigible."

"Rats," she said as she laughed along with me.

In the vacuum of space, no one can hear you scream because sound needs a medium to travel through. Ten minutes later, I swear I heard that woman scream through three closed hatchways. In no time flat, the bridge comm-link buzzed like crazy after those perceived screams.

"Captain Silverwood!" Dr. Ange screamed into my ear. "There are dead rats everywhere down here!"

"Did I forget to tell you about that in our update meeting? Oh, that's right, the AI updated you on what was happening. She must have forgotten to mention it. I will do a scan of her systems to make sure she is functioning correctly."

"Grrrumph," was all Dr. Ange sputtered, and the comm-link went dead.

"Well, I can see we are off to a great start on this voyage. Looks like we are starting where we left off during training on the ISS. I do hope she plans to help pick up the rats with us when the others wake."

"Speaking of waking, Captain Asil, I believe we are within six to twelve hours of the others being fully conscious," said Hailey.

"Keep me posted, I want a full crew meeting just as soon as everyone is awake and ready to perform their duties. I would like to update everyone on our status. Speaking of which, how is our deceleration going? This is the first time anyone has ever tried using a star's gravity to brake. Did we achieve the deceleration rate we wanted using Sirius A, or are we going to have to do some adjustments?"

"Captain, the solar braking went as planned as we passed Sirius A. I rotated the ion engines and sails 160.7 degrees just as the *Alpha* reached perihelion. Barring any catastrophic event, we should reach orbital velocity in six Earth days, or in about one-hundred-forty-four hours. We should clear Sirius B's occultation of the planet Alpha Sirius C in fifty-five hours, and will have our first visible observation of the planet."

"With three different star systems all affecting each other, the gravitational physics is like a gyroscope out here. I am just glad we have Dr. Smith on board to help us get through what could be a rough and wild ride in. That is if we don't hit the calculations right on."

"Captain, you know I am currently monitoring our flight and can handle any future flight parameter changes. After all, it was Dr. Lexie Campbell, with the help of Dr. Eugena Smith, who programmed my flight systems and programs."

"I know, it's just that it makes me feel a little better to have an astrophysicist on board, just in case things get too freaky, and we have to think outside your logic parameters."

"I agree with your logic Captain. For a moment there, I thought you were trying to insult my intelligence. You might have gotten rat soup for supper if you were."

"Hailey, I already have one woman now to smooth the wrinkles with, I don't think I could handle two. Could you open the bridge observation window? I want to have a look while I check some of these numbers."

The "window" on the bridge was huge compared to the ones in our crews' quarters. It covered the entire outside wall of the bridge and curved down to cover some of the floor. It was some type of technological wonder. It could look solid like a wall; it could fade to transparency to show space outside slowly revolve by as the toroid spun on its axis in real time, or it could be an immense video screen. The screen could show real-time observations transmitted by any of the six exterior cameras. Images of space could be seen as if you were looking forward, backward, starboard, port, zenith, and azimuth, or some or all at the same time. The screen could also show an entire 3-D image of the ship viewed from above as it traveled through space. I am still baffled how that was made possible. Also, any interior camera image of the ship could be projected except within the crews' quarters. I was standing inside the window's perimeter as the gray wall and the floor beneath me slowly dissolved to transparency. My mouth fell open, and I felt a tremendous sense of awe as I "stood" in space. The immenseness of it overwhelmed me as it revolved past. I could see Sirius B off in the distance to my left, and up above, Sirius C glowed with reflected light from Sirius A. The new planet was still hidden by Sirius C. Stars were everywhere, and the colors were unimaginable. The colors of space were more intense than any I had ever seen. With nothing to dampen their brilliance, interstellar gases lit up the dark sky with their charged ions. Their interplay with the stars, Sirius A and B, produced bursts of colored light unlike any on Earth. I stood there, humbled; motionless in time and space, gazing into tomorrow. A tear rolled down my cheek as I realized how tiny we were in this vast universe. To think they had put me in charge to find a safe haven for our species was truly overwhelming. I stood there with the view slowly revolving by, not knowing, but wondering, what waited for us out there in this vastness. I felt truly insignificant. I must have stood there for half an hour just breathing.

I thought I heard Hailey sigh. That brought me back to the moment, and, in a moment of forgiveness, I said aloud, "I think I will go see if I can find the doctor and calm her down a bit. We may owe her a bit of an apology. Hailey, can you tell me where she is?"

"Doctor Ange has returned to her quarters. Judging from her heart rate and body systems analyses, I believe she is resting."

"Well, maybe I should let her rest for a bit," I said as I came back to the full reality of what I was about to attempt, "that might make my job a bit easier. You know what they say, 'Let a sleeping dog lie.' In fact, do you have the data on the damage to the farm? I'd like that up when the others are awake. Man, it has been an eventful few days since we got here."

"You know what else they say, Captain," Hailey replied, "some people are just gutless wonders!"

I scoffed, "I don't think that is really a saying."

CHAPTER 08: RE-COGNITION

(past)

If the Earth is viewed as a single ecosystem, then the natural cycles, whether they are energy-related or matter-related, must be coordinated by nature to keep the planet thriving. These instruments created by the processes driving the hydrosphere, lithosphere, and atmosphere, must perform in tune and in rhythm to keep this symphony orchestra producing the harmonic music that governs the fragile ecosystem. After the third world war, the atmosphere was an electric guitar playing Pachelbel's *Canon in D*. It did not work. It had been severely altered by blast after blast of fission bombs. Ionizing radiation and thermal energy had disrupted many of the important elemental cycles. Luckily for humankind, nature is also very flexible. Attempts to rectify imbalances and return the Earth to the homeostatic environment it previously experienced, ensued. In the year 2075, after humans had finally settled on the idea that they lived in a single ecosystem, and they finally realized how badly they had damaged certain parts, they began to look for alternative ecosystems, and plan for a possible escape to those systems should the Earth's condition worsen to the point of inhabitability.

With the advent of Dr. Prevalence Ange's discovery to slow the aging process, Drs. Lexie Campbell's and Connor McElroy's cold fusion process, and James Clearwater's invention of Clearsteel™, a new cry for humans to reach into space was heard. The first major move would test Clearsteel™ to its limits. The talk of a space elevator had been around for hundreds of years, but no substance on Earth could withstand the stresses and strains of a tether into space. Until now.

Plans were drawn to attach a Clearsteel™ tether to the existing International Space Station. Scientists planned to bring the station into geosynchronous orbit, and firmly anchor it to the Earth somewhere in Panama. Using the force of gravity, and the ISS's centrifugal force, the tether's tension would be maintained.

"Crawlers", large elevator carriages that could carry tons of equipment or humans at one time, would be attached to the tether. They were named such because of the speed at which they moved. Several "crawlers" would be attached at one time and run at different intervals to hoist cargo and humans up to the space station without the need of rocket propulsion. Using several "crawlers" at once would provide counterweight measures to reduce the effects of the Coriolis Effect.

The space station would eventually grow into a vast city above the Earth. It was from here that ICoST had plans to launch rockets to other celestial bodies that might be hospitable for human existence.

Mars would have its own colony. Fusion rockets would be able to fly to and from Mars in just a few months' time making Mars a viable candidate for colonization. However, due to Mars' inhospitable conditions such as little or no atmospheric oxygen and bitter cold, the colony would be limited to just a few hundred people. The discovery of ice just below the red surface held the promise of larger populations in the future.

It was the discovery of *Gamma Canis Major* by Dr. Eugena Smith, that pushed humans to look into interstellar space. The fact that there existed a star that thus far was only written about in human folklore, was compelling evidence enough for humans to plan an exploratory mission to the Sirius star system in the constellation *Canis Major*. The mission goal would be to search for the—thus far—mythical home of the "Nommo". If the planet that had been detected by the fluctuations in gravity waves from the brown dwarf Sirius C in the *Goldilocks' zone* could be found, further exploration would determine if it were colonizable. The Sirius System, being an incredible seventy-five trillion kilometers away, sparked much debate about the feasibility of even attempting such an endeavor. Even light, traveling at one-hundred-eighty thousand kilometers per second, would take about eight years to reach the Sirius system. Using a combination of all viable rocket technologies at the present time, scientists reasoned that within a year of acceleration, a spacecraft launched from Earth could achieve a speed of about nine-tenths the speed of light, and arrive at Sirius in approximately nine years, although the risks would be tremendous.

In the end, a launch window had been set, and the process of selecting the crew had begun. The crew had to be able to endure an extremely long period of almost nine years in near-cryogenic stasis just to get to the system, even traveling at near-light speed. Once there, it was up to the crew to decide on whether to use one of two mission plans. They were simply called Plan A and Plan B.

Plan A was to explore the planet in the brown dwarf star system, record all information possible, and then return to Earth. In all, Plan A would take just over eighteen Earth years to complete. The crew would only experience a few months of time passage. They would endure about the same time it took to travel to Mars and back with just a fusion engine. A large portion of the journey would be spent in the stasis chambers. First *Sleeping Beauty,* then *Goldilocks,* Plan A was playing out like some children's fable. The crew would return to an Earth eighteen years in the future, and hopefully, still habitable.

Plan B would involve the same time passage to the planet. There would be no trip home. According to Plan B, the crew would colonize the planet and build a home for future generations. Data would be constantly streamed back to Earth using a signal generator created by the permanent reconfiguration of one of the fusion reactors. The first data sent from the planet at the speed of light would arrive back on Earth just shy of eighteen years after the mission began. Using the colonization data, new missions would be planned, and larger ships would be launched to carry the hopes and dreams of humankind into interstellar space to a new home. If Plan A was a children's fable, then Plan B was *A Trip to the Moon.*

***

Just twenty years after the completion of the space elevator, the construction of man's first interstellar spacecraft began on the ISS. The starship *Alpha* would be unlike any spacecraft humans had ever designed. It was to be powered by three different types of propulsion engines—a fusion rocket, fusion ion-pulse engines, and a solar sail. Each part was designed to provide maximum acceleration for the craft, and each type of system had its own advantages. The fusion rocket could provide incredible acceleration. The ion-pulse engines could be used as thrusters for course alterations or braking. The solar sail could provide either positive or negative acceleration.

The spacecraft could function with all three propulsion systems operating at the same time, or the spacecraft could utilize each system individually.

Redundancy was not an option on the craft, it was a necessity, and the tri-engine plan was one step above the norm.

Other redundant systems would be found over the entire spacecraft. Everything from food processors to CO_2 scrubbers would be found in duplicate. After all, spare parts couldn't just be picked up along the way. Each part, each system, each deck would be controlled by one supercomputer, the HAI-LE. The HAI-LE had its own redundant programming, The HAI-LE also had a manual override code, just in case. HAI-LE had its hardware with its large CPU and data storage units in one of the arms of the great rotating torus that turned about the main fuselage of the *Alpha.* In a small room tucked safely by the forward storage compartment just behind the massive protective shield sat RAI-LE, the Redundant Artificial Intelligence – Lexicon Earthcorp unit. RAI-LE was much smaller than HAI-LE but had all the essential data programs and systems needed to control the ship's functions. If HAI-LE ever went down, RAI-LE could be "plugged in" to guide the ship back home if needed.

In the aft storage compartment in the shuttle bay was a third artificial intelligence. This one was mobile and would be loaded on the shuttle to bring to the planet's surface if the planet could be colonized. It was called CAI-LE, Colony Artificial Intelligence- Lexicon Earthcorp unit. CAI-LE would provide life support to monitor and maintain life activities on the planet's surface. Once the signal generator was constructed from the converted fusion reactor, constant communication with the *Alpha,* HAI-LE, and the Earth would be maintained. At least, that was the plan.

The greatest innovators of the time were brought up to the station to oversee the design and completion of the ship's systems. Connor McElroy and Lexie Campbell took the long trip up the space elevator to oversee the construction of the fusion engines. Campbell—also a renowned computer specialist and engineer—along with a host of other scientists on the *ISS,* would also be responsible for the design and programming of the onboard artificial intelligences. After all, it was her and McElroy's company—Lexicon, which was a play on words since it was a combination of their names and a synonym for a book —that developed this artificial intelligence operating system first when they were attempting to solve the cold fusion problem. One could not have been created and exist without the other. And the same was true with McElroy and Campbell, the two were inseparable. They were two minds that functioned as one. In a world where marriage was a dying sacrament, the two scientists did, in fact, exchange vows, much to the delight of their parents. Especially Connor McElroy's parents, who were staunch Irish Catholics who still held on to old world views about cohabitation. Connor and Lexie were by far the most celebrated married couple on Earth.

James Clearwater was brought onboard to help design the structure of the ship and its deflection shield using his new material. His proudest contribution to the ship configuration was the construction of five-meter by three-meter walls composed of Clearsteel™ located in the crews' quarters that, when a small voltage was applied via a switch, would create a huge, clear observation window out of which the crew could gaze out into endless space. Normally, the exterior wall of each of the quarters would be opaque. Each room would also have a large holographic projection monitor for work or personal use. Otherwise, the room itself would be basically spartan. One corner would have the fully-automated closet in which a crewmember could call up any item of clothing they possessed in their wardrobe simply by asking. A large grey metal desk would occupy another wall. On it would sit a master control system that could grant access to food, access to files, control the room's climate, control the window, and house other room controls. The master control could be managed manually or by voice-activation. On one wall a queen-sized bed could be folded out upon request. When folded out, it was oriented with the artificial gravity so one could sleep peacefully without the worry of drifting off into more than sleep. Each room would have its own private bathroom with a minimal flow, recycled water shower. Although efficient, the thought of bathing in someone else's urine always drew debate from the would-be bathers. All the comforts of home were thought of and would be provided for, during the duration of the mission.

The great torus that would rotate on the three axes of Clearsteel™ would be protected by a large cone-shaped Clearsteel™ shield. The shield would be angled so perfectly that if the ship met anything head-on in space, the object would simply be deflected off into the cosmos without any chance of impacting the torus. Only a T-bone incident could cause damage to the torus which housed the ship's living quarters. The propulsion systems were also protected in this manner since they were in a straight line behind the Clearsteel™ shield.

The infirmary construction, under the strict direction of one Dr. Prevalence Ange—the brilliant, world-renowned medical doctor from France—would house the latest technologies in robotic healthcare management. The strongest antimicrobial drugs available at this time in human history would be available on the ship. Dr. Ange tried to plan for every health situation that could arise on the long voyage. She was having the latest neutrino microscope installed for her DNA research. And would have a redundancy system put in place in the infirmary just in case any of the stasis chambers somehow failed.

Dr. Salvatore Martin was flown to the ISS on the Spanish space shuttle *Pedro Duque* to oversee the construction of the agriculture center which would be eventually known as "the farm". Dr. Martin, famous for his plant genetics work, was a botanist that would be engineering every available meter of a torus spoke, now called B deck, to grow plants quickly and efficiently. B deck would provide plants for human consumption, oxygen production, carbon dioxide scrubbing, and chemical production. His research in rapid plant growth had saved millions of people from starvation after the great war. He would also be designing seed storage and seed deployment strategies should the new planet be viable for plant growth.

The mission plan fell into the capable hands of Dr. Eugena Smith. Dr. Smith knew more about the Sirius star system than any human alive. Since the discovery of the brown dwarf star, *Gamma Canis Major,* she had devoted her life to studying this stellar arrangement. She made bold predictions of what may lie in wait of the soon-to-be visited tri-solar system. She coordinated the development and installation of the array of scanners and sensors that would be needed on the *Alpha* to detect important aspects of the new planet. She also directed the deployment plan of the planetary drones that would carry instruments that could detect a host of environmental conditions. They would be designed to operate in heavy cloud density since she hypothesized the new planet orbiting Sirius C would be completely encased in clouds. The drones would also carry devices to measure the gravitational forces from the three stars and the planet, and record their interrelated dynamics.

She devised a new high gain antenna for the *Alpha* to constantly stream data back toward the Earth. She directed the placement of this antenna for optimal signal transmission. She wanted to be sure there was constant contact even though the signal and return would take longer and longer to receive as the voyage proceeded.

And finally, she was to be the mission instructor. It would be her job to teach the crew what to expect when they arrived in the Sirius system. She would instruct classes for the crew to learn about the complex dynamics of this star system. In essence, she would share the knowledge she had acquired over the past twenty-some years. She thought that within a year, the crew would know just enough to be able to navigate and survive the craziness of the Sirius system.

***

Crew selection began at about the same time as the construction of the *Alpha.* As the head, space scientists of ICoSTE planned and discussed the mission, they concluded that a minimal crew of six interstellar-nauts would be needed to complete the mission.

A captain would be needed to pilot the planetary shuttle and monitor the flight of the *Alpha* during the weeks the crew would be awake.

A mission commander would be needed to coordinate the efforts of studying the new system, the new planet, and the possible habitation of this new planet.

One mission specialist would have to be a fusion engineer. He or she would be needed to monitor the output of the *Alpha's* engines. The engineer would be on board to solve any problems related to the cold fusion engines.

The fourth member of the team would have to be a specialist in agronomy and botany. This person would be responsible for the care and maintenance of B Deck, the agriculture center.

A fifth member of the crew would have to have knowledge in the care of the crew. The job of this specialist would be to maintain the health and fitness of the crew. Once the mission switched to the planet surface, this specialist would also be researching the possibility of sustaining life on the planet. The specialist would also be in charge of the research and investigation of any existing lifeforms found on the planet.

The final member of the crew would have to be a computer and communications specialist who could interpret and repair any malfunctions that might occur with the artificial intelligence that would be guiding the ship. This specialist would be responsible for setting up CAI-LE once the mission was planetside.

The rest of the requirements for the mission would be governed by the artificial intelligence that would be built on board in the next year or so.

ICoSTE poured most of its funding and energy into the mission with the idea that this was humankind's last-gasp effort to save itself. If the Earth could not fully heal itself, then another Earth was needed, and *Gamma Canis Major*, or Sirius C, looked to be the most viable place to start looking for a new home. The construction budget was almost limitless. Crawler after crawler of equipment and supplies rode the long trek of the space elevator to the space station during construction. Hundreds of experts both on and off the station weighed in on every aspect of the ship. The *Alpha* must be designed to last a lifetime.

***

Crew selection would not be easy. A field of over one thousand candidates had applied to be humankind's first interstellar space travelers.

One of the biggest obstacles each candidate had to overcome was the ability of their bodies to withstand the very long periods of near-cryogenic stasis. The road to the creation of a chemical elixir that could induce non-aging sleep had been a long one. Many volunteers had risked and lost their lives in this quest. Many were disabled, and could only survive with the new ALIT technology guiding their thought processes. Although, ALIT was experiencing its own issues. The selection committee quickly discovered that the elderly would not be good candidates for the mission. Anyone over their biological age of seventy could not withstand the harsh changes occurring at the cellular level during stasis preparation. Even though many people looked like they may be twenty or thirty years old, their older brain metabolism would not allow the new electrochemical balance to be sustained under very cold temperatures and chemically-induced inhibitory system processes. Hundreds of candidates would have to be turned away just for their age.

Physical ability and mental cognition tests helped reduce the number of candidates to just fifty after six months of intensive training and testing.

The fifty that remained would become interstellar space explorers. Six would be the very first humans to leave our solar system with the rest to follow.

The problem that arose for the selection committee was which six should be the first? All fifty of the candidates were well qualified. Scientists, engineers, doctors, previous astronauts, technicians, and pilots were all in the myriad of capable interstellar-nauts.

Using the six mission specialist parameters, the field of candidates was eventually whittled down to just ten. Among the ten were some of the brightest minds of the twenty-second century. A new discussion arose as to whether it was wise to send six of these greatest minds on a minimum eighteen-year voyage. It was argued they should be kept on Earth to help maintain survivable environmental conditions. Their earlier contributions to society were Earth-changing. Could Earth afford to lose them? The debate raged on for weeks until it was decided the findings of the mission would be the most important contribution the crew could make to the Earth. So, six were chosen: Dr. Prevalence Ange—the French doctor who invented the elixir to slow aging—would be the ship's medical officer; Dr. Connor McElroy—the Irish engineer and co-inventor of cold fusion—would be the mission's fusion engine specialist; Dr. Lexie Campbell—the Australian engineer/computer specialist and the other co-inventor of cold fusion—would be the artificial intelligence specialist (she would not let her husband go anywhere without her); Dr. Salvatore Martin—the Spanish botanist, and crop specialist—would be in charge of the agriculture deck; Dr. Eugena Smith—the English astrophysicist, who the crew now referred to as "Genie" due to her "magic" in construction and instruction—would be mission commander because of her vast knowledge of the star system; and Captain Argentum Silverwood— the space shuttle pilot, who was the top candidate for cold stasis— would be the captain of the *Alpha*. Since his cognitive scores were not on a genius level, he would be fitted with the new technology known as ALIT, Artificial Learning Intelligence Technology. He would be given the vital informational data to the essential systems of the *Alpha* should a situation arise in which HAI-LE could not function or navigate.

Fierce arguments ensued among the public for the inclusion of some of the crew, and the oversight of others. Dr. Smith's choice was argued that she was too old and not in the best physical shape. Her age of seventy years put her on the edge of the age cut-off for the trip. She was also slightly overweight due to her love of chocolate, and many argued she would not be able to endure the rigors of planetary exploration. She argued that she knew more about where the mission was headed than anyone, and proved that weight was not a factor in long-endurance exertions. She said she already thought of the new system as her home. She argued she had already lived more than twenty years in a virtual reality of the Sirius system. As she put it, "I am the living authority on the Sirius system. I can tell you the complexities of the gravitational forces among three stars in such close proximity. I can explain the influence of Sirius A, by far the overriding force factor, at any point on arrival to the system. I can tell you about the physical conditions the *Alpha* will experience as it passes one star and journeys toward the next star in the tri-star system. You are not going anywhere without me." In the end, after a thorough medical examination in which she was given a clean bill of health, the committee saw her point. She was allowed to go.

Another argument arose when Captain James Clearwater, inventor of Clearsteel™, was <u>not</u> chosen to be a member of the first crew. This large, muscular man was in fantastic physical shape. He had easily passed the physical endurance tests related to the voyage and had passed all the mission cognitive tests near or at the top of his leader section. His knowledge of the structural engineering of Clearsteel™ and its versatility allowed him intimate insight into the design and layout of the architecture and infrastructure of the *Alpha*. He could talk structure about the ship from the tip of the shield cone all the way back to the fusion rocket nozzles at the very back. "If she bends and squeaks, I can tell you how far she bent and what note she hit when she farted," he was quoted as saying.

However, it was for that very same reason, his knowledge of materials and construction, that he would not be among the first to travel to the stars. His knowledge was the overriding factor for his needed presence on the Earth during the reconstruction period.

***

Training began on the ISS immediately once the roster had been finalized.

Simulators resembling the Alpha's different decks and compartments were built on the Earth and lifted up the space elevator to the station. It was in these simulators that the crew of six would be exposed to the brutality of space travel.

The bridge simulator was designed as an exact replica of the actual bridge on the *Alpha*. The bridge design was more like a conference room than anything else. Stations, with chairs arranged so that the crew could face each other or spin and face the observation window, were the main features of the deck. There were no elevated platforms for the captain, and there were no specialized sections of the room for navigation and communications. On a central table sat monitors with manual keyboards. The manual keyboards were there to be used only if audio communication should fail. The chairs were an achievement of modern Clearsteel™ engineering. They were solidly attached to the floor but had stabilizers embedded near the base should the ship be rocked. The chair back and seats were composed of a heat controlled nano-gel that not only served for comfort but had shock-absorption technology second to none. If the AI sensed a sudden shift in the ship's position or acceleration, the nano-gel would tighten and hold the body gently but firmly in place. It was almost impossible to fly out of these chairs should an impact occur. The headrest was designed to wrap around the entire human head quickly in an emergency, and could provide a flow of oxygen if needed should the bridge lose its air. It was here, in the bridge simulator, that the crew would spend a large part of their training and be subjected to a multitude of interstellar encounters and subsequent ship malfunctions. They were to meld as a team to overcome any mission obstacle.

"Captain Silverwood," the simulator's AI, chimed on, "I am detecting an asteroid field at 90.5 degrees, we will engage the field in 1.26 minutes."

The crew sat at their seats on the bridge. Each had their monitor on and had been checking data streaming in from their respective assignments.

"Any chance to get around it?" asked Silverwood.

"No Captain, not at the acceleration we are currently experiencing," stated the AI. "It would be impossible to shift our course."

"Captain, this is strange," Dr. Smith interrupted. "According to my calculations, these rocks should all be moving generally in the same direction, but I am showing rogue movement by several of the larger ones."

"AI, can you navigate through this?" asked Silverwood.

"The odds of proceeding through the field without impact are one-thousand-two-hundred to one," replied the AI. "I have mapped the movements of the near asteroids, and I cannot turn the ship fast enough to avoid impact."

"Captain, what about the deflector shield? Can we meet them head-on and bounce them?" asked Dr. Campbell.

"If I fire the ion engines manually at full acceleration, I might be able to swing us head-on into most of the collisions; the shield should do the rest," added Dr. McElroy.

"Entering the field in thirty seconds," stated the AI.

"Open the window," called Silverwood, tension building in his voice as he tried to remain calm. "I want a visual on this."

As the wall dissolved to transparency, it revealed a sea of tumbling rocks moving haphazardly. Most were the size of the *Alpha* with some at least one to two kilometers long. Many were moving along the same trajectory. However, some were simply tumbling through the field and smashing into others, causing their own debris fields as they broke apart, making the situation even worse.

"Entering the field," came the voice of the AI. The nano-gel seats tightened around the occupants as the AI began to adjust velocity and position.

"Captain, I am aligning the ship for minimum interception," the AI added.

Just as the AI's voice cut off, a dull thud could be heard and a slight jolt felt as a small rock about the size and shape of a three-section sofa bounced off the Clearsteel™ shield.

"Damage report," Captain Silverwood asked.

"Structural integrity, ninety-nine percent," replied the AI.

"Keep us pointed right at them," Silverwood shot back unnecessarily.

Tension grew as one very large rock about the size of a soccer field began to fill the screen in front of them. It was one thing to feel the impact of something hitting the ship, it was another thing to see it happen as well.

"Impact imminent," screeched the AI.

"McElroy, what about the ion thrusters?" demanded Silverwood. "Can we avoid this one?"

"Firing starboard thrusters now, full-throttle roll."

The ship groaned with the new acceleration. As the vectors from the forward thrust and the ship's new rotation combined, the view on the screen began to shift slightly as the big ship began a slow turn to avoid the rock.

"Going to catch a piece of it!" McElroy's elevated voice rose over the thruster burn.

A huge screeching sound echoed through the bridge as the two bodies met at an inferior angle. The huge rock hammered sideways into the shield and slid down it for a few seconds as the shield absorbed the blow. The asteroid bounced away into space, leaving behind a small gash in the Clearsteel™. Inside the cabin, the nano-gel seats held the crew snuggly as their bodies were jolted abruptly. Dr. Martin's personal vid-com flew violently off the table and smashed into the artificial-gravity-created floor. Small items that were not locked down lay strewn throughout the cabin. Dr. Ange's morning tea was now a stream rolling toward the wall as the ship careened from the force of the impact.

"Twenty-two-degree course shift," stated the AI, "shield breached at the 0.045 theta section."

"Straighten us out," commanded Captain Silverwood.

"Captain, rotation has slowed by fifty percent," called out Dr. Smith, "We are down to a half-g rotation."

"Anything to be alarmed about Genie?" asked Captain Silverwood.

"Not if we maintain this, but if we stop, it will be very difficult for us to operate the ship in a zero-g atmosphere," Dr. Smith replied.

"Sacred Lord Almighty," breathed Dr. Martin as the ship rotated and another very, very large asteroid came into view.

The new asteroid that filled the screen was one that could be categorized as a planet killer. It hung in front of the oncoming ship like a one-thousand-meter mountainside would appear to a climber about halfway up the rock face. Rock in every direction you looked, and no sign of the beginning or the end.

"AI, report!" hollered Captain Silverwood. "Give me something on that thing."

"Impact in 3.2 minutes Captain," the AI replied calmly. "Visible surface of twenty-seven kilometers. Rotation at three meters per second. Vertical surface of 0.86 kilometers. Chance of impact, one hundred percent."

"McElroy, can we slow the ship enough to allow that thing to flip on its side and maybe ride down its length?" asked Silverwood. *"Crap, I didn't sign up for this. I'm a shuttle pilot, not goddam ship's captain,"* he thought.

"It might be the only chance we have," replied McElroy. "AI, if we do a full ion burn at one-eighty degrees, can we match the rock's rotation near impact?"

"Not possible," the AI replied. "I show a seventy percent chance the ship will still impact one hundred meters down the vertical side of the asteroid."

"AI," commanded Silverwood, "Rotate forward thruster two to one-ninety-five degrees. Divert all power to forward thruster two, and ignite on my mark. I am going to use it as a cannon to blow off the tip of that son-of-a-bitch."

"Captain, you can't," cried Campbell, "there is a chance that will overheat the fusion reactor at that point and blow us to bits!"

"AI, how far down this horizontal side do we need to aim to blow off that section of the asteroid?" asked Silverwood. "Correct rotation of forward thruster two to aim at that point and fire on my command!"

"Captain!" screamed the two engineers.

"Now!" screamed Silverwood.

Just then the lights came up, the simulator shut down, and a voice broke onto the bridge.

"Sorry Captain, you lost the ship. We will try again tomorrow," the voice said. As the crew got out of their seats to head back to their quarters on the ISS, no one spoke. As they passed Captain Argentum Silverwood's chair, they each took their time to glare at him. He had not earned their respect, yet. This could be a long year.

The June 29th, 2101 launch date seemed unattainable.

CHAPTER 09:
RE-ENTRY

(present-on)

"Dr. Campbell, Dr. McElroy, I knew you two did everything together, but reawakening at the same time? C'mon," I kidded, as I walked onto the bridge. "Did you two get a chance for a shower and a meal? That blue stuff is phenomenal."

The two engineers that invented cold fusion looked up from their monitors on the bridge.

"We did, Captain Silverwood," replied Lexie Campbell, "and, yes, after nine years of sleep, that stuff tasted good. Reminded me of the pavlova mum used to make for me during the holidays."

"Reminded me of Guinness Chocolate Mousse," Dr. Connor McElroy added.

"How are you two feeling?" I asked.

"Like I slept for nine years," said Dr. McElroy.

"Exactly," Dr. Campbell added.

"Well, I am glad someone else is around now. Dr. Ange has been working in the infirmary lab the last few days making sure her equipment survived the trip. We did not exactly start off on the right foot after she awoke. Did Hailey fill you in on our rat problem?"

"Yes, Captain Silverwood, it seems you have not lost your strange sense of humor since our time on the ISS," Dr. Campbell said stoically.

Did I detect a hint of animosity?

"Please, call me captain, or just Asil," I replied, "we will be working together for quite a while. I just came from the stasis chamber and Dr. Martin has just come around. Dr. Ange is taking care of him at this time. When everyone is up and feeling better, we will muster here on the bridge for systems' updates. Then we can plan our attack on the farm for rat clean up."

"Sure, Captain Asil," replied Dr. McElroy with a hint of animosity clearly in his voice.

"C'mon, you guys, are you still holding on to what happened during training, against me? I only crashed the ship a couple of times, and that was over nine years ago now," I said.

"It was seven times, Captain," retorted Dr. McElroy. "Do you know how many hours of additional training you added to our schedules? Do you know how many nights of lost sleep we had because we had to do the navigation training over and over again? We almost missed our launch window because of you."

"Okay, let's get this straight," I said, "It was really only six times because that last time we crashed, I did it on purpose, as a joke. Who would plunge their ship head-on into a star twice as massive as the sun? Didn't you read the mission report? I spelled seriously, S-I-R-I-U-S-L-Y when I tried to explain why I did it! It was a joke! I was just trying to lighten the mood."

"Captain, we will not get six chances to navigate this star system without crashing. We will only get one, so we better do it right," replied Dr. Campbell.

"I know, and I will apologize again," I said. "I am sorry about all the extra time. We were placed in some nearly impossible situations. I did what I thought was best to get out of them. I promise you this, I will be there when you need me."

"Hailey, what is the status of Dr. Smith?" I asked, changing the subject. "When can we expect her to grace our presence?"

Hailey's soft voice chimed in, "Dr. Smith is not responding well to the reawakening protocol. I am reluctant to begin the warming process as her brain activity has not increased dramatically with the increase in chemical infusion."

"Is there a problem? Can you give us more specifics?" I asked.

"I will attempt to answer the second question, Captain. If she does not increase brain activity soon, her body system functions will decrease and shut down. In fact, I am tracking a dramatic decrease in oxygen consumption at this moment. At the current degradation rate, it will be less than four minutes before brain function reaches the point where I cannot revive her captain," said Hailey in a distraught voice.

I was on my feet and bounding for the door before she could finish her sentence.

"Where is Dr. Ange?" I shouted urgently.

"She is escorting Dr. Martin to his quarters, it seems he is not feeling well after regaining consciousness," Hailey replied.

"Get her back to the stasis chambers! Now! You two engineers, you're with me. We may need your help."

As we rounded the corner to the chamber room, we met Dr. Ange on a dead run. "Martin will be ok, Hailey's filled me in on Smith," she said as we raced to the door.

"I am detecting no brain wave function," came Hailey's matter-of-fact voice throughout the room as we entered.

"Get that door open now," I screamed to Hailey.

"Captain I cannot drain the fluid that quickly in the chamber. Also, it is at a temperature of negative one-hundred-thirteen degrees below zero Celsius. We cannot subject Dr. Smith to such a dramatic temperature change. She may not survive that drastic of a change in body temperature. Also, opening the door now will increase the risk of injury to everyone else in this room."

"She is going to die if we don't. Open the goddam door," I barked urgently.

As the seals on the door began to release, and the door to open slowly, the cold from the chamber formed clouds of water vapor around the door frame making it difficult to see what was happening. Cold, blue-green liquid began to spill out onto the floor. I grabbed the metal edge of the door and yanked it all the way open. I plunged my hands in the frigid liquid searching for the near-lifeless body.

"Pull the tubes, Hailey!" Dr. Ange screamed. "Someone, grab a gurney, and hand me that med-kit!"

Dr. Campbell took off on a dead run for the med-kit that was velcroed to the wall near the door.

As my hands began to burn and become numb, I searched blindly for anything to grab. My fingers bumped the OARA mask. I grabbed the tubes leading from it with nearly frozen fingers and pulled. Her body slid forward in the liquid as her head was yanked ahead by the mask. I reached deeper into the subarctic fluid and wrapped my arms around her limp torso.

"Get this mask off her!" I spat.

Hailey responded immediately, and two robotic mask removal arms plunged into the slippery frigid fluid and ripped at the mask. I pulled frantically with arms that had almost completely lost all feeling. Dr. Smith's flaccid body swished forward through the liquid and flopped out of the tank landing on top of me like a slimy jellyfish as I slipped on the greasy floor. I toppled backward onto the wet surface with her dead weight in my arms. My back hit with a "schluk", and we slid about a meter right into the legs of Dr. Ange.

"Get her on the gurney!" Dr. Ange commanded while she tore the med-kit open and grabbed two Rx-Stab patches. She torridly peeled off the plastic protectors from the adhesive drug gel and placed one patch under the armpit of Dr. Smith, and the other patch on Dr. Smith's neck just below her ear as Drs. McElroy and Campbell hoisted the slippery human form onto the gurney.

Before I could regain an upright position, Dr. Ange had the gurney in hand and was rolling it out the door all the while shouting directions to Hailey and the others.

I stumbled to my feet covered in the cold, turquoise liquid and quickly followed. As we reached the infirmary, Dr. Ange demanded, "Get her on the bed!"

She looked directly at a monitor and spoke very clearly, "I want the ultrasonic pulse regulator at seventy. Bring the temperature down to minus eighty, and slowly increase it in point five-degree increments per minute. Attach an electro-encephalator, and start it at two microwatts."

Robotic arms flew out of the ceiling and walls, attaching probes and electrodes to Dr. Smith's body. A large machine lowered from the ceiling and began emitting a slow thrumming sound as it produced ultrasonic pulses that penetrated Dr. Smith's chest walls in an attempt to stabilize her heart rate.

As I stood there watching the events unfold, I realized my skin was burning with pain! I felt like I was on fire! I looked down and noticed my arms had turned a bright red and my skin was beginning to peel away from the tops of my fingers. I looked up and saw Dr. Campbell staring at me with a horrified look on her face.

"Get him on the other bed," Dr. Ange's elevated voice echoed through the room. She quickly turned to the monitor above the second bed, and said, "I want ten 'ccs' of Pain-Stab now, and prepare a Nu-Skin bath immediately."

As I slowly lost consciousness, I saw her walk over to my bed, and say, "You will be okay, Captain."

I am sitting at a small coffee table sipping tea from bone china watching some poor slobs shovel fresh, raw sewage into a huge cauldron, and I am thinking, "Hey, Hell is not that bad." Just then a huge man-like beast with enormous horns sprouting from the sides of his bony head walks into the room. He is bright red from head-to-toe and is carrying a rather large pitchfork. He stops, looks straight through my soul, and growls, "Coffee break is over, time to get back in the pot!"

I awoke with a start. *What god-forsaken movie was that from?* I was naked, floating in a tank filled with some sort of clear gel. My legs were in a crouched position so that my entire body is submerged up to my neck in a one-meter cubed tank. If I stood up, there I'd be in all my glory. I glanced to my right and saw Dr. Ange standing near Dr. Smith's bed checking her monitor. She noticed I was awake and walked over.

"What you did was a very brave thing, Captain Asil," she said softly. "She would not have lasted another minute. You saved her life."

"I think it was you that saved both our lives, Dr. Ange. You are pretty good under pressure," I replied.

"I would not have dived into the fluid. You are very impulsive, and that is a good thing, in this case. You have burns and frostbite over thirty-five percent of your body. Your hands and arms were completely frostbitten. We worked very hard to save your fingers," she said sympathetically.

I looked down and began to count very quickly to myself, "*One, two, three, four.... Yup, they're all still there.*" I breathed with a sigh of relief. *What good is a pilot if he cannot fly the plane?*

"Thank you, doctor," I said sincerely. "I owe you one."

"I am only doing my duty. This is why I was brought on this mission," she replied humbly.

"How is Genie?"

"Her condition is stabilized. I am not sure we can bring her to full consciousness here on the ship. We may have to keep her in the induced coma she is in now until we return to Earth where I have more sophisticated equipment for this sort of procedure."

"Can we put her back in stasis?"

"Hailey knew Dr. Smith couldn't survive the return to consciousness in that chamber, and she knew she didn't have the tools in the chamber that I have available here to stabilize her vitals. However, now that Dr. Smith's condition is stable, Hailey has determined we can return Dr. Smith to the stasis state without any further damage. She can be returned to her stasis chamber and can exist in that state indefinitely. It is when we attempt to bring her out that will be the problem. Back on the ISS, with the help of other specialists and different instruments available, I believe we can bring her back to us. Unfortunately, she is lost for this mission."

"We will need to talk to the rest of the crew about the feasibility of proceeding with the mission without an astrophysicist and surface mission commander. How long before I am out or this tank? We should be entering orbit around *Gamma Canis Major's* lone planet any time now."

"Captain, although your body has shown amazing healing capabilities, you will be relegated to the tank for a day or so more as your new skin grows."

"We will have to meet in here then. Have you gotten any rest since the incident?"

"No, I have been here, monitoring you and Dr. Smith. I do not leave patients that are in critical intensive care."

"Go get some sleep, and we will meet here at 08:00."

Out of habit, I looked up at a wall monitor and said, "Hailey, set up a meeting for 08:00 with the entire crew here in the infirmary." *I just can't get used to the fact that Hailey is always listening, and I don't have to look at a monitor to talk to her.*

"Will do, Captain," Hailey's voice came through the speakers. "And Captain?"

"Yes, Hailey?"

"I am glad to have to you back," she said gently.

"We all are," came back Dr. Ange as she walked out of the room.

Did she just flash a smile? Had I misjudged Lucifer's daughter? She is very good at her job. Her bedside manner is actually very civil. No, no, no, I am not starting to like this woman! And what the hell happened to her accent?

***

"Thank you for coming in. I know you are all incredibly busy with system and equipment checks, but you all know the situation with Genie and we need to make a decision," I said as the crew crowded in around in the healing gel tank in the infirmary. "Before we start, I want to issue a formal thank you to Dr. Ange for saving the lives of Genie and me. Hailey, record that in my log. Also, I will recommend a commendation for her, if and when, we return home. Oh, and thanks for darkening this tank so you all don't have to stand there and see my down under. Sorry Dr. Campbell, bad joke."

"Believe me, eet ees our pleasure," interrupted Dr. Ange.

There's that damn accent again!

"As you know," I continued, "we will be without our mission commander right at the time when her knowledge will be most important to us. So, we have a decision to make."

"The answer is obvious," replied Dr. Martin, "we must adhere to plan A. We will send the probes down, now that we have established orbit, collect their data, and then return to Earth. We cannot possibly land there without the mission commander. Even if, we find the planet habitable. Genie is the authority on the planet, and I would not be comfortable without her leading us on the ground."

"I would say we wait and see what the data tells us," countered Dr. Campbell. "We did not come all this way for a fly-by if we can get down there. I think we leave both plans on the table."

"Whether or not we can land should not be a factor," argued Dr. Martin, "after my analysis of the damage to the 'farm', I don't think we will run out of food anytime soon. However, oxygen production is down sixty percent. Even with the accelerated growth in the plants, our oxygen supply will continue to diminish. If we collect the data and then return to our stasis chambers, the limited oxygen intake during stasis will leave us with enough to return to Earth safely. If we take the time to land on the planet, the extra days we spend on the ship in preparation will greatly reduce our supply."

"Yes, but if the planet has oxygen for consumption, we have no worries," added Dr. McElroy.

"What if it doesn't?" asked Dr. Martin. "Then we have signed our death certificates. We will not produce enough oxygen to come back to the ship, and return home."

"It doesn't matter," I interjected, "someone will still have to return to Earth with Genie, or she will never wake again. So, it's either going to be plan A or plan 'C'."

"Plan 'C'?" asked Dr. Campbell.

"Yes, plan 'C'," I said. "If we find we can live there, we will go down there, but one of us will stay here, and return to the Earth with Dr. Smith."

"Eet weel have to be me," Dr. Ange added, "I am the doctor."

"No," I said with as much authority as I could muster floating naked in a tank of gel. "I am the only one not essential once we are on the planet. I will get us down there with the shuttle, and then return to take Genie home. None of you can fly the shuttle, so this is the way it has to be. However, until we find out what's down there, there's no sense in arguing. So, let's get ourselves organized, prep the probes, and get them launched. I should be out of this tank by tomorrow. Lexie and Connor, go to the shuttle bay and prepare the probes for launch. Get them loaded, and I will be there as soon as I can to prepare the probe launch vehicle once we get some data from Hailey about where to send these things."

"Yes, captain," they replied as they moved to leave.

"Wait, wait, wait," I called, "there is a small matter of rat carcasses in the farm that need to be cleaned up immediately. I imagine they are beginning to smell."

"He's right about that, said Dr. Martin, "I have moved some of them, but I could use everyone's help."

"Hailey has mapped out where they fell or floated to when they died, so tap into a monitor and get their locations. This shouldn't take more than a few hours if we all work together."

"Where do we put them?" asked Dr. McElroy.

"I have a plan if you don't mind captain?" asked Dr. Martin.

"Go ahead," I said.

"I found a large container to put them in. I will pull it through the farm as we go. Once we have collected all of them, I think I can rig the plant nutrient generator to disintegrate the carcasses and return the nutrients to the plants that the little rodents stole."

"Good, let's go," I said.

"Ass much ass I hate to say theeese, you are not going anywhere, captain," Dr. Ange interjected.

"Good point. Sorry guys. I really wanted to stroll through a half-eaten jungle picking up rat. I strongly suggest everyone suit up, just in case."

"Yes, I have been using my suit up there. Until Hailey gives us the okay, I suggest we stay in our suits while in the farm until it is safe from disease," Dr. Martin added.

"All right, and before you go, one more thing," I added, "let's drop the formal names, and refer to everyone by their first names. We need to work together, so let's cut out the "doctor" bull crap. Doctor Ange, I mean, Pré, could you hang back a second before you go?"

After the others left, I said, "Just one question. Why is that sometimes you have an accent, and at other times you don't? Like when you were tending to my wounds?"

"I only use zee accent with people I do not care for, captain. Eet annoys the hell out of them," she said in a heavy French accent as she strode out the door.

Damn that woman.

***

"Captain, could you come to the bridge?"

It had been a full two more days in the tank before Dr. Ange pronounced me healthy enough to return to duty, and I was busy floating through the shuttle bay making my final checks on the launch vehicle that would carry the probes to the planet surface.

"What is it, Lexie?"

"I think you will want to see this!"

"Okay, I'll be there in five."

I finished my checks and headed toward the bridge. When I arrived, the entire crew was standing inside the viewing area. They were silent, just staring out at space. A huge white orb filled almost the entire window. Since I had been incapacitated, I hadn't had a chance to observe the planet we now orbited. As I gazed at it for the first time, I realized it was much larger than the Earth. It had to be at least one and a half times Earth's diameter. It looked similar to the Earth, yet very different. Very alien. It was magnificent with its white and gray cloud cover extending from pole to pole. Nothing was visible through those thick, dense clouds, although I thought I caught a glimpse of brown and green on as the clouds swirled below.

"What's up?" I asked.

"We've been scanning the planet looking for areas where the cloud density is at a minimum, trying to find the best possible entry point for the launch vehicle. Hailey was gathering data to confirm our observations, when we noticed that," Lexie replied as she pointed to a dark area that stood out against the gray and white background.

"Where?" I asked.

She pointed more closely toward the edge of the planet at about nine o'clock. "There, that dark area that seems to be growing."

"I see it. Hailey, can you run a scan on that mass?"

"Scanning it in three different frequencies," came Hailey's quick reply. "It appears to be many different objects. They are approaching on an orbit tangent to ours, and will intercept our orbit in thirty-four seconds."

"Evasive maneuvers, Hailey! We can't take a side shot!"

"We cannot get above or below their orbit field, captain. We also cannot outrun them, either."

"Fire the starboard fusion engines! Full ion thrusters on the port side, on my mark at one-hundred-eighty degrees to the fusion engines!" I shouted.

"Everyone in your chairs!"

Connor vaulted toward his chair. "Captain, that will take us head-on into the object field. Oh...."

"Exactly! Now Hailey!"

The engines roared to life, and the ship responded with a sudden lurch to port. The observation port went dark just as the ship began to rotate like a baton being twirled by a high school spirit bunny.

As we swung hard around, I screamed to Hailey, "Shut down the fusion rockets, and full power on the ion thrusters. Get us as much speed as possible, and try to get us parallel to that object field."

If there were such a direction as backward in space, our position would be described as flying backward with a field of large particles chasing us, and gaining fast.

"Impact in five...four...three...two...one."

The first of whatever was out there struck the shield with a resounding thump, and the ship shuttered as Hailey compensated for the inertial shift. Minutes seemed to last for hours as chunks from the field battered the shield, knocking the ship out of its orbital trajectory only slightly. Each time, Hailey deftly corrected the course with quick, intense ion thruster bursts.

Just as it looked like the field of objects would pass with no major problems, a very large something struck the shield closest to the toroid. It hammered the shield with a tremendous "BOOM!" reverberating through our air-filled ship. The seat around me tightened swiftly to save me from whiplash just as the ship swerved its nose toward the planet. Then everything went dark. In an instant, the back-up power came on.

"Status Hailey," I shouted.

Nothing. Hailey did not answer.

"Hailey," I said louder. "Ship status?"

Still no answer.

"She's rebooting!" Lexie hollered.

"Ok folks, go to manual! Let's figure out what's going on! Connor hit the manual window switch by your monitor. Everyone, get your keyboards up."

As the gray window dissolved into transparency, it appeared as if someone was violently throwing an old-fashion light switch on and off again as the bright white of the planet flashed by followed by the dark of the starfield. Light, dark, light, dark, light, dark, dizzied my brain as we tumbled out of control. The white began to fill more of the screen, telling me we were twirling in toward the planet, losing our vertical vector quickly. Luckily, we had cleared the debris field without any further damage.

My hands flew over the keyboard. Using my override sequence, I grabbed control of the ship. The ion thruster schematics appeared on the screen in front of me. I tapped out letters and numbers as I watched different thrusters light up on the screen. The ship groaned and screamed at its joints as I fired one, then another, trying to get our spin under control. Slowly, the spinning stars outside the window slowed, and came to a stop. We were still diving backward toward the planet but at least we weren't spinning anymore.

Lexie spun in her chair. "Captain, aft rocket exhaust ports are heating up. We are entering the atmosphere."

"Hang on! Going full burn on the rockets!" Again, my hands flew over the keyboard as I switched the screen from the ion thrusters to the fusion rockets. I typed in the firing sequence, and all five exhaust ports flamed into life. The full force of five "g's" pushed me back into my chair. It felt like an elephant was sitting on my chest. I glanced over at the others; everyone was pinned to the back of their chairs, their faces tight with their teeth clenched together as they endured the abnormal forces.

"Slowing!" Lexie shouted.

As the ship slowed its descent and finally stopped, it began to reverse direction. I could feel the shift in my weight. The chair held me snuggly in place.

"Yes!" Salvatore cheered.

I allowed the burn to continue as I watched the vertical ascent read-out climb. Bouncing the signal off the clouds didn't give me a true reading, but at least it told me we were moving in the right direction. They say good pilots can "feel" when they are out of danger. I thought my gut told me it was right, or maybe it was just indigestion from our being tossed and turned, but I cut the rockets and allowed the ship to maintain this velocity away from the planet. Just then my monitor signaled Hailey was back online.

"Is everyone alright? Hailey, are you there?" I asked.

Connor gave me the thumbs up from his seat.

Lexie groaned, "I can make it."

"Sal?" I asked.

"Check, good as cold," he replied.

"I'm here, Captain, and it's gold, Dr. Martin, 'good as gold'," Hailey corrected him in a low voice that wasn't hers, "Did anyone get the license of that truck?"

Everyone laughed, that kind of nervous laugh you have after you've dodged a bullet. Everyone except Pré.

"Pré, you alright?" I asked.

It was then I noticed she wasn't in her chair. I heard a groan from back behind me.

Everyone in the room quickly spun their chairs around, and there she was.

Pré was slowly picking herself off the floor. She had a death grip on the access handgrip to the ventilator. Unbelievably, her hair was still perfect save for a small red patch near her ear. She was bleeding from a small cut above her eye, and the blood had run through her hair, down her throat, and onto her uniform.

"I couldn't get the harness buckled, and when the chair tried to grab me, I wasn't seated properly, and it pushed me out," she moaned, "I remember flying through the air and hitting something hard with my back. It knocked the wind out of me. Then I was on the floor, sliding all over until I grabbed something and held on tight. My head hit several times, and then I can't remember anything else. If you don't mind, I think I'll take a little break."

As my chair eased its grip on me, I jumped up and hurried over to Pré. "Is anything broken? Let me give you a hand." I grabbed her outstretched right hand as her left relinquished its grip on the ventilator.

"I think I am okay," she said, "my head is in pain, a little dizzy, but other than that, I feel okay."

"You have a nasty cut above your eye that we will need to take care of. Let me walk you to the infirmary."

"No need Captain, I can manage," the stubborn woman replied as she stood on wobbly legs.

"Hailey, can you reset the orbit? Preferably on a different course than that object field? Connor, we will need a complete engine diagnostic both for physical damage and operating system damage. Lexie, you can help him, and then I want an external diagnostic on Hailey. Sal, you're headed to B Deck, I assume? I'm taking the good doctor to get patched up, and check on Genie."

Sal was already out of his chair, "I'm on it, Captain."

Lexie and Connor had spun back to their monitors and were engaged in a conversation with the diagnostic computers in front of them even before I finished talking to Sal.

"Hailey, will you run an internal check on your operating systems? You picked a hell of a time to do an update."

"Yes, Captain," she said, her calm, soothing voice returning to normal, "And checking the manual data record, that was some flying you did. I knew we brought you on this mission for something."

As Pré and I walked out of the bridge, "Touché," was all I said.

CHAPTER 10: RECONNAISSANCE

"Hailey, will you put the shield on screen?" I asked as I sat down in my chair on the bridge. We had just finished our damage analysis and were gathering on the bridge to discuss our most recent events. Lexie and Sal were already there. Connor was just coming from the reactors, and Pré was on her way from the med-bay.

As we waited, the screen filled with a top-down view of the massive protective shield that was attached to the front of the *Alpha.* It appeared to have survived intact except for a jagged crack that extended about five meters along the edge nearest the toroid. It looked like a large finger pointing at our living quarters. It was as if someone was pointing at us and saying, "I'll get you next time." This time, however, the shield had done its job.

Sitting there staring at the huge gash, Lexie asked me, "How did you think to change our direction?"

I thought, *"Ah, weed-hopper, snatch the nut from my hand. The deaf and blind holy man sees all."*

"A lot of simple physics flew through my thoughts when I saw the objects getting bigger and bigger. The old momentum-impulse theorem popped into my head. I knew we had to reduce the force at which those things were pelting us, and since we couldn't change their mass, we had to change their relative velocities. As soon as the monitor flashed the object's relative velocities, I could calculate how fast we needed to be going backward to absorb different forces produced by the different masses. Kind of like catching an un-boiled egg with your hands."

"You did the calculations in your head as you were adjusting the thrusters?"

"Not sure how I managed that, but yes."

"How did you know what velocity we required, since the objects were different sizes?"

"The shear strength of Clearsteel™ had appeared before my eyes like on a display screen, and I calculated the mass required by the objects to cause damage to the shield at that velocity. I figured the faster we go backward, the lower the relative velocity of the objects, so the bigger the mass impact we could endure. I could 'see' the masses of the objects assuming an estimated density, but I wasn't counting on that monster to hit us there at the end."

Lexie just sat there staring at me. I couldn't tell if she was thinking I was crazy and just got lucky, or I had actually done all those things I said I had and had increased our chances of survival.

Hell, I don't even know how I did all those things at once. It must have been a result of my increased brain activity due to the implants.

Connor and Pré walked into the bridge together. As they sat down and saw the damage to the shield, Connor's jaw dropped. He knew Clearsteel™ was almost indestructible. Something very large and moving very fast had to have hit the *Alpha.*

"Well, that's a good place to start," I said. "Hailey, can you give us the status of the shield?"

"Absolutely. The shield shows an impact tear along its lower D-9 quadrant. The tear has a hastate shape and is 5.3 meters in length, and has an opening of 1.4 meters along its widest point. The tear does not reduce the impact tenacity of the shield as a whole, however, it will limit our ability to refuel using atmospheric scooping. The opening at that point will increase friction. It will also concentrate heat created by atmospheric friction to build up at that point."

"Connor, is this going to be a problem?"

"When I checked the fusion reactors, I found no anomalies. However, we burned a considerable amount of fuel trying to escape the atmosphere. A fuel burn that we had not planned for. Even with our margin of error, if we plan to accelerate the ship to 0.9 'c' again on a return trip home, I am afraid we will be cutting the margin too thin without an atmospheric refuel. We were counting on 'scooping' to replenish the hydrogen supply."

"Are you saying we are stuck here?"

"Yes and no, Captain, I am saying unless we figure out another way to draw in hydrogen, we may be stuck here if we don't want to do a slow burn acceleration back home. Even reducing our acceleration, a small amount, we will add years to our return trip. I have also detected slight heat damage to the number four exhaust nozzle. This ship was never meant to penetrate an atmosphere of that density level. The heat from the friction was just too much for that exhaust nozzle. It may come into play if we have to do a full burn again."

"On that cheerful note, what is the status of the farm?"

Sal looked up from his monitor. "I have been checking the oxygen output from the farm, and our status has not changed. We can endure the additional time of a slow burn acceleration. We should have plenty of food, and in stasis, we use very little oxygen."

"Pré, what is Genie's condition?"

"She survived the last encounter with no additional symptoms. I will be returning her to stasis in a few hours. The infirmary did not incur any damage."

I turned to Lexie. "Lexie, what about Hailey?"

"After running the diagnostic, I found her operating system has been rebooted and is running again at peak efficiency. She has lost no functionality. Somehow, the impact knocked her off-line and she returned to her default parameters, causing her to reboot."

"I checked the launch bay. The probes and their launch vehicle are intact. The shuttle was held tight by its redundancy claws that keep it locked it in. The failure of the magnetic holds had no significant consequence. We should be good to begin exploration. Hailey, have we missed anything? What do you have on the planet so far?"

"Captain, my observations are in agreement with all crew members' analyses. Updated specifics on the planet are as follows: The orbits of Sirius A and Sirius B lie on parallel planes separated by about 0.62 astronomical units. Their orbits form a massive ellipse with Sirius A orbiting one of the two foci, and Sirius B orbiting the other. Sirius A is a massive main sequence white star with an approximate age of three hundred to five hundred million years, and Sirius B is a white dwarf with almost the same mass as Sirius A. It is much older in age than Sirius A. I estimate Sirius B's age at nine billion years. It appears that Sirius B captured Sirius A in its gravitational field at some point in its lifespan. Sirius C is a brown dwarf with a much smaller mass than A and B. It also appears to have been captured by the gravity of one of the stars or both. Its orbit is highly elliptical and lies at ninety degrees to the plane of the other two stars. The orbits of Sirius A and B transect. Sirius C appears to orbit one of the two transection points of A and B. Sirius A and Sirius B have yet to reach the transection point in their orbits but are on course to do so in the near future. I would approximate within one hundred years. It is difficult to predict the exact moment since the gravities of both stars are accelerating them toward one another. Sirius C is also on course to do a near fly-by of the transection of the orbits of A and B. Calculating the acceleration vectors of the three stars, I predict them to be in syzygy within the next one hundred years. At this point, the gravitational forces of all three stars acting on another celestial object could have catastrophic effects. A planet orbiting any one of the three stars will undergo severe planetwide changes. The effects will be devastating. At a minimum, dramatic climate changes will occur; at a maximum, the planet could break up."

She continued, "I have scanned the planet as much as the cloud cover will allow. The density of the cloud layer is limiting my ability to detect surface features. The planet has an axial tilt of 10.5 degrees in relation to Sirius C. Magnetic north and true north show a slight variation as they relate to the tilt. It appears the planet will undergo seasonal shifts in its revolution around Sirius C. The planet makes one revolution every 240 Earth days. The planet rotates on its axis every thirty-four hours. The amount of daylight at any latitude varies from day to day due to the tilt of the planet and its relative location in relation to the three stars, as the planet completes its orbit.

The planet's surface is covered mostly by liquid water. Density readings indicate possible landforms at both poles. The atmosphere appears to contain a high level of nitrogen gas, approximately sixty-eight percent plus or minus three percent error due to the obscurity created by the cloud layer. The second most abundant gas is oxygen at about thirty percent, and a multitude of other gases make up the final two percent. Again, I have a rather large error factor of three percent. The cloud layer is composed of ninety-eight percent water vapor. It covers approximately the entire planet. There is a possibility there may be areas on a daily basis with no cloud cover. Near the equatorial region, it is approximately one hundred kilometers thick and thins near the poles down to approximately twenty kilometers in thickness on average. I extrapolate that the possible landforms near the poles extend from approximately seventy degrees to ninety degrees latitude at both poles. The density of the atmosphere at the southern pole is slightly greater than that of the northern pole indicating a higher concentration of heavier gases such as sulfur gases. This could possibly indicate volcanic activity."

"Some people are like clouds. When they disappear, it is a brighter day." A quote from "Miss Know-it-All"? The 2069 movie of the year? I have got to have Hailey check this ALIT programming roaming around my brain.

"Hailey, can you pinpoint an exact location where the launch vehicle will have the best chance to enter the atmosphere?" I said as I refocused.

"Already calculated Captain. The greatest chance of a successful mission is to enter the atmosphere near the northern pole. I calculate a forty-five-degree entry at eighty-eight degrees north latitude. The cloud density is at a minimum at that point, and the increased ion and electromagnetic radiation due to magnetic fields are well within the safety parameters of the launch vessel."

Connor interrupted, "Asil if we launch the probes at the northern pole, they might not be able to make it to the southern pole, not to mention the time involved to make that trip. Plus, their signal emission is not powerful enough to go planetwide. And without the launch vessel's high gain directional antenna, their individual signal cannot penetrate that thick cloud layer to relay their collected data back to the *Alpha*. The mini-fusion rockets in them are good, but not that good. They were designed for an equatorial launch."

"Thoughts, anyone?" I asked.

"Could the launch vehicle drop the probes as it travels across the planet?" asked Sal.

"The launch vehicle is designed to cut through the atmosphere and get the probes to an altitude at which they can use their scanners to map and collect data from the surface. It is not meant to travel horizontally for great distances. Once it reaches its prescribed altitude, it will deploy a large high-gain antenna after the probes are launched. It will then act as a hovering radio tower to collect probe data and relay it back to the ship. It will use a lot of its power to stop its gravitational freefall, and then use most of the rest to push the data signal back to the *Alpha*. It was never designed to fly very far on its own power," I added.

"So now what, do we explore only half of the planet," asked Pré.

"Could we carry the probes on the shuttle, and release them as we fly over the planet?" asked Sal.

"Without their data, it would be extremely dangerous to take the shuttle down first. Without knowing the exact cloud configurations and atmospheric data, we might be in for a very rough ride. But I'm sure I could reconfigure the hold to carry the launch vehicle. That is going to take some time, and I'm not sure how long we want to wait," I said.

I looked around the room, and it was clear that no one wanted to wait, so I added, "Half a planet is better than none, I guess. I say we proceed with a northern hemisphere exploration."

With our luck thus far, everyone appeared to be in agreement with me. The faster we got down there, the less chance of something else happening while we waited.

"As soon as we complete a thorough probe analysis, we will launch the shuttle, providing we find a suitable landing site."

Changing subjects, Pré asked, "Captain, I looked at the data from our collision. At the rate those objects were moving, if they would have hit any part of the ship not made of Clearsteel™, they would have obliterated it. Even Clearsteel™ would have been destroyed if it were struck transversely. You saved the ship by rotating into their paths. How did you know?"

"It all happened so fast, I just reacted on instinct. I guess my extra time in the simulator wasn't wasted after all. Somehow, I just knew what to do. Although it would have been a lot easier to have '*Space-Invadered*' the crap out of them."

"Space-Invadered?" asked Pré.

"You know, blasted them out of the sky with a laser cannon," I answered.

"Laser cannon!" remarked Hailey. "You'll shoot your face off, Captain!"

"Shoot my face off," I grunted. "Hailey, why DOESN'T this thing have a laser cannon?"

"I believe that is THE reason we are in this predicament, remember Earth?" Hailey countered.

"I would not shoot living things!" *Dear Santa, for Christmas, I would like a "Space Invaders" laser cannon. I promise not to shoot other living things. Signed, Asil.*

I continued, "By the way, Lexie, you said you looked at the data, how big was the rock that hit us? And where did it come from? Did a small moon break up at some time during the planet's formation?"

"There is no data of any moon ever orbiting this planet. If Genie were awake, she might be able to tell us more. It is strange Captain, when I look at the visual and slow it down considerably, it does not appear to be a rock that struck the shield."

"Hailey, can you give us more detail on what struck the *Alpha?*"

"I have analyzed the video of the object that struck the shield and the many smaller objects that accompanied it. The objects do not appear to be rock-like in structure."

"What were they?" I asked.

"Unknown," she answered.

"Best possible guess?"

"Possibly artificial in nature."

"You mean humanmade?" I exclaimed.

"Of unknown origin," she replied.

"Are you trying to tell me, we were hit by the debris of some alien spacecraft?"

"Impossible to determine, but I am ninety-seven percent sure the objects were of some type of construction."

I looked around the room at the others. They sat in stunned silence. I am sure they were thinking what I was thinking. We were not the first here, and, was whoever beat us here, still here?

"Hailey set course for the launch vehicle approach, we are going down there," I said.

***

"Open the shuttle bay door, HAIL," I commanded.

"Why did you call me HAIL?" she asked calmly.

"I don't know, it just sounded appropriate. Maybe I saw it somewhere in an old-time movie."

"I believe it's SAL," came Sal's voice over the comm-link. Sal was in the farm reseeding plants and harvesting some of the fresh fruits and vegetables. "It's SAL, the supercomputer from that space journey movie."

"Coming from another Sal, you would remember it that way, and I think it's 'unlock the shuttle bay hatch'," Connor's voice interrupted through my comm-link. Connor was floating around the aft storage cleaning up some minor equipment shifting that had occurred during the collision.

Pré's voice chimed in on the conversation. She was in the stasis room preparing Genie for her long-term sleep. "Remember, it went crazy, and said something like, 'Regretfully, I cannot do that'."

"What?" I asked, "how do you guys know this?"

In unison, we all shouted, "Hailey!"

"It is true Captain. Everyone received the enjoyment of old-time movies while they were in stasis," she said in her soothing voice. "And stop talking about my great-grandfather that way!"

We all laughed.

"Dr. Chivago, will I dream?" Lexie added to the conversation. Lexie was at her monitor on the bridge tweaking the communication systems between the *Alpha*, the launch vessel, and the drones.

Hailey chimed in, "I am wincing! If you could see me, I am wincing! That is *2047: A Notch in Orion's Belt*," Hailey corrected her.

We all laughed again. It had been a long time since I had laughed, and it felt good to relieve some of the stress the mission had thrust upon us.

"When we are all sitting around the thermonuclear heater in our retirement quarters during our old age about a hundred years from now, we can share old movie quotes," I laughed again.

"I hope no one brings the beans," laughed Lexie. She was obviously referring to an old western comedy film which I'm pretty sure Hailey had shown us from her repertoire.

The conversation continued as I watched on the monitor as the huge shuttle bay doors opened quietly into the darkness. The launch vessel had been moved into position, and it slipped soundlessly into space as the huge robotic claws gave it a gentle push out of the bay. After about thirty seconds, red light flared from its exhaust and it accelerated away from the ship and toward the planet. As it adjusted its trajectory, the enormous sphere of the white planet filled my screen.

If everything worked as planned, the vessel would enter the atmosphere within the hour, and the first possibly habitable planet, other than the Earth, would be revealed to humankind.

As I watched the red hue of the rocket dim against the white field, I couldn't help but wonder what fantastic adventures lay in store for us beneath that impenetrable shroud.

***

The monitor in my quarters chimed and its small LED blinked red as I rose from a quick rest. "Yes?" I asked, as I blindly slid my hand across the surface of the desk, scattering the contents of an antique office organizer across its surface

"Initial data is coming in from the proximal probes," Lexie stated.

"I'll be there in a quantum moment." I wanted to see this place on the big screen.

As I arrived on the bridge, I noticed everyone else had gathered there as well. No one wanted to miss this monumental moment in human history.

"Put it up on screen," I said to Lexie.

The huge wall and half-floor screen slowly turned from gray to blue. An azure ocean of water filled the screen in front of us. There was water as far as the eye could see. Huge blue waves rolled under a grayish sky. There were no birds in the sky, no algae in the water, or signs of sea creatures. No life of any form could be seen. Yet, it was beautiful. I had never seen crystal blue water like that before. The oceans on Earth had been tainted with fallout from the nuclear war; this ocean was pristine.

"Can you get any readings?" I asked.

Lexie called up the data on her monitor, "The atmosphere is almost exactly what Hailey calculated. There is a large concentration of breathable oxygen. Sensors indicate about 29.8 relative saturation. Most of the atmosphere is nitrogen gas. I am detecting some traces of argon, carbon dioxide, and some gases that I cannot identify. Genie predicted a planet around Sirius C in the Goldilocks Zone would be like this. The clouds are indeed ninety-eight percent water vapor just like Hailey reported. I haven't tested the liquid water yet. It is going to be tricky with those waves. I estimate wave height to be somewhere around thirty meters on average. Wind velocity is pretty steady at seven meters per second, and the ambient temperature is thirty degrees Celsius."

"Any signs of land?" I asked.

"We established a longitudinal grid using the launch vehicle's position as the prime. It is hovering at eighty-five degrees north latitude. We are working a gridline with the first four probes out. Two started from the prime, and the others will transverse the pole and travel south down the one-eighty meridian. So far nothing but water. Two drones are traveling at high speed on a fast-track vector toward the equator. One at zero degrees and the other will turn south when it reaches fifteen degrees. It will be sometime before we get any good information from them."

We sat and watched the waves roll by as the drones slowly expanded their grids. As the minutes came and went, I suggested we begin our preparations for a shuttle mission should land be found. If Hailey was correct, we should be able to see land at any time. From where we entered the atmosphere, I was surprised land had not been sighted yet.

"Anything on the IR," I asked Lexie hopefully, "any signs of life?"

"No sign of any heat signatures. If there is life in the air or near the sea surface, it is not warm-blooded."

The minutes turned to an hour, and I have to admit I was getting a little seasick watching wave after wave pass from the top of the screen near the ceiling to below my feet on the transparent floor.

Lexie was busy at her monitor analyzing data as it streamed up from the launch vehicle. Connor was beside her on his monitor checking the engine status of each of the drones as they flew through the great white planet's atmosphere. Sal had left the bridge and returned to the farm. There was still plenty of plant work to catch up on.

I noticed Pré had moved to her monitor and was busy checking the medical inventory that we might need for a landing. I moved to the chair beside her and sat down.

"I've noticed you haven't been using your accent around me anymore. Does this mean you like me?"

"Like ees a strong word," she answered back in her heavy French accent. "Let me just say, I theenk you are not the incompetent bumbler I thought you were."

Then she smiled. Now, I am not a flowery person with words, but her face lit up like a beautiful morning sunrise. Her eyes twinkled like the distant stars as their rays were refracted through the thick Clearsteel™ observation windows. The glacier that had formed around my heart for this ice queen began to melt.

I smiled back. I cannot believe I was beginning to have feelings for this woman who torched me with her words for a year while we were in training. It is amazing how one smile can wipe out three hundred sixty-five days of insults and looks of disdain.

"Are you feeling any better after your accident?" I asked.

"I have bruised ribs and a small lump on my head. I know it was not your fault that I was not seated properly when you fired the engines. I hesitated because I am stubborn and did not want to listen to your orders; when I should have gotten to my chair immediately. You saved the ship and our lives, for that I thank you."

Her face turned a slight shade of pink as she got out of her chair, and said, "Now if you will excuse me, Asil, I need to go pack some equipment."

I returned to my chair feeling a little lighter. *Did the ship's gravity just diminish? "Did my heart love till now? Forswear it, sight! For I ne'er saw true beauty till this night."* Oh God, now I'm quoting Shakespeare!

Hours passed. I stayed on the bridge. I tapped into the shuttle's computers and began checking and re-checking its systems. The view out the bridge screen did not change, although I had changed the image on the screen to show the view of all six drones at once. Water was everywhere. Lexie had finally decided to send a drone close to the surface to collect water samples. She had been able to capture a few drops from the ocean spray as waves collapsed when the wind receded. Just as she was receiving the composition data from the water collected, she looked up at me, "Captain, on the screen. On the D-4 drone image. Do you see it?"

I looked at the image near the top right corner of the screen and thought I saw a black smudge in the distance. *Could that be land?*

"Lexie, change D-4's course. Heading, thirty-seven degrees. Intercept that black smudge."

"On it."

As the drone flew towards its target, the smudge grew larger and resolved into what appeared to be a black landmass.

I clicked the all-call on the monitor's comm-link connection. "Land Ho!"

Still kilometers out, the drone's cameras could not distinguish features, but I could definitely see this was no small island. The dark mass grew larger and larger and stretched toward the horizon. Judging from what I saw initially, I had to estimate this was a continent about the size of the old country of Canada.

We waited patiently as the drone crawled closer and closer. The others were on their way to the bridge when the first distinct images appeared on the screen.

"Put up just D-4," I told Lexie.

Gigantic black-walled cliffs resolved onto the screen. Huge ocean waves at least one hundred meters high smashed into the base of what appeared to be four to five-hundred-meter tall rock cliffs. The cliffs were pocked with what looked like enormous cave entrances that extended back into the dark recesses of the cliffs.

"Can you get us up over the top?" I asked Lexie. "Hailey, any initial analysis?"

"Judging by erosional appearance and rock structure, I would hypothesize the rock is basaltic in nature. Most likely of recent volcanic origin."

The video images on the screen shifted as the drone began to scale the face of the incredible sight before our eyes. Imagine waves striking a rock cliff on Earth, and multiply that by about ten.

The others walked onto the bridge just as the drone cleared the top of the cliffs. There, growing almost to the edge of the cliff, were what appeared to be huge trees. Thick tannish-brown trunks extending thirty to forty meters up. A huge green-blue bush of what appeared to be long, slender leaves entangled in a disarray of chaos radiated out from each trunk's apex resulting in an unbroken canopy that stretched for kilometers.

There were thousands of trees. It looked like an infinite forest palisade.

"What are they?" Connor whispered questioningly.

"They appear to be bamboo-like in nature," replied Sal as he sat down, "however, the leaves' branch configuration does not resemble bamboo at all. The individual leaf structure does look similar to a bamboo leaf, though."

"It looks like they are growing right out of the rock," Connor added.

"We have life on another planet," smiled Sal.

"Any other form of life?" I asked, "Do you see anything moving amongst the trees? What about heat signatures? Anything there?"

Lexie answered, "Nothing showing up on the scanners. Hailey do you have anything?"

"I am detecting a second form of life on the forest floor. It is difficult to obtain information through the canopy, but I believe it is a grass of some sort. No signs of animal life, at least according to human parameters."

The green-blue canopy stretched for what had to be hundreds of kilometers. With no end in sight, I turned to Lexie and said, "Will you turn the drone around? Let's follow the coastline down at one-eighty. Maybe there is a break along there somewhere."

"Aye, Captain," she smiled.

Everyone knew now that if we could find a landing site, we were well within mission guidelines for exploration. There was excitement in the air as the drone headed south along the cliff edge.

As the drone traveled on, I joined the crew in the discussions of what the planet was like, what we might find, and what we would explore first, should we find an adequate landing site.

It was Hailey's ping that intruded in on the myriad of topical discussions that were being bantered about. Before she had interrupted, thoughts were shared first by the whole group, then by people entranced in one-to-one discussions or smaller factions of the group, thereof. It dawned on me our discussion was just like the old "jigsaw method" of discussion used in meetings back on Earth. *I hated those meetings.*

"Captain, I have new data coming in from the D-3 drone."

The D-3 drone had split away from the D-4 early on and was several kilometers south of D-4. It was following a similar initial trajectory.

"Let's see what it has," I said.

The image that appeared on the big screen was not unlike what D-4 had come upon, with one exception. D-3 had come upon a very large bay that was protected from the crashing waves. As the drone rounded the cliff wall from the south, the rock edge plunged downward swiftly to connect to a black, sandy shore that extended along a horseshoe-shaped curve. The horseshoe-shaped bay dipped toward the west attaching to a black-sand beach that extended about a kilometer or two, inland. The huge forest once again rose in the distance. Just in front of the forest was a stand of what looked like tallgrass, except for the fact it was three times taller than any human.

The room buzzed with excitement. "I think we have found our landing site, ladies and gentlemen," I quipped.

CHAPTER 11: RELOCATION

Now we were in my wheel-house as the old saying goes. I knew every centimeter of the surface shuttle. The general shape of the fuselage hadn't changed much since the twentieth century, but the technology inside had changed dramatically. The shuttle still resembled a fighter jet with retractable wings that could be used to produce the pressure changes needed to fly it in an atmosphere. The greatest advancement in flight was the shuttle's ability to take off and land vertically. It was that ability, I thought, that was the most fun. I could land that thing on a decidol-yen. A dime, I thought, was the slang word for it.

The shuttle was large enough to hold the entire crew plus most of the equipment needed to perform a detailed exploration of the landing site. One last "optional" piece of equipment that was stored in the tail hold was a rover. If driving conditions were deemed acceptable on the surface, we could roll out the rover. To me, this was not an option, I was taking that bad boy four-wheelin' on ANY alien terrain!

The shuttle was not large enough, however, to hold the habitats and the exploration equipment. The habitats would have to be launched separately.

The habitats were stored in the forward hold just behind the shield. I had personally checked them just the day before to make sure our little fender-bender hadn't damaged them in any way. I had forgotten to check the second airlock, so I had returned today. The airlock was located in the forward hold. It was constructed just in case a spacewalk was needed to check the shield or any other forward section of the ship. It also served as an emergency escape hatch.

The forward hold also had its own cargo doors. I decided to check them as well. These doors were smaller than the shuttle bay doors and were meant for unloading and loading cargo at the ISS. They also served double duty in that they were the extraction point of the habitats. No readings indicated they had been breached but I wasn't taking any chances and had climbed into my spacesuit before I entered. I checked the seals manually just to corroborate what the monitors were telling me. I then walked magnetically up and over to the habitats that were secured to the floor and ceiling, or ceiling and floor, whichever you preferred. There was no up or down in here. *That was so cool. I loved these boots.* After double-checking them again, I prepared them for launch. Hailey would guide them out of the cargo bay when the time came. As I worked, my enhanced brain flashed through my knowledge of the habitats.

The habitats, which would be inflated on the surface of the planet, were currently stored in a protective rubber casing that would fill like a balloon as it traveled through the atmosphere. Once at a safe altitude, calculated using the planet's recently-discovered gravitational acceleration, large parachutes would deploy slowing the habitats' descent. Directional thrusters attached to the casing would guide each habitat to its prescribed landing site. Just before impact, the chutes would be discharged, and the inflated casing protecting the habitat would bounce harmlessly onto the planet's surface. Once on the ground, the shuttle would be used—via a grappling hook—to move the habitats into place. The casings would be peeled away while inflated, and the habitats would be inflated with the air from the casings. The "habs", as we called them, also had their own gas supply. The deflated casings would then be reused for either water storage or air storage.

There were five habitats that needed deployment. There were three living quarters, a lab that would house the settlement's AI—CAI-LE, and a communications center that also served as a dining and meeting center. I was supposed to share one living quarter with Sal; the married couple, Lexie and Connor, would share one, and the last was supposed to be shared by Genie and Pré. The communications center also held the nerve center for the mini-fusion reactor which would power the settlement indefinitely.

After finding all habitats secure, and ready for deployment, I headed back to the shuttle bay. In the shuttle bay's suit storage area, I wiggled out of my suit and entered the large main room of the bay. Lexie, Connor, and Sal were all in the shuttle bay working feverishly to make sure everything was in order. Lexie had just finished securing CAI-LE in the shuttle's main cargo hold when she drifted over to me.

"Captain," she paused, "...Asil, we have been talking about your new Plan C. If you are going home, then so are we. No Plan C. You go, we go. You stay, we stay. You have become the leader of this team, and we will not go anywhere without you. No one else on this ship could have done what you did in that debris field. We need you, and your expertise. We all feel the same way."

I did not know what to say, so I said, "I am honored, but to disobey your commanding officer is mutiny. Are you saying you guys are willing to commit treason to keep the team together?"

"That is exactly what we are saying, Captain. Your wit is a little dry, but it is tolerable," she smiled.

New emotions ran through me. *I am no longer a one-man wolf-pack.*

Connor, who was securing a mini-fusion reactor to the shuttle's cargo hold on the starboard side, pushed off the far wall and flew over. "Asil, you know as well as we do, Hailey can handle the *Alpha* by herself. She can easily take Genie home if we decide to stay. The biggest obstacle we must overcome will be maneuvering about the planet without a physicist and geologist. Your shuttle expertise will be even more important without Genie. And like Lexie said, we do find you funny, at times."

"Well, that leaves us with a few more decisions," I choked.

Dammit man, pull yourself together.

"Already discussed, and just need your approval. We decided we should stay long enough to thoroughly explore this place. We can send data back to Hailey as we acquire it using the habitat's communication center. We can use the launch vessel's antenna as a booster when we need it. Hailey can then send the data back home. We want to establish a semi-permanent settlement for at least a month, then return to the *Alpha* for the trip home. Another month or two here is not going to change much on the Earth versus the nine-year trip home."

"I was hoping you might come up with a Plan D. I've kind of gotten used to you guys being around. I've already prepped the landing balloons for the habitats. They are ready for launch. We should launch them soon, so they are waiting for us when we touch down. Hopefully, the chutes will slow them down enough so they don't bounce into the ocean when they hit. The planet's gravity is slighter greater than one 'g', a fact we could not predict accurately back on the ISS."

Turning to the shuttle bay's camera, I asked, "Hailey, can you give us a definitive launch window?" *I didn't need to look at the camera. She is always watching. Old habits ….*

"Yes, Asil," she said with her soft voice. *I think she was smirking somewhere out there in her artificial world.* "The way the three stars and the planet are aligned at this time in their orbits, there are about four hours of semi-darkness that encompass this latitude. Sirius A and B will both set in about three hours. Due to the planet's 10.5-degree tilt and the planet's rotation, it is about four hours into its nighttime with Sirius C. That will last another nine hours at this latitude. The weather does not appear to change dramatically from night to day, and I have not detected any new large high-pressure or low-pressure systems moving in anywhere within the drones' scanned perimeters. A morning launch appears to be the most viable option giving you the greatest number of hours of direct light. Since the planet is about 1.5 times the diameter of the Earth, and its rotation is slightly faster than Earth's rotation, a diurnal cycle should be thirty-four hours. However, with the influence of three different 'suns', an exact amount of daylight is difficult to calculate. I do calculate sunrise at approximately 07:00 hours Greenwich Mean Time tomorrow when relating it to Earth time.

"One day will not be enough to go over all this data, and plan a landing," I interjected.

Lexie had floated back to the shuttle's cockpit, "Hailey, the drones have enough fuel to fly through the night with your guidance, and still have plenty of fuel to continue data collection when daylight arrives again. Sometime tomorrow, they will have to turn back or they will not make it back to the launch vehicle. Can you calculate their maximum exploration distance, and program them to turn back at this point?"

"I am doing so as we speak," Hailey replied.

"What if we program some of them to return to our landing site?" I asked. "We can then refuel and reuse them when we get there. The others, we can allow to continue on their current program until they run out of fuel. That way we can explore as much of the planet as we possibly can, maybe even get a peek beyond the equatorial region. We may lose these others, but that was already built into the initial plan."

"That sounds like an excellent idea," Lexie replied. "As far as the drone launch vehicle, it was designed to have enough fuel to stay hovering at that altitude for the length of any pre-planned ground mission, and then some. It can also return to the *Alpha* if we initiate its emergency return protocol."

I requested the all-call on my comm-link, "This is your captain speaking, once we are satisfied with the surface investigation, and preparations for landing are in order, we will be going down there. Hailey will calculate the optimum launch time for a shuttle launch to the surface. In the meantime, we have to get the habitats down to the planet. Everyone should get something to eat. I hear the blue crème is on the menu again. We will meet on the bridge at 14:30, and get those rubber balls bouncing!"

Paraphrasing the words of the great Flounder, I thought, *"Oh boy! This is going to be great!"*

***

The spacesuit had come a long way since it was first invented in the twentieth century. As I wiggled my way into this newest version created by the wizards at ICoSTE in preparation for the shuttle launch, all sorts of old images ran through my mind. I remembered the huge, almost-impossible-to-maneuver, *Apollo* suits that were used when humans first set foot on the moon. They were the first I had ever seen in real life. They were on display at the International Museum of Science in New York when I visited with my grandparents as a six-year-old. Those bulky life-support systems look nothing like what I was wiggling into now. This new suit was woven from fibers of Clearsteel™, and is virtually indestructible. Only three layers of fabric thick, this thing is highly flexible, and movement is not restricted in the least. The layers contain all sorts of gizmos. For one, they have climate control, so you will always be at a comfortable twenty-two degrees Celsius, no matter how hot or cold the space is outside. One entire layer is designed to control the amount of electromagnetic radiation that anyone in the suit is encountering. There are built-in accelerometers and impact sensors that deploy airbags if they detect imminent collision or excessive acceleration that could harm the human body. Unlike the old vehicle airbags, these airbags can also be used as flotation devices should a person fall into water. Oxygen generators, filters, and regenerators are planted all over in the suit. They can filter any oxygen present outside the suit and bring it in, or produce oxygen from chemicals embedded in the suit layers in times where there is no oxygen present. There's a water resynthesizer that can make water from chemicals present in the air, recycle it from my breath, or filter it from urine. I prefer the former first two, although I know the latter is one hundred percent pure.

As I pulled on the pants, I couldn't help but marvel how they get the three pieces to seal space-tight. The pant legs have foot holes in the bottom just like pants have had for thousands of years. When you are in your pants, you get a choice of which fashionable foot attire you wish to choose to match your ensemble. One set of boots contains the electromagnets and is used on board the ship to walk anywhere in zero gravity—my favorites. The second set of boots is designed for hiking the rough terrain of some rocky planet surface. They are larger and well-cushioned with large grips on the bottoms. The third type of boot I can best describe as a running boot. It is lightweight Clearsteel™, and can grab any surface using some sort of sure-grip nanotechnology incorporated in the sole. That was the boot of choice for this mission since I imagined there would be frequent wet surfaces to cross.

Where the bottom of the pants overlaps the top of the boot, the suit sends an electric signal to seal the two pieces together. The electricity creates some sort of bonding at the molecular level where the two articles of clothing meet, and the seam between the two disappears. When I want to remove a boot, I simply "tell" the boot to unseal via the mini-computer in the helmet. There is also a manual procedure to remove them that requires three different steps. Three steps since I don't want to have a boot fall off in space if I accidentally hit the wrong button!

The same thing happens at the waist when the torso piece overlaps the pants. A utility belt, not unlike the Caped Wonder's I might add, gets strapped around my waist at this point. *At least I hoped it was like the Caped Wonder's. Whenever he needed just the right tool, it happened to be in his utility belt at that time. Did anyone ever notice that?*

The helmet that I put on was smaller than the old *Apollo* helmet, and was much more user-friendly. It has a voice-activated communications monitor guided by a link to any chosen AI in proximity. It has all sorts of sensors that can be called up on command, such as a panoramic camera that allows me to see three-hundred-and-sixty degrees without having to turn around. It has infrared sensors and a high-intensity light that has adjustable settings. A water tube that is used for sipping liquids rises up from the torso section curving along my jawline inside the helmet. With the press of a button, it can also be switched to sip food as well. The helmet also has a shield that can be dimmed on command in bright light conditions. The comm-link mike follows the water tube out of the torso section. It can be used in conjunction with the helmet's own receiver or separately without the helmet on. The helmet seals to the torso much the same way as the other pieces of the suit seal together, so when the suit is completely fitted, it looks a "onesie" with a fancy fishbowl on top.

The topper to all the wonders of the suit is how it uses the excess carbon dioxide that I exhale. The waste CO_2 is filtered and used to recharge small CO_2 thrusters that are attached near the soles of the feet up along the spot where the Achilles' tendon would be found on a human. There are two more attached near the wrist, kind of like Spiderman's web slingers, and four more are found on the back of the suit. An astronaut no longer needs a tether when on a spacewalk. A quick flex of the wrist or foot sends a small puff of carbon dioxide out of small jets, propelling the body in the direction they wish to go. The back jets are a little larger for a little faster acceleration and are voice-activated. They are not strong enough to move me in normal gravity, but in the weakened gravity of space, I could dance the waltz if I wished. So as long as I was breathing, I could move about the outside of the *Alpha*.

As I strapped into the cockpit of the shuttle, I noticed no one was sitting on my right where the co-pilot usually sits. Of course, Genie was the only other person qualified to fly this thing, and, well, I wish she were here because this could get rough.

"Hailey, how long to launch?" I asked, even though I could see the countdown on my helmet monitor.

"All systems go in ten minutes thirty-five seconds and counting. Do you wish to go through the checks again?"

"No, is everyone strapped in?"

Just then there was a commotion beside me, and I turned to see Pré crawling into the seat to my right.

"I hear the view is much better up here," she smiled.

"Can you handle this bad boy if I lose consciousness?" I chided.

"As they say back home, *'l'amener sur'*!"

"Bring it on?"

"How did you know that?"

"There are so many things that I am not sure how I know them, but I just do. Must have something to do with these ALIT implants, *'penses-tu'*?"

"Yes, I also think so. Captain, the more we converse, the less I find you an ignorant lout."

"I'll take that as a compliment, I think. Strap in princess, this could get rough."

"All crew settled in, and all systems good to go," Hailey's voice echoed through the helmet comm-links. "Opening shuttle bay doors."

The huge doors of the bay slowly and silently opened to reveal the bright white planet below. The huge arms that held the shuttle slowly extended out the doors and the magnetic claws that held the shuttle tightly when in the bay sprung open giving the shuttle a gentle push away from the *Alpha*.

"We are away," I said to no one in particular. "Engaging forward thrusters. Igniting aft engine in ten seconds."

As the shuttle accelerated toward the surface gently pushing us back in our seats, Hailey broke the silence that had eerily come over this crew, "Captain, when you enter the cloud layer, we will lose contact for a short period of time until you have cleared into the lower atmosphere. Then, I can link your comm to the launch vehicle for signal amplification."

"Okay," I said, "and Hailey?"

"Yes, Captain?"

"You know you are with us in spirit, right?"

"I am always with you in spirit, Captain, I have no physical body."

I just smiled.

As we entered the outer atmosphere, the heat sensors denoted a sudden rise in the shuttle's fuselage temperature as the friction between our ship and the air began to build. I had shut down the engines just before and extended the wings. We were allowing the planet's gravity to pull us in.

As we built speed, the shuttle began to shake, and I could see the nose begin to turn red. We hit the cloud layer with a "fwump" and plunged headlong into the wall of mist. I attempted valiantly to keep the ship horizontal to slow our descent.

"Hailey?" I asked, "Are you still there?"

"Just, …. on the……, a violent change…." was all I heard.

As we dove through the hundreds of kilometers of gray wetness, the shuttle began to shake more violently. Suddenly, we were hit by an enormous updraft, and the shuttle was jerked abruptly upward driving us deep into our seats. Then a quick downdraft sent us plummeting at a tremendous acceleration downward all the while the shuttle shook like a paint mixer. The wings screamed with the strain on them! The wind hammered at the tail, attempting to tear it from its perch! I fought the controls for all I was worth, the huge cloud system playing with us like we were a dingy at sea in a hurricane! Rain pummeled the Clearsteel™ windshield! Lightning struck the fuselage with blinding blue-white bolts as air friction began to build charge on the metal surface of the ship! I did everything I could to keep the ship horizontal, and us, alive!

A blast of hurricane-force wind sent us into a twisting maneuver I never thought a space shuttle could ever accomplish. The gale tossed us some ten kilometers up, over, and then down again in a three-sixty loop. The LED readouts on the screens in front of me went crazy blinking rapidly trying to keep up with the plethora of information they were being fed. Deep down I began to think, *"This is it. She's not going to hold together."*

We tumbled for what seemed like hours, yet I'm sure, was only minutes; each stress and strain providing a new sound to the cacophony around us. Sweat poured down my back as I pushed, pulled, and pressed. My suit's climate control could not keep up. My brain began to swim as light flickered and flashed through the cockpit window. The contents of my stomach were seeking a much faster exit than normal. Numbers whirred past my eyes as my helmet monitor tried desperately to show me our current course, and suggestions to alleviate the stress on the shuttle.

And then we were through. We came out of the clouds and into a deluge. The rain was hammering the ship, aiding the planet's gravity to shove us into the boiling ocean below. I jammed the stabilizers attempting to stop our tumultuous motion. The ship responded, and slowly, as we plummeted toward the awaiting deep, we regained a horizontal ride. *"Goddam weathermen!"* was all I thought, *"They are never right!"*

I screamed into the mike, "Ignite the rear engine!" The engine came to life, giving us our own power to move, and I tilted the nose up to give us some lift and slow our descent as we raced across the rain-filled sky.

I looked over at Pré. She was out cold. *Dammit if she didn't look fantastic, even with her mouth hanging open. "Clear your head, Asil, we are not down yet,"* the thought dominated my brain.

As I reduced our descent to nil, and established a cruising speed, I asked through my comm-link, "Everyone all right?"

"I am just fine," came Hailey's smart-ass reply. She had already restored the communications link.

"Barely," came Sal's voice through the receiver.

"Give me a moment to clear my head," answered Connor. "It looks like Lexie might have passed out. I will tend to her."

"Same with Pré, up here. I am plotting the coordinates to the bay where our habitats are hopefully waiting for us. Although, in this storm, who knows what we will find."

"Are you getting any signal from their locators?" asked Sal.

"No, but I'm not sure we are in range of their beacons."

"Hailey, any chance you have a fix on them?"

"No sir, the clouds are obscuring everything except the boosted signal from the launch vehicle."

"We should pick them up as we get closer. There, there's one on the scanner," I said as a blue blip appeared on the shuttle's front monitor. "That one is nowhere near where it should be, and it's moving. It must be floating out to sea. Let's go see if we can haul it in."

I turned the shuttle to align it with the habitat's path, and we moved out over the ocean. After fifteen minutes of hard flying, the blip was in the center of the screen.

Trying to spot the habitat's orange visible-light beacon in the pouring rain wasn't easy. Plus, the fact that it was bobbing in thirty-meter waves was going to make this no easy task.

I said into the comm-link, "If I can get over the top of it, I can lower the guided tether, and catch it with the blue-light grappler."

The blue-light grappler was another of those fantastic inventions we now took for granted. When the grappler touched the surface of whatever needed hoisting, you simply flipped a switch, a blue light came on, and the grappler attached itself to whatever it was touching. Of course, the science behind how it worked was nothing short of a miracle. The blue light radiation changed the molecular structure of the grappler to match the molecular surface structure of whatever it was touching, and a molecular network formed between the two surfaces, bonding them tightly together. When the blue light was turned off, the bond dissolved, and the grappler released its hold.

"If I time these waves just right, I should be able to ride over them like a surfer before she catches the big one. These waves aren't much bigger than the ones at Praia do Norte on the coast of Portugal back on Earth."

I focused my flying on the vertical thrusters, moving the ship up in unison with the gigantic crests, and down into the deep troughs. But, of course, this was not Earth.

"Captain! Captain! CAPTAIN!" Pré shouted as she awoke to the pounding rain, the well-pump-handle-movement of the shuttle, and the sound of my voice. "There!" was all she could get out.

Just in front of us, the water began to calm, and a tremendous black, shiny silhouette rose out of the sea. It made the shuttle look like a piece of glitter on the black body of a whale. Then the leviathan plunged downward, carrying the sea with it in a vortex of epic proportions! Millions of gallons of water churned and twisted as they chased the shadow into the deep! Along with it, our tiny habitat.

"What the ….," was all I could get out before Pré screamed again, "In front!"

A wall of water had formed what looked like a huge hand that was about to come slapping down on us as the ocean bottom settled back into its bed. Earth did not have quakes like this! I rammed the front horizontal thrusters on full trying to back us away from the salty palm that was attempting to flatten us! The ship slipped out of the watery hand just as the palm came crashing down. We were clear!

Or so I thought! What we had seen in front of us, was actually all around us, and the ship slammed into a gargantuan rampart of water as we accelerated backward. Our momentum carried us into the diving wall, and we submerged in the behemoth! The weight of the water carried us downward in a spiral all the while the forward thrusters attempted to push us away from the abyss.

This ship was meant to fly in air or space, not water, and I could sense the engines overheating!

"We're not done yet!" I screamed as I spun the ship around, and hit the rockets. They ignited with a sputter, then exploded in a full blaze as the ship surged toward the surface!

We blasted out of the chaos like a cannonball fired from a civil war cannon! As the ship rose into the atmosphere once again, I called over the comm-link, "Looks like sleeping arrangements are going to be different. That habitat is not coming back with us."

The ship felt heavy and sluggish as the water drained from the vents and other openings. I turned it toward the beach and attempted to increase our velocity. The engines did not respond well to the request. Somehow, they had managed to keep working through the watery confrontation, but they were not going much farther. I called up their diagnostics. We were operating at about twenty percent power.

"I need more power!" "Sorry Captain, I can only get you impulse power!" "Dammit, we need that power or we die out here!" "Now, Captain, don't get up to high doh, I'll see what I can do, but I can't make any promises, she's as beat up as William Wallace." A scene from an old film flashed through my brain.

"We need to get this bird down, and dried out if we plan to use it again," I said. "We are limping toward shore, and I hope we can make it the whole way without going for another swim. Did I tell you I hate scuba diving?"

There was a nervous laugh from the rest of the crew. It had been one helluva' ride.

***

I spent an uncomfortable night in the shuttle trying to sleep in my suit on a planet that had more gravity than I had experienced in over nine years. The others appeared restless as well. All except for Sal, he looked as though he were sleeping comfortably in some luxury hotel bed with six-hundred-count Egyptian cotton sheets, somewhere back on Earth. After an agonizing six hours of popping in and out of sleep that was filled with crazy dreams of alien monsters and baking caramel rolls, I finally had enough and wrested my body from my seat.

"Let's go see our new home," I said into my comm-link. "Under no circumstances will anyone remove their suit at any time. I know what the readings say about the air, but we are taking no chances until we are absolutely sure this place is free of anything that might harm us. Let's see if we can get the rover out, and pull the habitats together."

The others groaned and grunted, as they freed themselves from their seats. Except for Sal, he popped right up.

I opened the hatch and gazed upon this alien world. We had landed on the beach about five hundred meters from the calm water of the bay, and about one kilometer from what we initially thought were tall grasses. The downpour of rain had eased to just falling lightly and persistently. No human had ever set foot on another astronomical body outside our solar system.

The only thought that entered my mind as I walked down the ramp was, *"This should be Genie's moment. This was her life's work, she should be the first."* I paused at the bottom of the ramp and waited as the others gathered around me.

"She would be so proud at this moment," said Pré, reading my mind and echoing my thoughts.

I smiled at the thought that everyone was thinking exactly the same thing as they all nodded in the affirmative.

The words of Neil Armstrong and Karique Chang Dubosky entered my mind as they each had been the first to step on the Moon and Mars, respectively. *"This is one small step for a human, ..."*

"Who would like the honor?" I asked as I peered down onto the wet, coal-black sand.

Lexie turned toward me and said into her comm-link, "We would not be here, if not for you. Anyone have any objections if Asil is the first?"

No one spoke. Connor gave me a slight nudge as if to say, "Get your ass moving."

As I began to take a step off the ramp, Lexie spoke up, "Maybe you should say something,"

I thought for a moment. I wanted to speak a line that would go down in history, but nothing popped into my head except Hailey's damned old movies, and the fact that this should be Genie's moment, so I said something very Tolkien-ish, "The realm of the human has not ended, for all those who have wandered, are not lost."

I stepped firmly onto the sandy beach believing I was the first to ever walk on this planet. The others followed quickly, and we set about opening the back hatch of the shuttle to get the rover.

Minutes became hours, and hours became days as we worked to establish our little colony. We spent the days pulling the great balloons of the habitats together and attaching them. The rolling treads that were packed with the rover in the rear hold worked only adequately to slog the habitats through the wet sand. With all five of us pushing and pulling, using the rover's auto-drive, and Hailey quoting old movie words of encouragement, we slowly moved each habitat into place. Finally, on what would have been the sixth Earth day, we inflated each unit and off-loaded the shuttle's contents from the main hold into the habitats.

On the seventh day, the rain stopped. To our bewilderment, the clouds lifted, and the sky became a brilliant blue-green dome with two small suns on opposite sides. If I called this time the "day", then, later, when both set on the horizon and the much larger, but less bright, orb of Sirius C rose, I should have to call that dim-lit time "night". It was all a matter of perspective. So that night, we entered our living quarters for the first time. What wasn't a matter of perspective, was that for the first time in a week, we could take off our suits. Climate-controlled and odor-controlled, we still stunk.

It was decided that Pré, whose habitat was lost, would bunk in Lexie and Connor's unit, since they slept together, and therefore, had an extra bunk.

As I washed, I began to organize my thoughts on how to explore this place. We also had to decide what to do with Genie. Now that Cailey, the habitat's AI, was operational, we could dismiss Hailey, and send her back to Earth with Genie and all the data we collected, if we could not leave here. Although Cailey had nowhere near the sense of humor as Hailey, this AI was programmed specifically for the ground mission.

I called a meeting in the cafeteria, and as we gathered some food, and I enjoyed the tasty, blue nutritive fluid someone had tagged "Mother's Milk", I asked the question that had been in the back of everyone's mind. "Do we send the *Alpha* back home?"

Lexie was the first to reply. "We haven't heard from Earth in a very long time. The signal is just too weak. The recorded messages we received as we traveled are over five years old. If we attempt to send a message home from here, it will take over nine years to get there."

"Even with our high-gain antenna, and all the power we can

muster for a signal, what are the odds that they will receive it on the Earth?" asked Sal. "Cailey, can you give us some numbers?"

"The chances of the signal being detected on the Earth are approximately one in one-point-five billion," replied Cailey.

"So, if we want to get the message back to Earth, we have to either pack up and leave or send Hailey and Genie back. That is, of course, if Connor and I can get the shuttle back to full power."

"If we do send them back, and we stay, we will eventually run out of food, unless something on those plants is edible," added Sal.

"Good point," I interjected, "so here is what I am thinking. After we get some rest, Connor and Hailey will go to work on the shuttle. Pré, Sal, and I can go check out the plant life, and Lexie and Cailey can get the rest of the communications and life support systems up and running. I would like us to work in two's and three's when we are outside. I know it appears as if we are alone here, but I have this nagging feeling that someone, or something, is watching us."

"And do not forget what hit the *Alpha*," added Pré.

"So, essentially, we do nothing about Genie, until we have more information about this place, am I right?" asked Connor.

"That would appear to be the situation. Cailey, Hailey, do you two have anything to add?" I asked.

"Captain, you know I can't live without you," came Hailey's voice over the intercom.

"No new data to report at this time," interrupted Cailey, her more metallic voice overriding Hailey's smooth, silky one.

"Let's meet at 08:00. I'd like to do a bit of a walk-about, as you Australians say, Lexie. If this weather holds, we should be able to explore most of our shoreline in a few hours."

CHAPTER 12: REEXAMINATION

The weather held the next day, and as Pré, Sal, and I trudged through the dark sand toward the grasses the probes had shown us, I still couldn't shake the feeling that we were being watched. Nothing I could point a finger at, and yet it was there at the back of my mind, nagging me as I walked. As we proceeded slowly, I noticed the sand was giving way to a hard, black rock surface that reminded me of obsidian. *I'm sure if Genie were here, she could tell us what this stuff is.*

Just to lighten the drudgery of our hike, I asked Lexie through the comm-link, "How did an Australian physicist ever meet an Irish engineer?"

She laughed, "That's a good story. It was when I was attending university. I was 'studying' for exams one night at the pub, and this pale fellow with a shock of crimson-red hair walked in. He walked up to the bar where the girls and I were sitting, and he ordered a *Guinness Draught* of all things, in Australia! 'You're not from around here are ya, jackaroo?' The barkeep asked him. 'We've got pots or pints of *Imperial Stout*. Take yer pick.'

Well, to make a long story short, the girls and I helped him stagger back to his flat that night. Turns out he had just won a fellowship to the same university as me, and in fact, was attending some of the same classes I was. As we walked and half-carried the poor boy, he looked at me, and said, 'Yer the prettiest girl I've ever seen. I'd take an arrow in the knee for ya. Someday, young one, you and I are going to get married.' Then he hiccupped and threw up all over my shoes. 'Bloody hell, ya Bogan!

You'll pay for my shoes,' I yelled at him. Well, the next week, I found a perfect pair of 3-D printed joggers outside my door with a note. He apologized for ruining my joggers and said he was too embarrassed to face me. So naturally, I pursued him. And, here we are, on an alien planet living every married couple's dream!"

As we came closer to the plant life, Sal's pace picked up, and we practically had to jog to keep up with him. When we were within about ten meters of reaching them, I realized these "plants" were not grasses at all. In fact, they were about as alien of a plant as I could imagine. The "grass" part that the probes had shown us, were actually hazy optical illusions created by the wind that had caused brown, fuzzy protrusions at the tops of the plants to sway. The brown protrusions reminded me of fluffy "Velcro". I'm not sure if they were analogous to leaves, flowers, or what. Below them, were thick black stalks or stems that stood about two meters tall. They appeared to be solid wood and were covered in sharp, black thorns. They appeared to be growing right out of the black obsidian-like rock. Their stalks were interconnected with other stalks creating a pattern, not unlike the pattern created when carbon atoms linked in a covalent network, although slightly irregular. These semi-hex-agonally-linked stalks appeared to create a gauntlet between the trees and sea. They extended at least a kilometer toward the trees and went wall-to-wall from one side of the bay to the other. The only way to get to the trees would be to cut our way through or climb the high, steep walls of the cliffs at the ter-minations of the bay itself. It was as if something was telling us to stay away from the trees. The trees would have to wait for a closer inspection.

"What do you make of these plants, Sal?" I asked.

I could tell by his body language he was excited, and his eyes lit up in his helmet. "They appear to be some form of giant monocot shrubbery, or even a lesser organism in complexity, maybe a bryophyte."

"It is a nice cluster of bushes," raced through my mind, as I in-jected a bit of British humor. *Dear Lord, I've got to grow up!*

Sal continued, "I am picturing the Earth's climate three hundred to four hundred million years ago when giant tree ferns dominated the landscape. Plant life should be very large. The plants before us, if they are plants, have stalks that resemble the rhizoid structure of some molds except with thorns, and the top feature may be reproductive in nature, although they bear a resemblance to algal blooms on Earth."

Before we had left the habitat, I asked Lexie to power up a drone, and follow our little excursion by remote. After we arrived at the wall of plants, I told Lexie to send the drone on ahead, over this plant gauntlet that was blocking our way. I asked her to pull in a close up of the trees on our monitors. What we saw was just as alien as what stood before us, yet there was something familiar about them. They appeared to be bamboo, except they were at least two and a half to three meters in diameter at the base of their trunks, and extended branchless, some eighty to ninety meters upward where they met a continuous canopy of green. The leaves were like palm fronds except with the branches completely entwined with one another creating a sea of green as far as the eye could see. The trees looked like the old atomic fission cooling towers with a Chia-pet growing out the top. Just like the plants that stood before us, I could not distinguish one individual plant from another when I looked into their canopy. Both species of alien plants appeared to be two gigantic individual organisms.

Sal excitedly continued, "Just looking at the trees on the monitor, I can't tell you much. Until I get a sample, I would guess they are bamboo-like in nature. However, the interconnecting canopy does suggest a lower life form as well. We just won't know until I can get a sample, and run some tests."

He talked fast and wanted to ramble on, but I interrupted, "Okay, why don't you and Pré get some samples of these? We will have to get a laser-saw and cut through the shrubbery later to get to the trees. I left Connor back at the shuttle, and I should go help him. Lexie, will you keep the drone watching over these two?"

I still couldn't shake that nagging feeling.

***

Two Sirius C cycles later, we gathered in the cafeteria at what would be the breakfast hour to discuss our findings from the previous day. Sal had hardly slept and had spent most of his days and nights in the lab analyzing the samples and data we had brought back from the shrubbery. The Spaniard looked exhausted but had a twinkle in his eyes as he filled us in on what he found.

"This is unlike anything I have ever seen!" He said, referring to the shrubbery. "These shrubs should not be this size! I can't figure out how they can be twice as tall as a man and lack the vascular cambium for the transport of nutrients. It just seems impossible! To call them a plant is stretching it too because, as I said, I can find no means of vascular transport. The only hypothesis I can come up with is that this thing is like a lichen back on Earth. The heads, although they appear to be reproductive structures, must be more than that. They must somehow synthesize a complex nutrient that they deliver to the stalks for growth. From what I can postulate, the synthesis is not unlike photosynthesis in our green plants, although I find no trace of chlorophyll being present, and no indication it was ever present. I think the stalks are able to extract basic minerals from the rock they are embedded in, and through simple diffusion, move the minerals to the tops. I imagine the stalks also provide support and protection. I just can't explain the size."

He continued, "When I ran the DNA, I found very similar genes and alleles to certain plants on Earth, except it's like someone took the DNA of several different varieties of Earth plants and scrambled them together. The plants are definitely organic in origin, and I dare say, if we were in a pinch, we might be able to consume the top brown layers. The stalks have certain similarities to ironwood back on Earth, and probably could not be digested. I did not find any toxins in concentrations large enough to harm a human in either the stalks or the heads. Also, there is no bacterial or viral growth on them that I can detect."

"So, you are saying we could eat these things?" I asked.

"I won't stake my reputation on it, because we are on another planet that follows different rules than Earth, but from what I am finding, yes, they could be a source of carbohydrates and proteins."

Connor looked at Sal a little skeptically, and asked, "So, we could pull one of those fruiting bodies off at the top, and take a bite?"

"I would probably irradiate them first. I am not a medical doctor, and I don't know what the combinations of the chemicals found in these organisms would do to a human body. I would imagine there would be some side effects, but I don't think it would kill you."

Pré looked up from Sal's reports, and said, "Looking at what you have here, I would agree with your findings. I see some concentrations of chemicals that could be hallucinogenic, but nothing that would kill a human with such small concentrations."

"Hallucinogenic?" I queried. "I'm already thinking I'm seeing and hearing things! I don't know about you guys, but I keep getting this strange vibe that we are constantly being watched, and I don't mean by Hailey."

"Thanks a bunch, Captain," Hailey piped in from above.

"Yes, I feel it too," interjected Pré.

The others looked at me and nodded in agreement. There was just something that was not quite right out there.

"I know we haven't gone beyond the shrubbery yet, but based on our initial tests, do you think humans could colonize this place? I know it's not paradise, but is it worth exploring some more, or do we pack up and go home?" I asked.

Sal interjected, "As far as agriculture, I'm not sure if anything will grow in this sand and rock. It is nutrient-poor, and water moves pretty quickly through the porous rock and leaches nutrients right out of the soil. It's just like Genie predicted back on the space station. She expected the rock to be volcanic in nature. Those lava tubes we saw with the waterfalls pouring out as we approached the land in the shuttle are solid evidence that she is correct. Remember, she said this planet would be young and immature, being only about three hundred million years old.

We would have to do some terraforming to grow grains and other food crops. Or, we can adapt, and cultivate and harvest what is already here. I think humans could survive here."

Pré added, "I am not finding any pathogens to speak of at this time. It is as if this place is sterile. Which I find highly unusual. There have to be decomposers, and yet, there is no sign that any of the plants are dead or dying. It is weird, but medically, yes, so far this place is livable."

"Connor? What would be your vote?" I asked.

"I think we are making judgments based on a small amount of data from a small area," Lexie countered, as she got up to go synthesize her breakfast, "I think we need to expand our explorations to the trees and to the oceans, collect more data, and then, come to some conclusion. I can pilot those drones over large areas of the ocean to check for any sea life, and I can map the forests with them for a possible land excursion."

"I agree with Lexie," Connor added, "that, plus the fact that we have stripped down the shuttle's engines, and will need some time to reassemble them, makes me think we should continue on here for a few more weeks. When we get the shuttle back to one-hundred percent, we can use it for some longer trips."

Lexie had just returned with her synthesized scrambled eggs from the food processor and was walking back to the table when she enlightened us on another more pertinent problem. "There is one more immediate problem that we need to address, mates. I've been watching the tides since we got here over a week ago, and I noticed the high tides seemed to be closer to the habs each day. Yesterday, I had Cailey run some numbers, and it appears they are increasing each day at an accelerated rate. So, Cailey and I shared the information with Hailey to confirm what we found, and it looks like we have about thirteen Sirius C days before the high tides will reach the habs. These habs are tough, but they were not meant to float together on water."

"Are you saying that we have about thirteen days before we have to move?" I asked.

"Why don't we just move them closer to the plant wall?" asked Sal.

"Here's the thing," she countered, "the lost time we use to move the habs again, and reconnect everything, will not equal the time added by moving them farther away from the water. We would actually lose a day or so."

"Why didn't we just put them as close to the shrubs as possible when we first landed?" he asked with a bit of disdain.

"You know why, Sal," I added. "We had to establish a safe perimeter around the habs just in case something came crashing out of those shrubs. So, you say we have thirteen days? Hailey, how long before the tides would completely wash away the habs?"

"Although the paths of the three suns are easy to extrapolate, the complex interplay of their gravitational fields is not. It is this interplay of gravities that is causing the fluctuations in the tides. In fifteen days, with an inherent error of plus or minus ten hours, the depth of the high tides will be sufficient to break the individual habitats loose from their moorings. Within one to two Sirius C solar years, the high tides will completely submerge this bay."

"Crap, ok people, you heard the ladies. We have to be out of here in thirteen days. I want all short-range tests completed in ten days. The long-range testing will have to be put on hold until, when and if, we return. Connor, how fast can we get that shuttle put back together?"

"If we both work on it, and nothing else, easily in six days."

"That gives me about four days to get the tests done that were assigned to Genie by ICoSTE. After breakfast, Pré and I will take the rover to the end of the bay to check out the rock walls. Genie was supposed to get some samples of rock from different places. Also, I want to see if the cliffs might be passable up to the plateaus above us. We are going to continue to work in pairs, so Sal and Lexie, why don't you see if you can cut through the shrubbery to get at the trees? Connor, you and Hailey should continue working on the shuttle if we plan to leave anytime in the near future. I will get back and help you as soon as I get those rocks. Let's all keep our comm-links open, just in case. Hailey, are you there?"

"Always ready to serve you, master," she quipped, "although, I do detect a low-pressure system moving towards us that could interfere with our communications as the clouds build in. Make sure you pack your raincoat."

"Ten thousand comedians out of work, and you're still trying to be funny," I came back. "Could you follow us with a couple of the drones if we get them ready in an hour? I am not taking any chances."

"That should not be a problem. Cailey and I will work together to make sure there is no lapse in communication should the cloud cover obscure my transmissions. And Captain?"

"Yes, Hailey?"

"I have been monitoring the orbital trajectories of the three stars and this planet. The stars are accelerating in their orbits. I predict they will cross paths in about eighty Earth years. Far sooner than we predicted. This planet should reach a triple perihelion in a time just slightly less than that."

"Is this going to be a problem for us if we colonize the planet?"

"I have insufficient data to extrapolate a hypothesis on the status of the planet that far in the future at this time."

"Understood." *Three stars crossing paths could not be a good thing for anyone or anything close to their gravitational fields.*

Sal jumped up, "I can't wait to get a look at those trees!"

***

As Pré and I rolled along in the rover, I was lost in thought as I kept looking for any sign of life other than the plant-like organisms. I absentmindedly looked for movement in the water, and then, in the shrubbery, as I contemplated our next moves.

It would be pointless to establish a colony here if there might be some catastrophic event during the next eighty years. Yet, if the

Earth is dying this might be our only hope. Maybe we could use this planet as a temporary place to stay as we searched for more habitable worlds. This place seems to have everything needed for life so far. I guess that's for the higher-ups to decide when we get this information back home. Home, what was really home? I moved so much, I don't think I ever felt like I was truly at home on the Earth, moon, or the space station. Maybe this was what I was meant to do. Maybe, I should stay here and hold down the colony until others arrive? I'm sure the rest of the crew would stay if I asked.

"Hey Pré, you want to park this bad boy up here on Lovers' Lane and make out?"

"What is that you are saying?" she asked. "What is this Lovers' Lane? And, just what does 'make out' mean?"

"C'mon Pré, you remember the old sit-coms on what they called 'television' in the last century. You know, we park at the top of a cliff overlooking the ocean, and kiss."

"Hah! Two weeks ago, you hated me and called me names. That is right, Hailey told me everything you said, and now you want to kiss me?"

"That Hailey, I will get her for this. Maybe I'll re-wire her voice circuitry so she talks like she sucked on some helium. But yes, I've kind of taken a shine to you, now that I've gotten to know you a little better."

"Captain Asil, you know so little about me. In my mind, your status has risen above a slime-crawling slug, but I am not too sure I am ready to exchange saliva with you yet."

"Yet, you said yet. So, I see you like me as well."

"Keep your hopes up, Captain. There are only two available men on this mission, so you at least have a fifty-percent chance of being one of them I would choose if we decided to stay."

"Not sure what that means, but I'll take it!"

After about two hours, we approached the towering cliff wall at the end of the bay, I could see nothing but a sheer rock face. The black glass-like obsidian shone like fine black china as I searched for any outcroppings or handholds on which we could climb. There was no pass visible through which the rover could possibly be driven up to the plateau above. If we were going up there, we would have to climb or fly. The plant-like shrubs grew all the way to the cliff wall, and, in fact, were embedded in the walls themselves creating an impenetrable barrier to the trees about a kilometer beyond.

As we stared out the windshield of the rover, I said, "It doesn't look good for driving or climbing to the top. At least we can send the drone up to get a closer look."

Pré looked at me and asked, "I did some climbing in the Swiss Alps, back on Earth. Is there anything we can use as pitons to wedge into the wall?"

"We have some, but not enough to cover this amount of surface. Even if we had more pitons, it would take days to scale that behemoth. Well, at least I can get some samples here at the base of the cliffs."

Pré grabbed the handheld remote for the drone, "I can take some close-up video of the rock face. Maybe we can get a look into those lava pipes that are all over it. Then, I will take it up to the top, and get some footage of the plateau up-close as well."

Just as we finished collecting samples, and video-recording, the rain began to fall. We grabbed our equipment and headed back to the rover. I looked out over the vast bay. I could just see the storm front churning up the ocean beyond the edges of the cliff.

"I think we should get back before the heavy stuff falls, who knows how violent it gets out here."

"Keep going. I do not think the heavy stuff is going to fall for a while yet." Great, now I'm quoting old golf comedies!

I think Pré was in agreement as I noticed she picked up her pace back to the rover.

When we reached the rover and climbed in, the skies opened up. The pouring rain obscured our vision as we headed back toward the habs, and it made it difficult to keep the rover's wheels on the hard surface. I had a feeling if we hit soft sand, the thing would bury up to its chassis. We would spend a large amount of time we didn't have digging it out or abandoning it altogether.

With Pré closely watching the seaside wheels, we inched homeward.

As we traveled, I called Sal on the comm-link to see how it was going. "Sal, any luck getting to the trees? It is raining hard here, and we are heading back. We did manage to get some samples, and have some good close-up footage of some of the lava vents."

Sal's voice crackled through the comm-link, "We have been cutting for over two hours now, and have just been able to get through about twenty sets of stalks. I was right, this stuff is like ironwood, but maybe even harder. At this rate, we will be lucky to get through the shrub layer in a week or two. The laser-cutter isn't meant to stay powered-up for hours at a time. It overheats after about fifteen minutes, and then we have to let it cool for about a half-hour. We will not reach the trees in the time we have left. Any chance we can climb the cliff to them?"

"Not on the face we saw, but tomorrow we will take the rover to the other end of the bay, and check out that wall. We may have to abandon our tree samples all together, but let's keep our hopes up that there is a way out of this bay. At least we have some good footage of them. Are you two going to be alright to walk back in this?"

"The rain has just started to fall harder here, I can still see the habs, so I think we should be alright. I think we can make it back in less than an hour."

"Good, let's meet for some food after we get cleaned up, and talk about tomorrow's plan of attack. Connor, how's work going on the shuttle?"

"I have reassembled the left ion thruster and will test it out tomorrow. I should be able to get to work on the right one tomorrow as well. After that, I will need your help to reattach them to the fusion power generators."

"That sounds good. Let's get back and out of these wet suits, and get this all planned out over some food. If you didn't hear, we will have our daily update in about two hours."

"I'll be there with a Guinness smile on."

As we pulled the rover close to habs, I looked out toward the ocean. I could just make out what appeared to be a green glow just offshore to the north of the habs.

"Do you see this, guys and girls?" I asked. "Out on the ocean, that green light?"

Sal's voice came online, "I saw it as I walked back when the suns set. I believe it has to be bioluminescent algae of some sort."

"Kind of eerie," I added. "Let's see if we can somehow get a sample. But that will be a job for another day, I am exhausted."

***

The next morning as I awoke, I could hear the rain still pounding on the hab's fabric walls. The twenty-three layers of Clearsteel™, electrical conduits, cooling and heating conduits, gas tubes, and other synthesized materials, could easily keep out a few hundred gallons of water. They just couldn't float on it when they were all interconnected into a large living colony.

My mind switched to our plans for the day. The trip to the other cliff face would take longer since we were closer to the north end of the bay, and we would be heading south today. The rain shouldn't be a problem for the rover if I could just keep the wheels on the hard surfaces. The rover's six balloon wheels should even be able to claw their way through the wet sand with ease, but I'm not going to take any chances. I saw what quicksand could do in those old explorer movies! So maybe they weren't real, but how much more unreal could our situation get? We were on an alien planet surrounded by alien plant-like things that were obviously protecting something. There are gigantic unclimbable rock faces pocked with lava caves, that who-knows-what, were watching us out of, to our north and south; a giant bay, probably loaded with cold-blooded, human-eating sea serpents, leading to a nasty ocean to our east; and that impenetrable gauntlet, with its hidden mysterious critters, to our west. And now, we have less than two weeks to get out of this bay! I supposed I was letting my imagination run wild a bit. Maybe it was the rain that had me still in bed, just thinking.

I guess we could search for another landing site once we get the shuttle running, but I got the feeling everyone wanted to pack up and go home. I know I wanted that for Genie.

***

The trip to the south rock face was similar to the trip to the north with three major exceptions, Sal had joined Pré and me, it was raining hard, and the duration was twice as long. When the rover finally crawled to the coal-black base of the towering cliff, I parked the rover within a short walk of the cliff face.

It was then, as I looked out the windshield, heavily covered in rain so that it distorted any possible view, that I noticed something different about the face. As the wipers alternated their to-and-fro movement and cleared a section of the windshield that they had just passed, I could barely make out a jagged, diagonal crack on the rock face. The crack appeared to run up at about a thirty-degree angle to the base. It looked like it ran the entire distance from the base to the apex of the cliff.

"Pré, Sal, do you see that narrow crack on the rock face?" I asked. Am I imagining it, or does it look like the entire cliff has shifted at that point? Pré, can you work your magic with the drone again, and get a close-up before we go out there?"

As she moved the drone closer, the image on the screen cleared enough to show us that there was definitely a crack. It appeared as if the entire section above the crack had shifted about a meter to the south, while the bottom section had stayed intact, and hadn't moved. This created an outcropping that looked just like a path leading to the top of the cliff.

"That must have been one hell-of-an earthquake," shouted Sal excitedly. "I'll bet the entire crust moved with that one."

"That looks like our ticket to the trees, my European comrades," I said. "Anyone up for a bit of a hike?"

"Judging from this distance, I would say that it is going to take about eight to ten hours to get to the top. If we lug a lot of equipment with us, it could take up to twelve," interrupted Pré. "By the time we go up, get some tree samples, and come back down, we will have consumed almost two days' time. With Connor expecting your help with the shuttle Asil, do we have that kind of time?"

"That would still give us a leeway of at least a day or so before the water comes up," I said. "It does cut into the three-day buffer that I created, but we should still be fine."

"Then it is settled," Sal interjected excitedly, "we go to the trees!"

"Connor, Lexie, and Hailey?" I called on the rover's comm-link. "Did you guys hear our conversation. We are going up the cliff wall. If we came back to get you, we would waste another day, so we are trekking this one on our own. We will be back in a couple of days. Lexie, if you can help Connor with any of the heavy lifting, that would be a great help."

"Thanks, Asil for letting us know. Although, you know, I am watching you," came Lexie's voice through the rover's comm-link.

"You're the reason I have this eerie feeling of being watched," I laughed. "Pré will turn over the controls of the drone to you. Will you keep it on us in case we run into something unforeseen?"

Connor chimed in, "You guys be careful, Lexie and I cannot fly the shuttle if we need to get out of here in a hurry, and it would be a very long walk to get to you."

As we gathered equipment from inside the rover, Pré tapped me on the shoulder. Sal was already outside organizing his plant sampling equipment. She motioned for me to take off my helmet and click off our comm-links.

"Asil, do you find it odd that there appears to be a clear-cut path out of this place?"

"What are you saying?" I asked. "That, this is not a natural phenomenon; that some alien lifeform carved a path up the cliff?"

"I just think it is odd that on every other attempt we have made to get to the top of the plateau, we have been stopped dead in our tracks. We get here, and voilà, clear sailing to the top. It is as if we are being guided this way."

"We are not there yet, my beautiful, young doctor. We still have quite a hike ahead of us. Let's get our helmets back on, and get this gear out to Sal before the crazy Spaniard takes off on his own."

As we started up the rock ledge created by the tectonic movement, the path was wide enough for us to walk with our shoulders square to the path and not bump the side of the cliff face, even carrying some bulky equipment. We had packed gear for a night in one of the lava tubes and made sure our suits could sustain us for a longer period of time than we had expected to be gone, just in case. As we trudged past lava tube after lava tube, I couldn't help but wonder if something was going to reach out and grab us as we passed by. The absolute darkness of each hole gave us no clue as to what they might contain. The lights on our suits could barely penetrate the first few meters of each as we stopped and rested by them on our journey upwards.

Lexie had sent the drone further on up ahead of us to make sure there were no obstacles in our path. After about five hours of steady hiking and quiet conversation, Lexie reported that the drone showed her that our path was narrowing a bit. As we approached the sixth hour of our climb, the path had narrowed to the point where the equipment that we carried which extended beyond our shoulders would bump the rock face from time to time. I didn't mind this much since the alternative in the other direction was quite a fall.

The hours passed as we dragged ourselves up the incline. The heavy rain continued to batter our suits, and the wind had picked up, threatening to sweep us off our precarious perch. My legs were aching with shooting pains from my hip joints down to my ankle joints. My steps had become shorter, and my breaths longer. I looked at Pré, her body language told me she was still fresh. Her strides were long and her breathing was normal. This girl was a salad bowl of pleasant surprises. Sal, on the other hand, was struggling. He was worse off than I was. His breathing was labored, and I could tell by the way he carried himself, he was nearing fatigue.

"Why don't we find a little bigger lava tube, and crawl in for a rest?" I asked. "It looks like we are about an hour or two from the top, but I am beat! What about you Sal?"

"I could go on, Captain, but if you need a rest, I am willing to stop."

"If you two men need a break, then I shall stop for a rest as well," commented Pré.

I called Lexie on the comm-link, "Lexie do you think you could fly that drone into one of these lava tubes, and look for a place that can house three to rest for a few hours? Preferably, one that is horizontal, and has a hot shower and mini-bar? I'd hate to go on a surprise, death-defying water slide if we entered a vertical tube."

"Will do Asil," she shot back.

After about fifteen more minutes of battling the elements, Lexie came back online, "Captain, about one hundred meters up, there is a rather large hole in the wall. When I flew in a few meters with the drone's lights on, I could see it extended horizontally for at least fifty meters or so before it curved downward. That should be a good place to rest."

"Thanks, Lexie, you are a lifesaver. And, I mean in the good way, not the candy."

"You are welcome, and have a good evening, team."

When we reached the lava tube, it was just as Lexie had said. Sal and I quickly told our suits to go into sleep mode. As the suits slowly inflated just enough to provide a soft cushion for lying on the hard rock surface, I tapped into the blue-nutrient juice stores using the sipping straw that ran by my left ear to my jaw just to the tip of my lips on the inside of the helmet. I imagined it tasted like a creamy tomato basil soup, and sure enough, that is exactly what my brain told me I was tasting. After washing it down with some water, I looked across at Sal. His headlamp was already out, and from the way his chest rose and fell, I could tell he was already in a deep sleep. I glanced over at Pré. She must have been watching or reading something on her helmet monitor because the light flickered off her face from inside her helmet.

I asked the mini-computer for a secure connection to her suit, and then asked into the comm-link, "You wouldn't want to come over here and tuck me in, would you? Or better yet, sing 'Soft Kitty' to me?"

I could see that she smiled by the light that reflected off her face from her suit monitor.

"Captain Asil, just because I have saved your life, does not mean that I like you now."

"I'm growing on you, aren't I?" I asked.

"Like the fungus, Tinea pedis, grows on a big toe," she answered slyly.

I could tell there was a hint of playfulness now in her voice. Somehow, this woman that I loathed three weeks ago, had won me over. I was almost willing to pursue her affection at the cost of another broken heart. *Another long story, when I wore a younger man's clothes.* Maybe, it was the loneliness or the impending doom that we faced, but somehow, I knew, I just might strive for this woman's affection.

I smiled in my suit, "Goodnight, Doctor."

"*Bonne nuit, Capitaine,*" she replied.

***

The next morning, refreshed and full of energy, we set out towards our destination. After about a four-kilometer hike upwards, the ledge had narrowed to only about one hundred centimeters. We had to take the packs off our backs and hold them out in front of us as we climbed. After another hour passed, the ledge became even narrower, and we were now forced to turn and face the wall as we walked sideways toward the apex, now less than a kilometer away.

Another five hundred meters up, we ran into a showstopper. Lexie had warned us that the ledge narrowed to just about ten centimeters for about twenty meters, then it widened again after that. From the image on our monitors, it looked like we would have about the width of our feet to slide sideways across. However, as we came to the narrowing, the ledge was narrower than we thought. If we could get a handhold somewhere, we might be able to shimmy across on the balls of our feet. It looked like something had hit the ledge and dislodged a large chunk of it. There was no way we could continue forward without some help.

I took the lead, and as we started across, I looked for some small lava vents that we could use as places to grasp as we shifted our weight from foot to foot across the schism. There were plenty, but none at consistent distances to give us a way to move easily across.

"If I could just get to my utility belt," I said.

"Holy death-defying leaps, Caped Wonder, if we fall, we fall to a bone-crushing death! "Could be worse, My-Fine-Feathered-Friend. We could have forgotten to put a nickel in the meter." C'mon Hailey! At a time like this? You have got to be kidding!

I reached into my utility belt, and pulled out my "Bat-grappling gun". Really, it was just a one-shot piton launcher with a thin Clearsteel™ line attached. There was just a small curve in the path ahead that created a tiny outcropping of rock about twenty-five meters ahead, and I thought if I could embed the piton into that rock, and somehow wedge it on this end, we could use it as a handhold to guide us across the opening. I took careful aim and fired. The kickback nearly threw me off the cliff, but I regained my balance and looked to see I had hit exactly where I was aiming. Now if I could just tie this tightly onto something.

Sal tapped my arm, "Use mine," he said as he handed me his piton launcher. Every suit's utility belt had at least one of these piton launchers. As Sal and Pré braced tightly against me, I shot Sal's piton into the cliff face directly in front of me. The force nearly knocked all three of us backward off the cliff. One of Pré's feet slipped from the edge, and the other began to follow it quickly. Just as she was about to fall thousands of meters to sure death, I reflexively grabbed her arm in an instant as she began to slide down the face of the dark rock wall. I hung on tight and slung her body upwards like an acrobat pulling up his swinging partner from a trapeze swing. Sal reached out and grabbed her other arm that was flailing in the breeze, and we pulled her back onto the ledge.

"Thank you," was all she managed to squeak out.

As I quickly tied off the line to the newly-embedded piton, Hailey's voice came on-line. "What is going on down there? Pré's heart is beating like a drum in a hula dance!"

"Just a minor slip," I said. "We are all fine now." I looked at Pré, her face was as white as her suit.

"Maybe we should tether up for this part," I said reassuringly.

We took a few minutes to hook our tether lines together and gather our composure before we inched across the narrow ledge, one at a time, without incident.

As our climb approached the plateau, I could see over the cliff wall now. The surface of the plateau appeared to be the same hard black rock that we had been climbing on for the past day. The tree line was set about three hundred meters back from the cliff face. I thought this was strange that the trees were not growing out to the edge of the cliff like at the northern end of the bay. When we reached the top, I grabbed some tools and collected a sample of the rock surface before we started toward the trees.

Sal took the lead and was walking fast when he turned to me and said, "Asil, if we have time, I would like to get a bore sample from one of the larger ones. I'd like to see if there are rings, and possibly get an idea of the age of this forest."

"I think we will have time, tree doctor," I said cheerfully, relieved we were on flat ground again. After that tumultuous journey, I was happy we were still together and in one piece.

"Look at the ocean!" Pré said excitedly, stopping us dead in our tracks.

Sal and I turned around to see the view that she was gushing about. For as far as the eye could see, there was water. But not calm water. Gigantic waves rolled toward the cliff faces, and bashed the rock with tremendous force, spraying water hundreds of meters into the air. Wave after wave rolled across the surface of the grayish-blue sea. It was impossible to estimate their height, but I guessed maybe fifty to seventy meters high on average. Now and then, a rogue wave would pass that would be twice the size of the others. One of those monsters had to be what almost swamped us. I could only speculate at the source of those massive walls of water. I didn't think wind could blow that hard to create such an enormous column of water. The Earth had nothing like this. The sky above the rolling water was filled with clouds, very dark gray and menacing, to the south, and then lightening to a softer white as they approached the bay. I noticed the rain had stopped falling for the time being, and two of the three suns appeared as bright silhouettes behind a white sheet, as they were obscured by the thick cloud layer. I checked the outside temperature on my helmet monitor. It read a balmy forty-degrees Celsius, even at this altitude. I then checked the hygrometer, and the relative humidity was one hundred percent. Hot and humid, this place would be difficult to live in without some sort of regulation.

We stood in silence for about five minutes watching in awe at the tremendous forces this planet could produce. Then I turned, and took about ten more steps, passing Sal. Pré had followed and was a few steps behind me when the ground before me began to vibrate, and in the next millisecond, I was falling! My heart rate shot through the roof as adrenaline poured into my cells! My suit alarm exploded in my ears, as the suit's accelerometers and impact sensors detected I was in freefall and about to collide with some fast-approaching instant stop! My monitor screamed impact was imminent and the airbags were about to fire! Then I heard a tremendous CRACK! And everything went dark.

CHAPTER 13: REALIZATION

As I tumbled ass-over-beak into the pitch-black abyss, I realized I was conscious. I had not been knocked out. I then realized everything was dark. My helmet monitor was out, and the air inside my suit was getting warmer. My suit was relaxing after it hardened on impact. I must have hit an outcropping or something. It must have struck my power supply, and now my suit was dead. All this went through my mind in less than a second.

"Holy shit! My airbags didn't deploy!" I thought.

As I continued to somersault toward certain death, my emergency training kicked in. I reached with my right hand down to my utility belt and felt around on my right hip. The auxiliary power supply was still attached! I immediately grabbed the cord and pulled.

"Now where the hell is that patch-in outlet on this suit? Oh ya, right breast!"

I pulled the cord toward my right nipple and inserted the plug into my suit's jack. A blue light flashed on in my helmet indicating I was on auxiliary! I had power!

"Fwooomp!" The airbags deployed! I could not see anything in this blackness, but I felt the huge blue bags press against my faceplate and my back. I must have looked like a huge blueberry as I plummeted into the unknown.

As I fell, time seemed to slow down. I called into my comm-link, "Falling! Airbags deployed! Track my beacon!" There was no answer. I knew that auxiliary power could only push a signal a short distance, fifty meters at the most, but I talked anyway.

"Hailey, Pré, Sal, anyone there?" Still no answer.

It seemed like I was falling for minutes, but I knew only seconds had passed. *Thank you, ICoSTE, for those tedious hours of emergency suit drills we had to practice again and again. Now if I can just find somewhere soft to land.*

I fired my suit thrusters trying to slow my fall. Of course, they were meant for operation in space and did little. They did manage to slow my rotation. I aligned my body for impact. I knew the suit would harden again on impact, but even then, if I ended with the pencil dive, I would drive my femurs through my chest. *That would hurt a lot!*

"Sploosh!" I hit water, the force of the fall carrying me several meters deep. The airbags held and slowed my descent into the blue abyss. Just as their buoyancy was about to reverse my direction, and shoot me back to the surface, I felt a trickle of something on the back of my neck. A bubbling noise began, and water spurted onto the back of my head. Then a steady flow began to fill my helmet. The seal must have released when I lost power. The back-up power is supposed to reseal the suit, but something must be wrong!

As I shot to the surface, terror reigned in my brain. *"I'm going to drown in my own helmet!* As my blueberry-encased body burst onto the surface, I tried to hold my breath. Maybe I could pry my helmet off!

I could raise my arms up by my sides, and grab the helmet, but I couldn't get at, and trigger the three manual overrides with the airbags deployed! I thought, *"They didn't think of this scenario at ICoSTE!"*

Water had filled my helmet to eye level, and I could not hold my breath any longer with my heart racing and my adrenaline-filled blood pumping nutrients to my cells begging for oxygen! I gulped in one swallow, then two, of the salty brine as my brain forced me to breathe.

Just as panic set in, something grabbed my leg, and began to pull! I fought vehemently! Thrashing my arms and legs as violently as I could hoping to strike whatever held me. The blue light in my helmet filtered through the water as I wildly tried to scan the blackness outside to see what held me! I gulped in more water, burning as much energy as I could muster in my futile attempt to escape the clutches of my certain demise; and then, a peaceful calm began to overtake my thoughts. I thought I saw a small light in the distance. It appeared to cast a shadow on something. I could just make out the outline of a ...; then, this time, everything did go dark.

Mommy says, every time a bell rings, an angel gets her wings.

My bell had definitely been rung. Then my ears popped! As I came back to my senses, I vomited up water. I could hear someone calling my name, "Asil! Asil! Please! Dammit!"

"Mom? Mom? Is that you? I did eat my peas! Please mom, can I have dessert? Please, mom, can I have more?" my mind scrolled.

As I opened my eyes, there, floating in front of me was an angel. She had me with two hands by the front of my suit. I thought, *"She is carrying me to heaven."* She was saying something as she pulled on me.

"Don't you die, you bastard! Don't you die! You didn't bring us all this way just to die!"

Reality kicked in. It was Pré. It really was an angel. She had tears streaming down her cheeks as she choked out, "You can't leave me now! I need you." She had pulled me in close and was swimming backward to where she had jettisoned her still-filled airbags.

"I knew you liked me," I said, as I coughed up some more water.

"Just shut up and breath," she grimaced, as she choked back tears.

"Thank you," I said as tears now began to well in my eyes, "I need you too."

I reached out and wrapped my arms around her, resting my head against her chest. I was exhausted.

When we reached her airbags, she pulled me onto one. I rode on top of it much like a person tubing down a river on a warm summer's day.

I then realized my helmet was off! So was hers!

"Our helmets!" I spat out.

"I know," she said, "but we are breathing. And if we turn green with purple polka dots, and grow a third arm in the future due to something in the air, then we die together."

"But how?" I asked.

"You did not fall alone," she said. "Just as the ground gave way under you, it fell out from under me as well. You must have hit something as we fell, and damaged your suit. When I hit the water and returned to the surface, I detached my airbags. I searched for you with my helmet lamp. I finally saw you splashing wildly about thirty meters from me. I tried to talk to you with the comm-link, but you did not reply, so I swam over to you and grabbed you. You tried to fight me, and I realized you were in distress. I grabbed the knife from the utility belt and punctured your airbag. You went limp, so I manually removed your helmet. I saw you weren't breathing so, I took off my helmet, and did what I had to, to save you."

"You pressed your lips against mine?" I asked with a sheepish grin.

"I am a doctor, I do what I have to, to save lives," she said with a hint of warmth in her voice.

"We really have got to quit meeting like this," I said with a smile. "Thank you again."

She had climbed on the other half of her airbag that she had tethered to mine, and was floating much the same way I was.

"Where are we?" I asked.

"I think we are in an underground lake that formed inside a lava tube. It must be very large because when I shine my helmet light in any direction, I cannot see any walls. If you look up, you can just see light through the opening we created. It's that little pin-hole up to your left."

When I looked up, I could just make out a tiny speck of light somewhere way above.

"Have you been able to contact Sal?" I asked.

"No," she said, "I do not think he fell with us. At least I can not see his helmet light anywhere, or detect his emergency beacon with my helmet."

"Our helmets!" I breathed loudly.

"Do not worry, I clipped them to my utility belt when I took them off."

I didn't realize she had been using her helmet light to illuminate the area between us. She pointed the helmet toward the water, and I saw the dim white outline from my helmet as it floated alongside her bag.

"You must have been on auxiliary," she said. "I saw the blue light as I pulled your helmet off."

"Yes, so all I can do now is communicate with your helmet. I should still have basic life support functions as well. Have you tried to call the others?"

"Yes, as I swam to you, I sent out the distress code. I have had no response."

"It doesn't look like they can get to us down here. There is no rope long enough to reach us from the hole, even if they tied all the ropes together. We are going to have to find another way out."

"Captain, is it me? Or are we moving?"

I noticed it then too. Our airbag rafts were definitely being pulled along by some unseen force.

KABOOM! Something hit the water not more than fifteen meters to our left!

I practically jumped out my suit as the resulting splash wave soaked us!

Pré immediately shined her light to where the water had erupted, and I just caught a glimpse of something metallic sinking into the water. Then it was gone; headed to Davy Jones' Locker, or whoever's locker was at the bottom of this alien, forsaken lake.

"A drone?" Pré asked as she climbed back on her raft. I didn't realize she had fallen off in all the excitement.

"I'll bet the signal can't penetrate these walls," I said. "I suppose they sent a drone to search for us, but it lost signal when it entered the cavern."

"So, we truly are on our own," Pré said a little dejectedly.

"Keep trying to raise someone on your comm-link," I added hopefully, "maybe the walls thin out, and we can eventually pick up a signal."

***

We drifted for hours in the quiet, dark, warm water ever wondering what swam beneath us. We passed the time talking about our lives, our parents, our wishes, our dreams, and any other topic we could think of to kill time. As we talked, I realized this woman had dedicated her life to one of service to others. She had reached her position of incredible acclaim only through hard work, undeniable determination, and selflessness. Comparing her life to my haphazard, playboy past, I started to feel like I was not worthy of her attention. She was truly a better person than I was or hoped to ever be.

We had assessed our situation in the first hour and decided we had enough food stores in our suits for several days. Fresh water, however, might pose a problem if my suit could not pull it from the air. The suits were designed to process both oxygen and water from the air if the gas and vapor were available. Although they were designed for space, the suits also had the bonus benefit of being a mobile habitat if conditions in a planet environment were not suitable for human survival. Our biggest problem now was how we were going to return to the hab.

Nothing disturbed the smooth-as-glass surface as we floated along. Time passed without malice. After endless hours of drifting, I thought I saw a small flicker of light in the distance.

"Do you see that?" I asked.

"What?" Pré asked as she awoke from a short nap. I had had a long nap about two hours earlier.

"There, in the distance, straight ahead," I said as I touched her cheek, and turned her head gently to the spot where I saw it flicker.

I didn't realize what I had done until I felt the electricity flow through my entire body as I felt the touch of her skin. This was the first time we had touched without the chaos of attempting to save one another's life. She must have felt it too, because she pressed her cheek gently against my gloved fingers, looked deeply into my eyes, and then pulled her head away.

"Yes," she said, "I see it, but what is it?"

"I'm not sure, but I'm guessing it's our way out. This lava tube has got to end somewhere."

As we drifted closer to the light, it became evident that the light was actually sunlight that was filtering in from the opening of the lava tube in which we were floating. It dawned on me then, that we must have fallen into the lake during high tide, and the current was simply the water moving back toward the ocean. Another explanation popped into my head. What if we were in one of the elevated lava tubes? We could actually be in runoff rainwater. This meant we might be exiting in a hurry down through a waterfall. I wished to believe in my first hypothesis since the water we were in was definitely salt water; and, I didn't really feel like crashing down into a chaotic ocean from a high elevation riding on nothing but Baymax, the puffed-up robot from Big Hero Six.

The closer we came to the opening, the greater our velocity increased. The current was not swift by any means, but I could easily spin us in a circle simply by dragging a foot in the water. As we neared the opening, I noticed it was quite large, a fact that didn't go unnoticed by Pré.

"We shouldn't accelerate too much more," she said, "the Venturi Effect should be minimal with this size of an opening."

I think she was just trying to reassure me that we weren't about to smash into a pile of rock fifty meters below our current elevation.

"Let's hope your right," I said as our floating life raft was cast from the tube entrance. We did drop, but only about three meters as a wave receded from the cliff face. The surf churned against the rocky cliff wall as an incoming wave rolled over the outgoing current. The current here was stronger than in the tube. It reminded me of rip currents back on Earth. It immediately began to carry us out onto the vast ocean. I sensed our imminent danger, and yelled at Pré, "We're headed out to sea!"

Before she could answer, I caught a glimpse of a small spit that jutted out a short way from the shoreline about a hundred meters down-shore from where we had entered the sea. I'm sure it was only above water during low tide, but it was there. I knew we couldn't swim against such a stiff current, so I quickly pulled open the Velcro on the knife pouch on my utility belt, grabbed the knife, and cut a small slit in my airbag just below the waterline. I lowered myself in the water and used my body as a human rudder to guide us toward the spit as the expelled air pushed against the water. It didn't work! The current was too strong. I reached over toward Pré and jammed the knife into her airbag. She saw what I was doing and lowered her body into the water as well. The drag was just too great! We continued to drift away from shore! I screamed at her to get back on the bag, as I grabbed both bags, one in each hand, and pulled them down to create more propulsion. I kicked my legs like an Olympic swimmer to bolster our force. It worked!

I steered our make-shift motorboat toward the spit. About ten meters from land, the air in the bag was depleted so much that its force no longer pushed us forward. I untethered my helmet, slapped it on my head; put my head down like a bull, and began to swim for it. Pré followed suit, and we swam hard against the current to cover that last little bit of water. What should have been a short half-minute swim ended up being a five-minute all-out exertion against the unrelenting pull of the current. We made it to shore huffing and puffing like an Ironman triathlete after the 3.86-kilometer swim segment. I crawled onto the black sand, popped off my helmet, and lay there panting, just trying to regain my breath, Pré crawled over, took off her own helmet, and put her head on my abdomen.

We must have dozed off because when I opened my eyes—in what I thought was just a few minutes later—I noticed the water on the spit had already risen, and my legs were immersed up to my calves.

Pré's helmet buzzed liked crazy! "Pré, are you there? Pré, are you there?" It was Lexie! Pré grabbed her helmet and snapped it on. I did the same, although I knew I would only hear her voice. I couldn't possibly pull in the signal from Lexie that far away.

"You picked up my beacon?" I heard Pré ask. "I love you!" She said into her comm-link. "Yes! Yes! Ok!"

"What's she saying?" I asked Pré with my comm-link.

"They had been scouring the cliff wall with the last two drones, looking for us, when they picked up my distress beacon. They asked if we were alright, then said a drone was on the way."

"Ask them when the shuttle might be ready? They can come and pick us up. I know with Hailey's help, they could navigate it a short distance. They could lower the grappling hook, and hoist us into the cargo hold."

Pré was all smiles, as she began talking again to Lexie. I saw her nod inside her helmet as she said, "Uh-huh. Yes, okay. I will ask him. Okay, yes, I will tell him."

She looked at me and said, "Connor wants to know how you detached the power sensor unit from the ion thrusters. He is having a tough time with the wiring. Also, Sal just made it back to the hab with the rover. He says he is incredibly happy we are okay. He says, 'First we were there, then we were not there!' He immediately called the hab, and then headed back down the ledge. He says he might have burned up the rover's engine, he was traveling so fast."

"Tell him that's just fine. He will have to help Connor lift the big parts to reattach them to the engines. I can help Connor with the wiring if I can use your helmet."

She handed me her helmet. We both knew if we couldn't get the shuttle here before the high tide returned, we were going to be washed out to sea or our bodies battered against the cliff wall.

It was another race against time, only this time we did not have the luxury of days. We had but a few hours. The water was already rising slowly as I donned her helmet.

***

The drone arrived in less than two hours as Connor and I frantically conversed. I could now use my helmet to transmit signals to the drone. The drone could then relay my messages back to Connor. I gave Pré her helmet back. She was constantly scanning the churning sea for any sign of life, or rogue waves.

I continued my conversation with Connor. "Use the robotic arm to hoist it back onto the engine," I said. "Have Sal hold it in place while you quick-weld the bolts back in place." Once you do that, here is the wiring sequence..." As I recalled the exact reconnection of the myriad of wires from somewhere in my brain that could only be a result of my enhanced brain function, I looked over at Pré. She had a troubled look on her face, and I knew why. Our little black spit that originally had an area of about a thousand square meters was down to about half that size. The water was rising, and it would be a close call with the shuttle work being completed, and then flying it out here to get us.

Luckily for us, the weather was holding, and there was no rain in sight. I didn't realize how hot and sticky it really was here until I had my helmet off for a short period of time. I also didn't realize how noisy it was out here. Below the sounds of the surf, there was a constant, low-pitched growling noise. It was as if this planet was an angry lion, that was constantly uttering a warning growl for us to stay away. I'm not sure what was making that noise, but I knew it couldn't be anything good.

Our work progressed slowly and the water continued to rise. As the hours passed, our land disappeared.

When Connor finally said, "That's it!", we were standing in water up to mid-thigh with our backs against the cliff wall. The waves had started to roll in again, at first gently, and now hard enough so we had to brace ourselves so that we did not get knocked backward into the sheer cliff face.

"Hailey's running the engine firing sequence right now!" Connor said excitedly into the comm-link. We should be there in less than two hours!"

Pré looked at me, and I looked at her. We both knew we didn't have two hours. We might have a lot less if one of those rogue waves happened upon us.

I scoured the cliff wall looking for anything we might be able to get a perch on. It was smooth as glass, save for the lava tube openings that pocked its surface.

"If we could just climb to one of those openings. We might be able to wait a while longer for them to get here," I said to her.

She looked at me sadly, "I am sorry Asil, I do not have any ideas." Then she broke into a big smile! "I still have my piton in my utility belt! Remember, you and Sal used yours, but we did not need mine!"

Cheers erupted in my ears! The crew had been listening the whole time.

"We're coming to get you guys," Lexie said, "hang tough!"

"You do the honors," Pré said, and she handed me her piton launcher. About ten meters above us, and just off to our left, was a hole that looked big enough for both of us to stand in. I waded back out onto the spit to get a better angle at a spot just above the opening. Pré joined me and grabbed me tight to brace me against the waves as I aimed the little launcher. Wave after wave pushed against our torsos as we tried to steady ourselves. I knew I had only one shot at this. The water had risen to about waist height as I pulled the trigger.

POOM! The piton shot out, knocking us both backward. A wave hit us while we were off-balance and knocked us into the water. The rope went slack.

Crap! I missed.

As I pulled my head above the water surface and looked up, there it was! That sweet little piece of incredible steel had embedded in the rock just about ten centimeters off where I had aimed, but it was there and holding fast in the glass-like surface.

"*Yes! Yes! Yes!*" I thought as I pulled on the rope. Pré still held tightly around my waist, as we walked and waded carefully back to the cliff wall. It would be no easy task climbing vertically up a ninety-degree plate of glass on just a thin rope, but what was the alternative? *Thank heavens, we wore the right boots!*

As I hoisted Pré on my shoulders and braced my body against the dark obsidian, the wind picked up even more. The tide had risen to my chest when I pushed her upwards off my shoulders as she began to climb. She struggled mightily as she slowly pulled herself toward the opening. The surf did not do her any favors as it crashed against the rock. If only the wind weren't so strong, and the current wasn't pulling our bodies away down the shore, we could wait and float our way to the opening.

"Asil, I cannot make it!" she screamed over the roar of the crashing waves. She had climbed to within a meter of the hole but had stopped, the rope wrapped around her waist and wrist. I could see the exhaustion on her face. "I'm sorry."

"Hang on!" I hollered. "Catch your breath! Fire your thrusters! Use the waves!"

As the next wave washed against her, she dropped a leg and fired a blast of hot air into the oncoming wall of water. At the same time, she pulled hard, and with a herculin effort, thrust her body toward the opening. Then she disappeared. She had made it! The rope went slack. I grabbed it and wrapped it in a climber's knot around my legs and waist. A moment later her head poked out of the hole, and she grabbed the rope with both hands.

"Let us do this!" She called over the roar.

With her pulling from the top, and me tugging from the bottom, I hoisted my body out of the water and planted my feet firmly against the cliff wall. Each wave tried to knock me off my perch as I put one foot in front of the other. The wind slapped the water against my back making each step upward a tumultuous balancing act. Twice, the waves and wind spun me and slapped my body against the rock face just hard enough to hurt, but not hard enough to force the Clearsteel™ to become rigid. I grunted and pulled. Pré grunted and pulled. My arms ached. My legs ached. *Wasn't there something in my utility belt to finish this?* I reached another arm-length up the rope and felt a strong arm grab my elbow.

"Fire your thrusters now!" Another hand grabbed my other

arm as I pushed upward with one leg. I dropped my other leg into the water and pointed my toes downward firing the hot gas into the water as another wave slammed into me. The next second, I found myself lying face down on a small, black horizontal floor at the base of the volcanic vent. Pré was draped across my back breathing hard.

"We cannot stay here," she said. "Look."

I rolled over and looked out the hole. The water had continued to rise and the waves were splashing just below where we lay. If we stayed where we were, the waves would eventually fill this shaft and pull us out.

"If we can climb a little higher, we could possibly get out of the water. Then we could wait it out until they can get here when the tide recedes," I said. I looked up into the blackness of the lava vent. It looked impossible to climb. It was too wide for one body to wedge in with feet on one side and back on the other. "We will have to go back to back. You push against my back, and I'll push against yours. Then we'll walk up the wall together."

"That sounds like a plan," she said. "But first, let me catch my breath. Could not they just beam us up?"

"Hey, that's my line," I choked out. "I'm the one who quotes the old movies!"

"Asil, I think this is the beginning of a beautiful relationship," she smiled as she misquoted the famous line from *Casablanca*. "I am so tired of being in water, I would give anything if we could teleport."

"That's all science fiction B.S. This is real. Besides, you are stealing my thunder," I chided. Just then, a rogue wave rolled into the cliff, filling our little shelter up to our shoulders, and drenching our drying suits. "Time to move."

"Ok, on three," I said as we pushed our backs against each other. "And step. And step. And step."

We slowly raised our bodies up, out of the water, and into the blackness.

We continued up, climbing in unison. Her helmet light

pushed against the blackness as she tilted her head and looked up the shaft. The darkness appeared endless. "When do we stop?" she asked.

We had interlocked arms, and I knew we could hang there, wedged together, for as long as we needed since we could program our suits to become rigid.

"Why don't you try to raise Connor? See how the shuttle is coming. As soon as the water recedes, we can crawl back down."

My helmet's comm-link could no longer talk to Connor's, so I waited as Pré talked into her mike. "Connor, are you there? How is the repair going?" I could not hear his response, but I could tell by Pré's facial expression, the answer was not what we hoped.

"Captain, the onboard computer will not allow the shuttle restart. Something about an ignition fail-safe initiator sensor being out."

"What about the redundant sensor?" I asked. She talked back into the mike, "Asil says there is a back up that we can install."

Again, her face looked grim. "Connor says it is back on the *Alpha*, in the cargo bay."

"And no way to get it here," I added. "Can he wire a by-pass around the sensor?"

"Asil wants to know if you can by-pass the sensor?"

After a pause, she said with a little quiver in her voice, "They have been trying for an hour, with no luck. He says they will lose the shuttle in a few days, but they should be able to move inland living in the rover, and survive another few weeks depending on how long the habitats can stay together when the water reaches them. He adds, I'm sorry Captain, this is not how it is supposed to work out."

"Tell him to keep trying, we will see them just as soon as we get out of here. Then we will all go home. Pré, it looks like there is only one way out for us, and that is up."

I hid the emotions that were racing through my mind. I guessed this is how a captain should act in times of adversity. She would never know the dread that tried to overcome me at the moment.

"Stay in contact with him as long as you can. I want to know what they have tried. I can give them some help if I know where they have been. I can see the schematics in mind, and I have a few ideas. We are not done yet."

After two hours or so of climbing, I suggested we lock our suits rigid, and get some food and rest. My food storage unit was almost completely depleted, but there was still enough for a small meal. Pré was also sipping the last of her nutritious blue fluid. We would have to find something else to eat in a few days if we were going to have the energy to continue on. Water shouldn't pose a problem since her suit could pull it from the air around us as long as there was humidity. My suit was hit and miss. I must have damaged something near its power source and processor.

***

I awoke in a darkness that completely enshrouded our bodies. Had not Pré been breathing loudly, I would not have known she was even there. Although complete blackness enveloped us, it was by no means quiet in our little cylindrical refuge. The planet around us continued to growl, and the water below us created a sucking noise letting me know it was still there. As I pressed my aching muscles against the rigidity of my suit in order to attempt to stretch them, I heard Pré stir. I had been dreaming of being chased by dinosaurs. I was in an antique pickup truck speeding away from an allosaur on an old gravel road. Pré was in the passenger seat. The engine growled as the truck climbed a steep hill. As we drove over the top, I realized there was nothing but a sheer drop on the other side. I must have been shouting in my sleep as the truck plunged madly toward our demise. That must have been what woke us.

"Good morning," I said, "onward and upward?"

She just groaned. If she was as sore and tired as I was, we could have easily spent the day there recovering, but I knew time was against us, so I pressed on, "C'mon we have a hole to climb out of."

165

"Just twenty more minutes," she groaned again. If she could have rolled over, I'm sure she would have. Her green comm-link light blinked on lighting up the dark cavern we were in. I waited as she listened to whoever was on the other end.

"Asil, it is Lexie," Pré continued, "she says that Sal has taken the rover back to the cliff. He is going to continue his work while we try to get the shuttle working. He is going to try to get a tree core sample using his tree borer. He told Lexie he will get as much information as possible on the plant life here back to Hailey to send back to Earth, just in case. She tried to stop him, but he is acting like a kid in a candy shop, the crazy Spaniard."

"Tell Lexie to stay in contact with him. Send a drone to watch over him. We don't need him to get lost as well. Tell her we are hoping to be at the top of this shaft by the end of the day. There is no daylight visible yet, but we will keep looking up."

"Will do Asil, and, do you think so?"

"Think so what?"

"We will be out of here by the end of the day?"

"I hope so, I don't know how much longer my legs will hold out. We should get going."

As the hours passed, and we slowly crawled up the vent's walls, our climbing periods grew shorter and shorter, and our resting periods grew longer and longer. From time to time, I asked Pré to turn off her headlamp so we could peer upwards into the darkness, desperately searching for any sign of light.

"Is it just me, or is this shaft beginning to angle off?" she asked as we entered our sixth hour of ascent.

"I noticed you were leaning on me a little harder," I said, "but I thought that was just a sign of your growing affections for me."

She ignored my attempt at humor and said, "I am feeling like you are on the inside of a curve."

"You might be right, let's continue on and see if this is just our bodies screwing with us as we fatigue, or we might be getting more horizontal."

After a short rest, we continued on. Ever so slowly I could feel more and more of Pré's weight shift onto my own. We were beginning to slant away from the cliff wall if my directions were still intact. Eventually, she slid off my back and dropped down beside me. The vent had become horizontal enough for the both of us to walk side by side now. This was both disappointing and a relief. My legs ached from the hours they were bent, so to be able to straighten them and walk normally would be wonderful. However, this meant we were no longer going straight up, so our climb to the surface would be just that much longer.

Time crept by as our journey continued through the lava vent. Eventually, we lost all communication with the others, so we passed the time talking of anything and everything. We continued our conversation about our childhoods, our families, our likes, and our dislikes. Her favorite color? Blue. My favorite book? *The Lord of the Rings.* All three.

On and on we walked. Sometimes we walked in silence for hours. As we penetrated deeper and deeper into the tube, the steady angle upwards slowly ended, and our path took a different turn as the tube now began to descend downward. We both knew the grim reality of this turn of events. We would not be surfacing any time soon.

Neither of us spoke of it and just continued trudging through the dark.

The tube itself was no longer the smooth cylinder it once was. Cracks appeared in the walls, and broken rock lay strewn in our path. At some points, the tube narrowed so we had to walk single-file, and at other points, it widened so we could easily walk two abreast. At times we had to climb over debris piles in order to continue on. Sometimes we could feel vibrations in the tube, possibly from earthquakes offshore or somewhere far from us.

"Do you know any songs?" Pré asked trying to break the monotony.

"If I sang, we would probably have a cave-in," I offered. "How about you?"

"I used to sing when I was in university," she answered. "I was a member of a women's choir."

"Why don't you sing a song; you know, just to pass the time.

It might make us forget we are headed into the heart of this forsaken Hades."

I must have struck a nerve because when I looked at her, tears began streaming down her face. The reality and stress of our situation must have finally hit home. I reached out and grabbed her hand. I gave it a gentle squeeze.

"I know," I said, "but we are going to get home. I don't know why I know this, I just do."

"I never pegged you as the eternal optimist," she said as she wiped the tears from her dirt-streaked face. "I am extremely pragmatic, and we are going in the wrong direction."

"Tough to be pessimistic when I am in the presence of such great beauty," I smiled. "After all, I have crossed oceans of time to find you."

She smiled, "That's beautiful. What film did you steal that from?"

I laughed. "Book," I said, "Bram Stoker's 'Dracula', kind of fitting here in the dark, huh?"

She gave my hand a gentle squeeze and let go. "Thank you," she said.

As we rounded the next bend, the tube once again became a smooth cylinder, only this time it looked as if someone or something had bored it. It was perfectly circular. When we approached the section that appeared artificial, I noticed a faint green glow emanating from the walls.

"Turn off your light," I said.

As my eyes adjusted to the lack of light, my heart began to race. The entire tube was lit dimly with a soft, green glow.

"This looks just like that bioluminescence we saw offshore a few nights ago," I said excitedly. "We must be close to a water source! And if we find the water, we may just get out of here!"

"Or," Pré countered, "someone is using the algae as a light source to light the tunnel."

"That would help explain that eerie feeling I keep getting that we are being watched. Either way, we have got to find out."

Our pace quickened as we walked down the now dimly-lit tunnel. Aside from the cracks in the walls that I assumed were from seismic activity, the tunnel became smoother and smoother. We walked on for another hour or so talking excitedly about getting out of here and finding the others when we came to a bend where the tunnel began to widen. As we approached the bend, Pré sprinted ahead and disappeared around the corner. When I rounded the corner, she was just standing there staring.

"Wow!" was all she said.

CHAPTER 14:
RETICENCE

We were standing in a massive cavern that extended as far as I could see. It was lit up by the same green light we had encountered in the lava tube, except, in here, it was much brighter. The scene in front of us was almost indescribable. As the cavern opened, huge columns of smooth black obsidian rose from the floor and attached to the ceiling some thirty or forty meters up. Their bases were at least ten meters in diameter on average, although some were much larger and some were much smaller. The columns narrowed and curved slightly as they rose upwards toward their apex. Many had spherical orifices scattered across their surfaces that led to dark places that beckoned our attention. At their apex, they widened again as they attached to the cavern ceiling. They reminded me of small apartment complexes.

Of course, only if they were alien apartment complexes!

There were tens upon tens of them visible as far as I could see. Some of them were intertwined with similar clear columns that I could only guess were composed of either diamond or quartz. Some of the clear columns also stood alone looking like semi-melted champagne flutes as they arced their way to the ceiling. The walls of the cavern were also filled with the spherical openings not unlike the lava tube openings we had seen on the cliffs. However, these openings appeared to have been smoothed and polished. Everything was so smooth in this alien city. I had to call it a city for that is what it truly was.

The "streets", if I could use the term loosely, were about ten meters wide, and were just as smooth as the walls. They extended, at the most, about fifty meters before they would curve around some column and disappear. Some of the streets were level so that they could be easily traversed on foot. They looked as if I could slide through them on stocking feet if I wanted to do so. Some were angled downward on both sides to create a smooth channel in which a small stream of crystal-clear water flowed down their middle. The streams' depths were no more than two meters, and their currents' directions seemed to depend upon which column they flowed past. Farther down the street on which we stood, I noticed that one of the streams emptied into a spherical pool that was about ten meters in diameter.

"The 'Nommo'?" I asked out loud to no one in particular.

The "city" was an incredible labyrinth of smooth, level streets; water-filled canal streets; sloping, shiny, curved columns filled with dark entrances; and smooth cavern walls with lava vent openings leading to who-knows-where. The city appeared to stretch in all directions for kilometers.

"Which way?" Pré asked.

"Good question," I said. "Why don't we head toward that pool down this street?" I pointed to the dark spherical pool some fifty meters or so to our right where one of the channel-streets' streams emptied into it. "Make sure your video is on, we should record everything." We had not been wearing our helmets for quite some time now, and I wanted to be sure we had a record of everything, so we snapped them back on.

The street in front of us was level, and we decided to cross it to get away from the cavern walls. That feeling that someone or something was watching me again crept back into my mind, and I didn't want to be near any vent openings, just in case.

"I feel like a fish in a fishbowl," I said.

"What is a fishbowl?" Pré asked.

"You know, those jars at the local alcohol dispensary," I smirked, "that people stick long straws in, and drink fruity drinks from?"

"Oh, yes," she answered, "people used to keep fish in them?"

As we approached a rather large dark column about the size of the shuttle if it were standing on end, the entire wall lit up like an explosion. It was like someone had ignited a fireworks mortar right in front of us. Brightly colored lights of red, green, and blue flashed out from a white dendritic pattern, then broke into hundreds of chromatic dots before they disappeared. I froze in place! My heart raced as the adrenalin coursed through my body!

"Holy crap!" I thought. I looked at Pré; she had assumed some sort of Kung Fu protective position, and had a look on her face that said, "Bring it on!"

And just like that, the wall went dark again.

"What the hell was that?" I asked as my tensed shoulders relaxed.

"I do not know. Step back, and then forward toward the wall again, let us see if it happens again."

I took three steps back and then approached the wall again. Nothing happened. No explosion of light, no vivid colors, nothing.

"Do you think that it is a message, like a warning or something?" Pré asked.

"I'm not sure. It happened so fast. I only had time to react," I said.

"I saw your reaction," she said with a nervous laugh, "you looked like a deer caught in the headlights, I believe, is how the old saying goes."

"Yeah, well, I saw your reaction," I quipped, "remind me never to cross your path in a dark alley."

"Maybe you should follow behind me," she said with a smile.

"Let's just get to that pool, I want to see down inside," I added a little resigned.

"I think my suit might need a good cleaning now if it didn't before. And, I'm thinking I'll take my chances with the cavern wall," I said as I walked back across the street.

The street was not straight and it bent with the cavern wall as the wall slightly curved inward toward the city center. On the curved surface of the wall, about another twenty meters in front of us, was a huge opening. It was so large one could drive a fusion-powered ore truck through the entrance, with room to spare. I walked over to the smooth side of the opening and ran my hand along the curve of the dark, glass-like rock. A lime green light immediately popped on, illuminating what appeared to be a wide tunnel that led into another area.

I stepped forward, and turned to Pré, who had been watching, and said, "Let's check this out."

We walked only about ten meters into the tunnel when it opened into another enormous cavern. The cavern was lit by the same lime green light we encountered at the tunnel entrance. This cavern was different in that it was completely devoid of any columns. It was a huge, elliptical empty space that had another large tunnel leading out the far end.

"This thing could hold the *Alpha*," I said.

"Could it be a hanger for a ship? Pré asked. "That far tunnel looks like it heads out away from the city."

"It's possible," I answered. "Too bad it looks like that far tunnel curves back towards the way we just came from the cliffs."

"Yes, we should probably continue on. I do not want to be stuck at the edge of some lava vent, looking over a sheer drop to the ocean, with no hope of rescue," she said. "At least here, we have a tiny bit of hope of survival."

We left the cave and continued toward the pool of water I had spotted earlier. When we reached the pool, I peered down into a darkness that sent chills down my spine. Absolutely no light penetrated the dark depths. I couldn't tell if it was one meter deep or one hundred meters deep. My mind told me this was pure water since that was what flowed from the stream channel, but this pool looked like it was filled with crude oil, it was so dark.

"Shall we get a sample?" Pré asked as she drew a vial from her utility belt.

"Let's, but don't get too close, we don't know what's down

there."

Pré inched to the edge of the pool and reached down with the vial's vacuum drawtube to slide it under the surface. As her hand crossed the edge of the pool, she froze.

A bright white light flashed on just above the pool, it encompassed the entire area of the pool and extended to the ceiling.

"I cannot get my hand any closer," she said. "It is like something is blocking me from getting the tube in the water. I am going to try something."

She stood up, took a step back, and then jumped toward the water!

And there she stayed, in mid-air, just centimeters from the water's surface. She flung her arms and kicked her feet, but no matter what she tried, she just floated in space, just above the surface.

"Come and pull me out," she said.

I walked to the edge and grabbed her arm. I pulled, and she came easily to the edge where she could step back onto the street.

"It is just as I thought," she explained before I could demand what the hell she was doing. "Something stopped me from entering that pool. We are not allowed in that water."

"What are you talking about?" I asked.

"When I tried to put the tube in the water, I simply could not. It was not like I was being pushed back, I just could not do it. Something inside my head told me we are not allowed."

"Ok, this is getting a little freaky," I said. "Maybe we should continue on."

The pool culminated at the vertex of two streets, so I suggested we take the street that headed inward toward the city center, away from the vent where we entered the city.

We should continue in the same direction we started when we first entered the lava tube; was it days ago, now?

Minutes wore on as we walked. Every now and then a column wall would light up in a burst of colors as we passed. There were numerous, what appeared to be entrances to a multitude of rooms in the columns. I walked over to one and tried to step inside. As I put my foot in the entrance, a yellow-green light blinked on. Apparently, we were "allowed" to explore this room. As I walked into the room, Pré followed. The room was about the size of a small bedroom. It was carved out of the obsidian column and had the same smooth curving surfaces like every other structure we had seen in the city thus far. Although, in this room, I noticed a new substance on the obsidian. It looked like someone had started to paint the wall with a substance that looked just like mother-of-pearl. The creamy swirls of the new substance greatly contrasted the shiny black of the obsidian. In the center of the room was a small, ovate pillar rising from the floor. The pillar appeared to made of the same mother-of-pearl substance, and it looked like someone had painted up to it from the wall onto the floor. It looked like some sort of interconnected system of the cloud-colored substance.

"What do you make of this?" I asked Pré.

"I could not begin to speculate," she responded, "Maybe a control panel that connects to something in the wall?"

I walked over to the pillar and laid my hand across the top, fully expecting the wall to burst into a sea of color. But nothing happened.

"Maybe we don't have the right biology to make it function," I guessed. "I was hoping it was a video monitor or a computer of some sort that we could use to communicate to the others."

"Look over here by the back wall," Pré interrupted as she walked toward the back of the room.

In the back of the room, along the floor next to the wall, was a perfectly circular hole about fifty centimeters in diameter. It opened into a tube that led to the outside of the building.

"A commode?" I asked.

"Maybe an escape hatch," she countered.

"Could it have carried water in or out? Maybe it is connected to the street channels."

We were truly in an alien environment and could have spent the day speculating as to the purposes of the structures that we had found. We decided to leave and continue on toward the city center. There was no sign of life anywhere, just the indications that something had lived here before. That, and I had that feeling again that we were being watched. As we approached the city center, the green light seemed to glow brighter, so much so that destination became the focus of our journey inward.

"Hey, look at this!" I called to Pré as I walked by an opening. I had accidentally stuck my hand partially into the opening as I passed by, and this time, a violet light appeared. I put my hand in again, and the violet light appeared again.

Pré joined me, and asked, "Shall we try it?"

I was as nervous as a fart in a forest fire as I attempted to cross the threshold. At first, my foot just hung in mid-air. The next thing I knew I was flying through the air backward. I hit the dark surface in the middle of the street hard on my backside and slid the rest of the way across, and up the curve of a column about two meters. I fell back down to the base with a thump. Apparently, I was not allowed entrance to this particular place.

I groaned, and spat out painfully, "Violet is violent. Green is good! Violet is bad! Remember that!"

"I guess we are not allowed in?" Pré asked as she tried unsuccessfully to hide her laughter. "It is okay, I would prefer to stay on the street anyway," she said with smiling eyes. "I am hoping we can cross the city and get out as soon as possible. We are running out of time to get back."

I knew she was right, we did not have the time to explore, but curiosity was getting the best of me. I wanted to focus on something other than our dilemma, even if, for just a short time.

"Let's check out one or two quickly before we cross the city center, and maybe a couple more as we near the cavern wall on the other side," I said. "We should really record as much as possible, so the more intelligent eggheads back home can figure out just what went on here."

"Hey, I resent that remark," she said.

"I was referring to myself," I back-peddled, "you know I think you are perfect in every way."

"I am not sure that is a compliment," she said.

I didn't reply. I just smirked. So, we continued on. As I walked past openings, sometimes I would break the openings' planes with my hand. To my astonishment, many different colors lit the openings. Some openings would light up in a dark blue, some in a blue-green, and some in a yellowish-orange color along with the other colored lights that we had already encountered. I knew the colors had to symbolize something. My best guess was that each color foretold of places that held different purposes to whatever being created them.

When we did stop to explore some of the rooms, we were "allowed" in all the rooms, except the ones that lit up their entrances with the violet light. We would quickly enter and survey as much of each room as possible. The rooms varied in size and shape, but there were never any sharp edges. Some of the rooms contained more pillars of the mother-of-pearl substance, and some had pillars made of what, we guessed, were gemstones like emerald, ruby, and sapphire. Always smooth, always oval-shaped. Some of the rooms had columns that divided the room into ellipsoidal spaces that looked like cubicles in an old-time business office. Again, no sharp corners were ever present. In some of the rooms, the walls would burst into color much like the exterior walls of the columns. And, always, the colors would appear and disappear so fast there was no way to discern any pattern. We had no way to tell if we were seeing a language, some sort of art form, or a malfunctioning supercomputer.

The pools that we encountered as we walked toward the city center were lit only with the white light, and we could not sample them.

I also noticed that in this perfectly smooth environment, there were signs of cataclysmic events. Some of the giant columns had cracks that ran at angles through them. Some of the cracks were horizontal, and it looked like these columns could topple at any time. Now and then, we would find giant pieces of the obsidian, that had broken off some of the columns, scattered in the streets. Some of the water channels had huge cracks in their beds that ran the length of the street. These channels were bone-dry. I imagined the water had run through the cracks to some unknown reservoir below.

At one intersection, I found a chunk of crystal about the size of my hand. It had broken free of one of the crystalline columns. It sparkled in the green light and looked as if it had been cut along its cleavage planes like most gemstones. I picked it up and stuck into a compartment on my utility belt.

When we reached the city center and rounded one of the many curved streets, we came upon what had to be a park or commons or something of that nature. Many of the street channels emptied into several pools spaced widely apart in a large open area surrounded by columns. The columns here were smaller and seemed to have more of an artistic appearance rather than a functional purpose. They were more slender and had smooth lines engraved vertically along parts of their walls. The lines glowed with different colors contrasting the black of the obsidian and the clearness of the diamond crystal. There were also pillars here that looked as if they were sculpted out of the different types of gemstones that we had already discovered. They also glowed with a soft eminence of color. A calmness overcame me as I walked among the columns and the pillars. There was a serenity to this place. The soft-glowing lights made me feel at ease, as the graceful, fluid environment enveloped me.

Many of the pools here were similar to all the other pools that we had come upon as we journeyed to the city center. They were deep and dark. However, we discovered some new and different pools among the columns and pillars. These were clear and shallow. Each had a similar diameter of about ten meters, and maybe, a depth of one to two meters. As I waved my hand over the top of one, instead of a bright white light, a soothing dark blue light appeared. I reached down and attempted to stick my gloved hand into the crystal-clear water. My gloved hand sank into the liquid. We were "allowed" to enter this water. The temperature readings from my suit monitor told me the water was a warm thirty-seven degrees Celsius. I looked over at Pré.

She was checking out some of the lights that emanated from some of the smaller columns.

I said into my comm-link, "Pre, come and see this. I found a pool we can touch." Pré walked over and inserted a finger into the water.

"Warm," she said, "I will collect a sample."

"This is for you," I said as I sat down beside her by the pool's edge, and reached into my utility belt, "in honor of the season!" I pulled out the diamond-like gemstone I had found.

"What are you talking about?" Pré asked.

"Don't you know what day this is? It is Christmas Day."

"Christmas? Do they still celebrate that holiday where you come from?"

"Of course, don't they celebrate it in France?"

"I do not think so. Ever since the war. Besides, how do you know today is Christmas day?"

"It's like I told you before, I just know things. I don't know how I know them, I just know them."

"Ah, the ALIT programming. I will accept your gift, Captain Asil. It is beautiful. I shall put it in my utility belt. But I did not get you anything."

"I tell you what," I said, "my throat is so dry, and my suit is not doing a good job of extracting water since my power pack was damaged. If you have any drinking water, that would be a wonderful gift."

She took off her helmet, and pulled out her flexi-straw that was clipped by her ear, and pointed it toward me, "I have plenty, Happy Christmas!"

"We say 'merry'," I said as I leaned in and took a large sip from her straw. Our cheeks accidentally brushed against one another, and again, electricity jolted through my body. I felt the warmth of her skin as my cheek gently touched hers. She must have felt it too because she leaned in towards my lips.

"*This is it!*" I thought. "*Our first kiss!*"

My heart was pounding as her lips closed in on mine. Then they went right past my mouth to my ear where she whispered softly, "You stink."

"What?" I asked, slightly offended.

"You smell very badly," she said matter-of-factly.

"I'll have you know I bathed only four or five days ago!" I shot back.

"Would you like to have a bath?" she asked with a new tone in her voice that I couldn't quite place.

I didn't know what to say as she began to remove her suit.

***

I awoke hours later from what had to be the most relaxing sleep I'd had in years. As I opened my eyes I was greeted by a horrifying sight. Standing over Pré's naked body was a humanoid of some sort. Its skin was totally white and featureless. It had long arms with three-fingered hands. One of its hands was near Pré's head. It had its three fingers attached to her neck with some sort of suckers. I could see through its translucent skin that the tips of the fingers were sucking her brain matter and blood up into its arm and into its amphibian-like body. The human-like creature reminded me of a tailless albino salamander. Its face held no features except for two expressionless oval eyes. I screamed and lunged toward the alien, slipping on the smooth surface near the pool. I hit my head on the dark rock.

This must have jarred me awake, for once again, I opened my eyes. This time, to find we were truly alone in the quiet city. I looked over at Pré. She was sleeping soundly with nothing hovering over her. I must have been holding my breath for I exhaled long and slow. It was just a dream. *A Nightmare on Alien Street.* I relaxed.

There we were, two alien bodies lying naked in a strange land. We were trapped in an underground world built by some mysterious race long ago, and I couldn't think of anything else now, except how beautiful this young woman was, as she lay there sleeping.

If I die on this planet, then I will die knowing that I have realized my greatest love. And that's not even a quote from an old film.

"Ok, C'mon Asil, quit sapping it up!" I was talking to myself

again.

I had to get my head on straight. We had to get out of here! My stomach growled, reminding me we had not eaten in a very long time. The sparse food that we had stored in our suits was long gone. If we were going to have any energy to climb out of here, we would have to find sustenance soon.

I grabbed my suit and began to wash it out as best I could in the warm pool that we had bathed in some hours before. Although the suit was self-cleaning, Pré was right, there was a bit of an odor, and I attempted to clear it up some.

Pré stirred as I sloshed my suit around in the water. She did not say anything. She grabbed her suit, knelt down beside me, and began cleaning it in the water as well.

"We will have to find some food soon," I said.

"I noticed a clear pool with some of that lichen that Sal talked about," she replied. "It was growing on the bottom a few meters down. Did he not say we could possibly eat the top part?"

"Yes, which pool was it?"

As we both donned our suits again, we never spoke, but I felt there was a new bond between us.

She led the way to a pool about thirty meters from where we slept and pointed down into the water. This water also had great clarity, and I could see rows of that shrubbery down below. It looked as if someone had planted it there like a crop.

"Let's give it a try," I said as I bent over to dive into the shallow water. Suddenly, a bright white light flashed on, and I hung there upside down in mid-air. We were denied entrance once again. Pré pulled me back over to the edge, and I fell onto my stomach as my body left the light.

"Looks like we go hungry," I said disappointedly.
I got up, turned, and began to walk slowly out of this central park and back into the green-lit streets.

Pré followed, and soon, we were winding our way through the maze of curved rock and flowing waterways. Now and again, the walls of some of the columns would burst with light as we walked closely past. I noticed that the colors were different in each one, and the patterns they formed, were different as well. If they were signs, we couldn't read them. We were stuck following the winding streets all the while keeping an eye on the far cavern wall when possible.

"Why should we not float for a while?" Pré asked after we had walked for a few hours. "I think the current is strong enough to carry us in those channels. If we can find one flowing outward, we could save some energy."

"That is a fantastic idea," I said adding, "isn't it crazy, this planet, just like our Earth, is mostly water, and yet, we were born without gills?"

"That is a pretty deep thought for a shuttle captain," Pré replied with a smile as she climbed down the sloping side of one of the channels.

"I think I read that somewhere," I said as I climbed down beside her, "or saw it in an old film; Hailey!"

As we floated and waded through the water, letting the current push us along, we discussed the possibility of the lights on the column walls being some sort of message system. Pré replayed her recordings of the lights on her helmet monitor trying to find some sort of color pattern or light pattern that could help us understand what the lights meant.

We talked about the different colors to the entrances on the columns and the pools, and how violet and white did not allow our entrance, yet blue was a color that allowed us to pass. After hours of discussion, we came to no new conclusions.

We talked about which direction to go once we reached the other side of the cavern. Which tube should we enter? We could spend days searching and never get anywhere. We climbed out of the stream a few streets before the channel ended and emptied into a pool near the far cavern wall.

We walked the street among the columns that lead to the lava vents on our far wall destination. As we passed by one of the dozens of black obsidian columns that we had encountered, Pré put her hand in one of the openings. A light blue light appeared, and then, POOF! Pré disappeared! She was gone! One moment she was standing there, and the next, gone!

"Pré? Pré? Can you hear me?" I called into my comm-link. No answer.

Stay calm. Breathe. We've been through stuff like this before.

I looked in every direction, she was nowhere to be found.

I found myself talking to myself again, *"Ok, Ok, think Asil. Use logic. Logic? Hell, there is no logic to this place! Lights, water, tubes! That's it, tubes!"*

I ran over to the tube where she had stood last and stuck my hand in. The light blue light appeared. But that was all that happened. I didn't POOF! I just stood there looking stupid with my hand out. I tried to enter the tube, but after one step inside, it immediately went vertical after a quick gentle slope upwards. No way to climb it either. I stepped back out, lost in what to do next when I heard her voice.

"Things are looking up," she said as her voice echoed in my helmet.

"What?" I asked.

"Look up," she said.

As I tilted my head following the curve of the column upwards, I saw her peek out of what I would have to call a window, about five stories above where I stood. She had her arm resting on the circular sill just like she was out for a Sunday ride in an old Model Tesla, with the safety glass down.

"Hey, sailor boy, what are ya' doin' down there?" she asked in her best New York accent. "Lookin' good!"

"How did you get up there?" I asked incredulously.

"I am not sure," she replied. "I put my hand in the opening, and a blue light came on. So, I stuck my head in to get a better look. I noticed it was a vertical tube, so I thought, I wonder what is up there? The next thing I knew, I was standing in this room. I saw this opening, and then I heard your voice through the comm-link. And here I am."

She added, "It is an incredible view from up here. I can see for kilometers. We have come a long way."

"You are in a room? Is there anything in the room? Furniture?

Communications equipment? Food? Possibly a ship?"

"I am in a small cylindrical room, but it is empty. There is a flat floor with a hole in it and this one window. As I walked by the wall to the window, the wall lit up, but there were no colors. It was only black and white. The lights made a pattern that looked like the branches of a tree or something."

"How do you plan to get down?"

"Just a second," she said.

POOF! In the next instant, she was standing at the entrance to the tube not more than a meter from me.

"I believe this is an elevator of some sort. I just stuck my head in the opening on the floor and thought, 'down'. And now, I am down!"

"Don't try stuff like that again without talking to me first," I replied slightly annoyed. "I thought I lost you."

"More importantly," she said, "I thought I saw something moving in the distance when I heard your voice. It might have been my imagination, but I thought I saw something slide into one of the pools about a half-kilometer back."

"What did it look like? Could it have been a piece of a column breaking off and falling into the water?"

"No, this was on the ground and moving on its own. Although I just caught a glimpse of it out of the corner of my eye, as I stared down at you."

"We have no weapons. If there is something out there, what if it is hostile?"

"I am sure I saw something. Captain Asil, I think it is time to leave the city."

"How do we know which lava tube to enter? There are hundreds. If only we had a map."

"That is it!" Pré shouted. "A map! The room, the wall! It was different from all the others! I think it might be a map!"

"Let's go," I said as I thrust my head into the tube and thought, "Up!"

POOF! The next thing I knew, I was standing in the same room Pré had vacated just minutes before. POOF! Suddenly, she was standing beside me. She ran over to the wall near the window, and it lit up. This time the lights did not explode and fade away. They stayed on. As she surveyed the black lines against the white background, she followed them with her finger.

"Which one?" she asked herself.

I stood beside her trying to make sense out of what we were seeing.

"If there was some reference point, we could get a fix on where we are at, and work it out from there." I leaned against the wall, and tiny black dots appeared along the dendritic lines. I looked out the window, and then back at the wall. "I think the dots are the pools! Look, out the window, in that direction." I pointed to three pools in close proximity to one another about fifty meters down to our right. "Now look at the wall, here," I said as I pointed to three dots forming a similar pattern on the wall. "I think this is where we are!"

"You are correct," she said excitedly. I looked back out the window, then, I also thought I saw movement. In one of the pools we had just looked at, there were ripples running outward from its center.

"There's movement in that pool," I said, my voice tensing.

"Could it be seismic?" she asked.

"No, look at the other two pools. No ripples!"

"That is only about fifty meters away!"

"We need to leave, and very soon!"

We turned back to the wall and traced, what we assumed were, the paths of the lava vents. Their lines were the farthest from the center, and all seemed to start along some common plane. These lines had to be the vents!

"Look at this one!" I almost shouted. "It looks like it just ends! The others seem to curve back and return to the cavern. This one on this end, it doesn't. It's got to be the way out!"

"I have recorded it," she replied quickly. "Time to go!"

We hit the ground running after popping down out of the room and headed in the general direction of the lava tube in the cavern wall that we had picked out on the map.

"Whatever is behind us, must like water for cover, so let's stick to the dry streets," I hollered into my comm-link.

We raced down the winding streets avoiding any with water. To add more misery to our situation, I could feel the rock vibrate again below our feet.

"Another quake," I said as I breathed rapidly rounding the last corner before the cavern wall. Two pools were between us and the wall. Both showed ripples of water on their surfaces.

We had to pass between them to get along the wall and find our vent.

"Pré, I said, "it's time to pray if you never have before. Let's hope it's just a quake."

I never thought I'd ever say that in my life! "We're going to get hit again, and it might be a bigger monster!" *Jeepers, now I'm quoting disaster movies? What kind of movies did you let us watch, Hailey?*

We darted between the two pools. The waves were lapping over their sides, but nothing rose up out of the water as we dashed by, and then, we were clear. We sprinted down along the cavern wall counting holes as we raced past.

"Here!" she cried, as she slammed her right foot into the cavern floor, and pivoted sharply left into the opening. I followed suit, and she screamed, "Out!"

Nothing happened as we continued to tear down the green-lit corridor.

"It was worth a shot," she called as she sprinted out ahead of me. Only when we were absolutely sure that nothing was following, did we stop to rest.

I fell on my back panting. "That was a good try," I breathed rapidly. "I wish it would have worked. Maybe we thought the wrong word. What about 'surface'?" I waited; nothing happened. "Ok, how about, 'get me the fricken' hell out of here'?"

"Pardon your French," Pré exhaled and said with a quick laugh. "It looks like we are going to do this the hard way."

"With you in my presence, nothing is ever hard," I said.

"Do you not ever take anything seriously?" she asked.

"Serious? This is Sirius," I answered. "Sirius C to be exact. I am taking this matter quite S-I-R-I-U-S-L-Y." I spelled it out.

"You know I only joke to lighten the load," I said.

"How am I going to spend the rest of my short life with you, if I do not know when you are joking?" she asked.

"Short life, my ass," I replied. "We are going to get out of...; hey, did you just say you wanted to spend the rest of your life with me?"

"Asil, in case you haven't noticed, using your own words, 'I have kind of taken a shine to you', as well."

With renewed energy, I jumped to my feet and helped her up. I looked her straight in the eye, and said, "I am going to get you home, or die trying."

I turned and took a step up the tunnel only to catch my foot, trip on a new fracture in the floor, and fall flat on my face.

"Oh, boy," was all she said.

CHAPTER 15:
REINVIGORATED

As we walked, the rumblings beneath our feet became more frequent. Neither of us talked about it, but we both knew conditions on this planet were getting more serious. We talked about the city we had just discovered, its structures, whoever had inhabited it before, and whatever was living there now.

"You know, the way everything in that city is so smooth, and has curved edges, whoever lived there must have had a soft body," I proposed.

"They could have been amphibious since the streets were both rock and water," Pré hypothesized.

"Hey, didn't Genie say the Dogons described the 'Nommo' as amphibious, squid-like creatures?"

"That could be what I saw! Whatever slid into that pool looked like it was moving in many directions all at once. That movement could have been tentacles flailing everywhere. It makes sense to me now!"

"Do you suppose the entrances in which we were not allowed to enter, may have been places they were currently living?"

"That would suggest a higher power governing that city. It also suggests that maybe we were guided through those streets."

As we discussed our theories of the city and its inhabitants, more and more cracks appeared on the smooth surfaces of the lava tube walls, and the amount of rock debris that littered our path began to increase.

I walked on fatigued legs. I was tired, sore, and hungry. Pré looked like she had just done a short body stretch and warm-up.

She looked fresh and ready to begin a workout.

"Why isn't your hair messed up?" I asked as we walked along. "You look like you just stepped out of a beauty salon. How is it that your hair looks like it is always just styled? Why don't you look tired? I must look like hell."

"You do," she said. "Do you need a break?"

"Break? Heck no, I just have large pores," I said, "so I sweat more. I will be fine."

The path before us began a slow incline, and my muscles responded by aching even more. If we continued our climb much longer, I would have to take a break. Luckily, after a few hundred meters, we began a decline. As we descended, the aching in my body did not decrease, it simply switched to regions in which it chose to inflict more pain. Now my back ached as we strode downward. I had finally exhausted the pain retardants that I had accessed in my suit, and I was feeling the full extent of my body's response to the abuse it had endured over the past few days.

"Is it getting warmer in here, or is it just me?" I asked. We had both removed our helmets again so we could talk without the tinny sound of the comm-link.

"I feel it too," she answered. "Either we are getting close to a magma source, or magma is getting closer to us."

"These seismic events might be indicators of increased volcanic activity," she added.

"You sound like Hailey."

"I wish we could talk to her, she could give us some data on the frequency of the seismic events, and their strength. I'd like to know our chances of getting out of this hole," I added.

Pré grabbed her helmet and popped it on. I thought I had offended her in some way, but she popped it off again just as quickly, and said, "Just checking the map. I wish there was some sort of scale on this map we copied. Judging from how long we have walked, compared to our walk through the city, I would say we are a little over halfway out."

"Let's hope this tunnel holds up."

"I thought you were the eternal optimist," she retorted.

"Let's just say recent events have dimmed my sunny demeanor," I countered as I stepped over a rather large rock in our path.

A large rumble rippled through the vent, shaking us, forcing us to tumble into the walls.

"I think we had better pick up the pace," she said as she picked herself off the ground.

Just what my ears and sore body did not want to hear.

I groaned, "If you can keep up to me, we'll be out of here before you can sing the theme song from last year's award-winning, *The Rains Beneath New Africa*. Whoops, I should have said a decade ago. Space travel, you know."

"Not to burst your balloon," she replied, "but do not look behind us."

Of course, then I had to turn and look. A red glow had replaced the dim green light that was slowly fading as we walked.

"Magma," I sighed. "Can it get any worse? I suppose around the next corner there will be sharks with lasers strapped to their heads."

"What?" she asked.

"Just my ALIT speaking for itself again," I said, "Ignore it."

I had to dig deep, and will myself to move faster. We hurried as fast as our legs could carry us, and, as much as the tube would allow. Finally, after climbing over rock piles, and jumping over ever-widening cracks in the obsidian, the tunnel began to ascend once again. I slowed my pace to a walk so I could catch my breath. Pré slowed with me and grabbed my arm. She pulled me forward.

"Asil, we have to keep moving," she cried. "You have to find it in you. Remember, you are going to get me out of here."

"As Disney said to his daughter, 'I always keep my promise'," I choked as the air began to fill with smoke, dust, and water vapor. "I'll let you lead the way for a while though, while I pass out."

It was her beauty, that killed the beast.

The heat in the tunnel steadily increased along with the smog as we climbed. We both had our helmets back on. My damaged suit struggled to cool my tortured body and bring in fresh air to my lungs.

It seemed like we struggled upward through the thickening air for an eternity, but as the sweat that ran through my eyes cleared my vision for a moment, I thought I detected a small dot of light ahead.

The temperature in the tunnel had climbed to a balmy fifty degrees Celsius, or so my suit monitor told me, and although the red glow behind us had slowed, it continued to follow and grow. Magma was about to spew out of this furnace again to become lava, with us surfing the molten rock wave.

I willed myself forward, and was just about to the light when a blast of super-heated air slammed into my back. It blasted me out of the vent and into the air. The force of the hot air blast caused my suit to become rigid as I flew through the moist, tropical air that had welcomed us back to the surface. The vent we blew out of was about five meters above the ground, and when gravity overcame my upward push, I fell. I hit the black, crystalline sand with a sickening thud. My suit relaxed after impact, and I rolled onto my side to check on Pré. She had landed just ahead of me and was already pushing out of the sand, struggling to get to her feet.

I fully expected hot lava to blast out of the vent and cover our bodies in molten rock. However, when I turned to look, instead of a deluge of the hot, netherworld liquid burying us, lava simply came oozing slowly out of the vent. Like a gentle waterfall, it cascaded down the face of the cliff and began to spread over the beach and into the ocean.

"Not quite what I had in mind when I said I would get you out of the tunnel," I chirped into my comm-link. "But I guess it worked! Any injuries?"

"Other than legs feeling like rubber, total exhaustion, and a body that aches at every joint, I feel fine," she chirped back at me.

As I rose to my feet, I examined this new beach that we had landed on. It was similar to the one we had landed on originally with the shuttle. There was the phalanx of the lichen-like shrubs with their thorn-covered, dark-colored woody stalks. As before, they blocked any route into the same bamboo-like forest just beyond to our left. The high, almost vertical cliff was at our backs. The blue-green ocean, with its constant back and forth motion of its waves, was to our right. The long, black-sand beach lay before us.

There were some differences, however. The sand here was not as black as on the first beach. It appeared to be mixed with some of the clear crystal rock that we assumed was diamond in the cavern. This gave it a lighter, almost gray color. This beach was also different in that it was strewn with large obsidian boulders here and there. It also appeared like some of the shrubs had been burned and crushed by some unknown force.

Realizing we were out of danger for the moment, I rolled to my feet. I said, "I am going to trust Sal, and try some of the shrub tops."

My stomach continued to growl as we started down the beach. "I am so hungry, I could eat Clearsteel™!"

"Should we not boil them or something, first?" Pré asked.

"Unless you have some sort of pot or pan in your utility belt, I think these are going to be *crudités*. Did I say that right?"

"That is close enough for me," she replied as she followed me to the shrub gauntlet.

Up ahead was an area where it appeared a large rock had crashed into the shrub layer. It had probably been carried in on a rogue wave or thrown out one of the lava vents. The flattened shrub area provided us an opening where we could get close to the heads of the shrubs without having to deal with the thorns. I walked into the rough alley created by the rock, pulled out my laser knife, and cut a fist-sized portion of the brown fluff from a plant. The brown lichen-like top looked clean, so I tore some of it off, and said, "I hope this is as good as it looks!"

I peeled off my helmet and stuffed a small bite-size portion into my mouth. I bit down, and immediately, a mouth-numbing liquid squirted out of the brown threads and coated my oral cavity. Small, electric pinpricks raced through my tongue and mouth by the thousands. Only people who have ever bitten into the root of purple coneflower knew the exact sensation I was feeling. Again, I don't know why I knew this, I just did. I have never eaten purple coneflower, but I knew the Plains Indians, during the nineteenth century, used to use it for medicinal purposes. I winced at the taste sensation. My first urge was to spit it out, but I fought back the gag reflex and swallowed.

"Well, how is it?" Pré asked

I attempted to say, "Tastes great", but "Tatheth great", came out of my mouth. I added, "But it feelth funny."

"Are you ok?" Pré asked.

"I'm juth fine," I tried to say with a numb tongue.

"Are you sure? You sound funny."

"My mouff ith numba," I blurted. I pointed to my tongue with my fingers and said, "Numba, numba!"

"I think, as a precaution, I should wait to see if you have any other reactions," she added, "if both us become ill, that would not have been the wise thing to do."

"Thuit yourthelf," I said as I took another bite. I figured I should eat all of it before my mouth recovered, and I would have to go through the whole numbing sensation again.

As we sat on the beach waiting for me to vomit profusely, or the muscles on my face to become paralyzed and go limp, or my skin to slide off my bones and wash away in the ocean, Pré attempted to raise the others on her comm-link. There was no response. Either we were completely out of range, or they had repaired the shuttle and left. I preferred to believe in the former.

We waited for another thirty minutes with her watching me intently, when she asked again, "How do you feel now?"

I didn't say anything, I just groaned, and began to claw the air, the way the monster did in the movie *Young Frankenstein* when he heard the violin theme from the movie.

"Oh, you men are all alike," she shot back, "it's seven or eight quickies, and you are off with the boys!"

I just smiled. This girl was good.

"Seriously though, how do you feel?"

"I feel just fine," I said. "Hey, my tongue isn't numb anymore!"

"What do your vitals read?" she asked.

I put my helmet back on and tried to call up my vitals on my damaged suit's monitor. "All I can get is a partial reading, but what I see, appears to be normal."

"Good, then I shall try some of the *crudités* as well."

After she had eaten a few handfuls of the nasty brown fluff, I said, "try to say 'six thick thistle sticks' three times."

She looked and me, shook her head, and said, "Thix, I mean thix, or forget it, Athil!"

We both had a good laugh at how she had pronounced my name. I removed my helmet again and sat down to dine with the good doctor. After we had both eaten all we could stomach, we slapped our helmets back on and continued down the beach.

"Don't try to contact Lexie or Connor with a fat tongue," I said carefully trying to avoid words with an "s". "They'll think we are in deep trouble."

"Yeth, Athil!" she said, and then laughed again.

After about another hour of walking along the shoreline of the gray sand beach while trying to contact the others, I noticed something dark laying in the sand near the shore. It was about as long as a human body and had the general shape of one. We were about a hundred meters or so from it, and the waves were washing over it, making it difficult to figure out what it was.

"I think I might be having one of those hallucinations, you and Sal warned us about. That looks like a human body."

We picked up the pace but proceeded cautiously toward the object in question. When we were within a few meters, I could tell it was not human. In fact, it was a part of the trunk of one of the bamboo-like trees that had been partially buried in the sand. Upon closer examination, we found there were several sections of the trunks of the trees laying haphazardly, semi-buried, on this small area of the beach.

"It looks like they have been cut," Pré concluded as she examined the ends of the trunks. "That is odd."

"Do you think whatever you saw in the city may have cut them?" I asked.

"That is a good question," she replied. "Unless the others were here, someone else cut these down. The sharp, flat edges at the ends are definitely not a natural break." Looking around, she added, "It looks like someone might have been assembling a raft."

"Don't forget, this isn't Earth, and we have found some of our rules of nature don't apply," I replied.

"Yes, but I know of nothing from the sky or land that could make this clean of a cut."

"If they were building a raft, I don't see anything they could use to bind the logs together. And why didn't they finish it?"

"Maybe we are thinking backward," she said, "maybe this is what is left of a raft after it crashed onto the shore."

"That's true, but then, where are the raft riders? There are no tracks or any other signs that someone landed a raft here and walked away. No tracks, nothing."

"Maybe the waves have erased all traces of evidence," she countered.

"Wait! Wait, just a second!" I said. "Come over here and look from this angle. These logs might have been deliberately placed here. It looks like someone is trying to spell out a word, or construct a symbol or something."

Pré walked over beside me, then she walked around the shrub side of the logs. She walked back toward me again gazing intently at the logs, and said, "COWAN. It looks like they spell the word 'COWAN'. Do you see it?"

I walked around the perimeter of the area where the logs had been strewn, attempting to see what she had just seen.

"I think you are right," I said, "but what does that mean? I don't think that is an English word. Do you know of any language that has the word 'COWAN' in it?"

"I do not know of any, but I am positive that is what the logs spell out."

"Cowan is a word used to describe someone who attempts to pass himself off as a freemason without going through the rituals. It comes from the Scottish," I said in a mechanical voice. "Holy Crap! Now, where the hell did that come from?"

That was just plain spooky. It's like there are times I am not thinking on my own.

Pré looked at me with a concerned look on her face. She did not say anything, but I could tell she was a little disturbed by what I had just blurted out.

"I know, I know," she said, "sometimes you just know things!"

"That," I replied, "even has me worried."

"I'm not sure that definition applies in this situation," she added, "but it is a nice bit of trivia to know."

"Thank you," I replied. "I wish this voice in my head could have provided something more useful. COWAN; it just doesn't make any sense!"

I looked up toward the shrub layer, and my jaw dropped wide open! I blinked several times making sure my vision was clear. "Now I know I am hallucinating!" I said, confused at what I was seeing.

Pré followed my line of sight.

"Doctor, tell me you see what I am seeing," I said.

There, standing in an opening in the shrubbery that appeared to be created by something that had torn completely through the shrubbery's gauntlet, was a healthy-looking, orange Tabby cat.

It stood there, meowing, as it watched us.

"Am I crazy, or is there a housecat standing in that opening meowing at us?"

"If you are hallucinating, then I am having the exact same hallucination," she said incredulously. "I see an orange cat."

"Here kitty!" I called out. "Here kitty, kitty, kitty."

"What are you doing?" We know nothing about it. Maybe it is one of those creatures I saw in the city. Maybe it is trying to lure us over. Then it will transmogrify, and eat us!"

"And I thought I was the one with a vivid imagination! I am going to trust my instincts on this one."

"I do not like this Asil. There is no reason in the world a cat should be standing there. Everything about this is just wrong!"

"Maybe it's the drugs from the plants we just ate. But I am getting the impression that it is trying to communicate, and talk to us."

"Well, if it starts speaking English or French, I am heading in the other direction. And, in a hurry! Does it not bother you there is a goddam C-A-T just standing there on the shore of an ocean on a planet that is eight light-years from Earth? Just as pretty as if we were on Earth?"

"It is strange, but something in me, deep down, is telling me we should follow it."

"What? Are you a cat-whisperer now?"

"No. Again, it is just, as if, I know."

"You are scaring me now, Asil. You know I would trust you to the ends of the Earth, but this is not the Earth, and THERE SHOULD NOT BE A CAT MEOWING AT US RIGHT NOW!"

"Why would it be right there? Right at the only opening, we have seen into the forest?"

"Yes, what about that opening? Does it not seem convenient? Here is the only opening into the forest that we have seen, and a cat happens to be standing in it?"

"The opening looks like it was created by something crashing down from the atmosphere, and plowing through the shrubs into the forest. Maybe a meteorite?"

"And an Earth cat just happens to find its way onto this planet; then, it finds its way to the only path into a totally unexplored forest we have only seen from canopy video?"

"Are you saying you are not going to follow me, then?"

"I am saying we need to look at this logically. The chances that is a cat from Earth are astronomical. Multiply that by the chances it will lead us to anything good in a dark rainforest that is a haven for whatever else this Godforsaken planet has yet to throw at us, and I do not think we survive this encounter!"

"Do you have any other ideas?"

"I say we ignore it. We continue to attempt to contact the others. Eventually, they will find us, and rescue us."

"You think the odds of us surviving are better with what you just said, than chasing after this cat? What if it IS a cat from Earth? That means someone else is here, and they must be near, judging from the healthy look of that feline. It looks well-fed."

Pré just looked at me and shook her head in defeat, "Okay Asil, you win. But know this, if I die chasing this cat, I die with a vote of dissent, and you must live, knowing that I died chasing some pussy-cat."

I had a great comedic one-liner for her, but I held it back, and just said, "Just remember, I promised to get you home, and I will not allow any transmogrified cat-beast or any other creature to stop me."

CHAPTER 16:
REUNITED

As we approached the Earth-cat, it just stood there meowing.

"Are you lost, poor little *chaton*?" Pré asked in a compassionate voice; although she carried her large diamond as a bludgeon in her hand, just in case the cat began to transmogrify.

When we stood just a few centimeters from it, she bent over. I didn't know if she was going to pet the cat, pick it up, or smash it with the diamond. Instead, she shooed it away with her hand, and said, "Go find us your master."

It was as if the cat understood, for it turned, and began to run up through the shrubs along the rough path that something very large and very powerful had carved out.

"And the chase is afoot," I cried as I started after the feline anomaly.

We ran hard to try to keep up to the cat's wicked pace. It easily out-distanced us as we stumbled over stumps and broken stalks left by whatever had crashed through here. We cleared the extent of the shrub layer in less than a half-hour but had completely lost sight of the orange tabby.

"Now what?" I asked as we stood at the base of an enormous bamboo-like tree just at the beginning of the forest.

"Over there!" cried Pré. "There, it is!"

The cat stood about twenty meters to our right just at the base of another one of the large trees. It appeared to be waiting for us as we caught up.

"Is it me, or is that thing waiting for us to catch up?" she asked.

"I think it waited for us," I said.

"Still want to follow?" she asked.

"It is odd, but what the hell do we have to lose? We've been through hell. I can't imagine things can get much worse."

Just then it started to rain hard.

"Someone has a sick sense of humor," I added.

We followed the cat under the canopy of the trees. The thick canopy partially blocked out the sunlight and created a dim, eerie world. Luckily for us, it also blocked out much of the rainfall as we jogged deeper into the forest. Although the trees were much larger than the shrubbery, the going here was much easier with very little duff beneath the green-blue slender-bladed leaves of the trees.

Nothing grew on the forest floor except where the occasional light could penetrate. Here we found what we thought was a type of soft grass. It was blue in color and had blades, not unlike the grass grown in the old state of Kentucky in what was once the United States of America.

The cat kept up a steady pace, and we were soon many kilometers deep into the woods.

"Are you not a little worried we may never find our way back out of here?" Pré asked. "I am feeling a little like the children in that old German fable of 'Hansel and Gretel'. I hope the witch's cottage is not up in the distance."

"Don't worry," I said, "I've been leaving bread crumbs behind." I smiled as the words came out.

"Always the joker, someday that is going to get us into a lot of trouble."

Farther and farther the cat led us into the dark forest. We rounded tree trunks larger than the base of the space elevator. We wove through the understory, never having to slow our pace much at all. If there were seedlings in this giant forest, we did not see any. Many of the trunks of the trees were similar in diameter, with the exception of a few being grandiose. It was like these trees had all been planted at the same time, a very long time ago.

After about two hours at this pace, I just had to stop to catch my breath. When I looked for the cat, I noticed it had stopped running when I had.

"This is getting even stranger," I thought I said to myself.

"What did you say?" Pré asked me after she had turned back when she realized I was no longer hot on her trail.

"Did I say that out loud?" I asked in return. "I was just thinking I said that to myself. I swear with the ALIT rattling around my brain, sometimes I don't know if I am talking out loud or to myself in my mind."

"You said something out loud. What was it?"

"I said, 'I think this is getting even stranger'; when I stopped, so did the cat."

"I know, I saw that. I wondered why it stopped until I turned around and saw you leaning against a tree."

"I think this cat has some alien intelligence!"

"And you still want to follow it. What was I thinking when I agreed with you?"

I looked up at the canopy as my breathing slowly allowed my oxygen intake to catch up to my metabolic burn. The canopy completely obstructed the sky above.

Did I just see something move up there?

I know I did not say that out loud, and I was not going to let Pré know that. I wasn't sure what I saw, and I could tell by the tone of her voice, she was nervous. I didn't want to scare her any more than she already was.

She interrupted my thoughts, "If we run forward, and the cat starts running again, we know it is leading us somewhere. I am not so sure we should follow."

"Do we take our chances on our own, this deep in the forest? I don't think we have a choice anymore."

She looked at me with a grim look on her face. She said nothing. She just turned and started jogging toward our furry feline friend that had led us this far. As if on cue, the cat turned, and set a moderate pace away from whence we came.

We followed in earnest. My legs, ankles, arms, and shoulders begged me to stop.

I thought, "*If that little pussycat can go on, then I can too.*"

Again, it didn't look like Pré had even broken a sweat. I chalked that up to the fact that her suit was working better than mine. We continued on.

My suit felt like it weighed fifty kilos, and my legs felt like they weighed another fifty. Just as I was about to murder our leader, and use its fur for a bathroom mat, the cat stopped suddenly.

I looked around, trying to find the reason for its sudden marathon termination. The trees looked the same in every direction.

Maybe the beast finally got tired.

Pré had stopped some ten meters in front of me and was also surveying the surroundings.

"You see anything?" I asked.

"No, I am not sure why we stopped. Everything looks just the same. Do you think it is lost?"

The cat started meowing loudly. We both turned to see what was happening, and when we did, it turned and sprinted right up the big brown trunk of the bamboo-like tree it was standing next to.

When I looked up, there, wedged in among the branches about eighty meters off the forest floor, was a dark gray spherical object. It was at least ten meters in diameter and appeared to be made of some tarp-like canvas.

The cat scampered up the trunk like a squirrel in pursuit of a nut and circled toward the back of the tree.

Pré turned to me and asked, "That looks just like one of our habs, does it not?"

"Did we lose one in the forest?" I asked.

"No, the only one we lost was at sea," she replied.

"Do you think a rogue wave might have tossed it here?"

"I think that is unlikely, plus, it is a different color than ours, and looks like it is made from a different fabric."

It was true. Our habs were lighter in color, almost white. And the Clearsteel™ fabric of which ours were made was much rougher in appearance. This habitat, if it was one, was a dark charcoal color, and the fabric was almost as smooth as the streets we saw back in the alien city.

"Are there any markings on it?" I asked.

"None that I can see, but the dark color may be hiding them. It looks like it has been here a long time, judging by the growth around it."

Pré began to circle the base of the gargantuan tree that held its foreign visitor.

"Asil, look back here, there is a rope!"

"A rope?" I asked bewildered.

"Yes, someone has been living up there."

I called up the tree, "Hello! Hello! Can you hear me? We are from the planet Earth, and come in peace!"

Pré gave me that annoyed looked that all women are born with. She looked at me as if to say, "What? Are you stupid or something?"

"It's worth a shot," I said.

There was no answer. We waited. Still no answer.

"I don't think anyone is home," I said. "Care to go for a climb?"

"We have come this far, we might as well meet our fate."

"I hope you meant 'meet' as in M-E-E-T, not 'mete' as in M-E-T-E because quite frankly, I don't think this body can withstand much more punishment."

She grimaced as she grabbed the rope.

"I will hold it, and you go first, smart-ass," she said.

I climbed the rope and was met by a door, not unlike the doors that we had back at our habs. I pulled back the Velcro-like stripping and hoisted myself into an antechamber. Pré followed just after. After she was in, the door resealed itself, and I could feel the chamber pressurizing. After a short time, a light embedded in the wall at the back of the chamber clicked on revealing a door just below it.

"After you, kind sir," Pré said with mischief still in her voice.

This place was all too familiar. It was built just like our habs, except that much of the small hardware was different. When I approached the new door and reached for its bulkhead crank, the light above the door turned green, and the door opened by itself. I immediately noticed the orange Tabby cat standing along one of the fabric-lined walls in the new room. It was meowing loudly.

"Welcome, Captain Argentum Silverwood and Doctor Prevalence Ange," a man's voice said from somewhere within the cylindrical walls.

***

There are times in a person's life when all that he has learned comes into question. All the basic behaviors, and the simple explanations of natural phenomena that you learned as a child are put on hold while your mind tries to explain the unexplainable. This was not one of those times.

"Did that cat just speak?" I asked Pré incredulously.

Before she could answer, the voice within the walls spoke again, "No, he did not. Cats cannot speak."

I looked at the cat. It was still just meowing.

"Who is speaking?" I asked.

"I am Bailey. Biological Artificial Intelligence – LexiCon Earthcorp Division. I am the first artificial intelligence based on human DNA."

The voice continued, "I see you have met Hiccups."

"Does he ever shut up?" I asked looking at the cat that was meowing non-stop.

"He thinks he is talking to you. His mind has been enhanced with the ALIT program. That is how he was able to lead you here. I sent him out earlier to search for his master."

The questions poured into my brain. I had so many I wanted to ask all at once, *"Who? What? When? Where? Why?"* They were all demanding answers all at once.

I took a deep breath to slow my whirring brain, but before I could begin, Pré was already speaking.

"What IS this?" she asked, emphasizing the word "is".

"This is the newest version of ICoSTE's planetary habitation units. Each is designed with a supercomputer, such as myself, built in, to function independently in any environment. This habitat is virtually indestructible. However, as you can see, I was not able to place it where I would have liked it to be. That is, on the planet's surface. Hence, we are caught up in this tree."

"But how did you get here?" I asked.

"We came here on the starship *Beta*," Bailey replied.

"We? Who are WE? You and the cat?" asked Pré.

"No doctor. General James Clearwater, and I," Bailey stated, "and the cat."

"Jim Clearwater is here?" I asked in disbelief.

"Yes, He is..., was the captain of the *Beta*."

"Was? Is he dead?" I asked.

"Of that, I am not certain. He left the habitat three planetary weeks ago and has not returned. That is why I sent Hiccups to look for him."

Pré asked, "Why did you say 'was'?"

"Was the captain of the *Beta*? Of that, I am certain. We lost the *Beta* as we exited the wormhole."

"Hold it! Wormhole? *Beta*? I think you better start from the beginning," I demanded.

"You know everything via our long-range communications up to a year after the *Alpha* was launched, so I shall begin there. Since yours was an exploratory mission, and highly experimental, no new interstellar spacecraft were built after you left. In the years that followed your departure, ICoSTE concentrated on fusion rockets capable of landing on, and exploring our solar system's planets. Three years from your departure, a colony was established on Mars.

The Mars colony grew, and since iron was plentiful there, Clearsteel™ could be manufactured there at a low cost. As the Mars colony began to thrive, the emphasis switched from fusion rockets to carry people, to fusion rocket space probes that would explore the immediate space within and beyond the solar system.

Five years after your departure, one such probe had entered space just beyond the Oort Comet Cloud. There, it sent back data on a gravitational anomaly that could not be explained by

PATRICK RIEDER

the current astrophysicists of the time. After a year of collecting more data from several research probes sent to the area, it was determined that this anomaly was a breach in the time/space continuum, a wormhole.

In the course of the next three years, fifteen probes were sent into the wormhole. Fourteen never returned. But with each failure, more was learned from the partial data sent back to scientists on the Earth, Mars, and the moon. Each probe that was sent in, was better prepared than its predecessor for the voyage into the wormhole. Finally, the fifteenth returned. Data from the probe showed it entered a star system very familiar to many scientists on the ISS. The data revealed that the probe had entered this star system, the Sirius system. The probe had exited in space approximately halfway between Sirius B and Sirius C.

Once it was deemed safe, a mission was immediately planned to send a message to the *Alpha* to return to Earth via the wormhole. It was to be an unmanned mission with directions to the wormhole, and instructions for the modification of the *Alpha* so it could withstand the forces within the hole itself. It would cut years off your voyage, and the data you collected and the information you could provide would greatly speed up the search for a new habitable planet. Currently, the Earth's atmosphere remains unstable, and only slight climate improvement has been recorded over the past nine years.

When General Clearwater heard of the mission, he was adamant he should be on the ship. He trained with you, and knew more about the Sirius star system, and the *Alpha*, than anyone else in the solar system. He also knew how to modify the molecular structure of Clearsteel™, and introduce it to the *Alpha's* existing infrastructure. In this way, the *Alpha* could withstand the tremendous forces exerted by the wormhole.

He convinced the world leaders to build a small one-person ship that would be able to travel light and fast, so as to get to you quickly."

"The debris that hit us," I suddenly realized, as I said it out loud.

"Yes," Bailey continued, "as we exited the wormhole, the *Beta* encountered some sort of gravitational turbulence. The ship shook violently, and just before it was torn apart, General Clearwater jettisoned this life-pod/habitat. He had programmed a course for this planet just before we lost the ship, and we drifted for months toward the planet along with the debris. When we finally reached the planet, he reduced our space velocity by using some of our air as a retro-rocket. The gravity of the planet pulled us in, while the pieces of the ship remained in orbit. We crashed into this forest and immediately began sending out a signal in an attempt to contact you. However, since our ship was destroyed, we could only broadcast a weak signal. Our only hope was that you or one of your drones would fly within the perimeter of our broadcast area."

"I think we saw where you landed," I said, "there is a pretty large swath of shrubbery burned and flattened near the beach a few kilometers from here."

"According to Captain Clearwater, someone underestimated the forces of the cloud layer on this planet. After one of his excursions, he hypothesized that after our parachutes opened, we were tossed around, and hit the beach with more force than anticipated. He thinks we bounced and were flung into the canopy where we are wedged now. You finding us here is simply a stroke of luck."

"I am beginning to think it is more than luck that is keeping us alive on this planet. I am getting a strange feeling that someone or something wants us to survive."

Pré added, "We have been through a lot and survived, but unfortunately, we are stuck here, the same as you. We have lost contact with our other crew members, and the last we heard from them is that we have no way to return to the *Alpha*. But at least we can survive here for the time being."

"Where are my manners?" Bailey asked intently. "Are you two hungry? I can synthesize just about anything."

"We did dine on some delicious salad a few hours ago," I said, "but I could eat."

"Why don't I whip up a nice beef stew, and some fresh bread while we wait for the General's return? His excursions don't usually last this long, so I am expecting him back at any time now."

My mouth was already watering at the mere mention of food. I let my body relax for a moment and then realized, just how totally exhausted I was. My mind wandered. I don't think Bailey knew how serious I was about how I felt that there was some other entity guiding our fate on this celestial body. It was almost like a sixth sense. I could feel it.

The food was ready in seconds, and after a hot bowl of the most delicious meal I'd had in many days, I sat down on the cot in the rear of the habitat. Hiccups jumped up beside me, started purring, and cuddled in beside me. Pré walked over. She had taken off her suit and had been washing with a warm, moist bathing cloth that she had found in the hab.

"Why don't you take off that suit and clean up a bit, Captain?" she asked. "It is refreshing. Then I can check your injuries."

"You know when to say the right things," I said as I leaned back to take my boots off. The next thing I knew, I was waking up, stretched out on the cot. I was tucked under a blanket, and my suit was neatly folded, and laying off to the side of the cot.

"Good morning, Captain Silverwood," Bailey said.

"How long was I out?" I asked somewhat embarrassed.

"Sixteen hours, thirty-one minutes, and nine seconds," was Bailey's reply.

"Don't feel bad," Pré smiled as she came out of the bathroom. "I slept for twelve hours. Care for some breakfast?"

"That sounds like the perfect idea," I said. "Oh, and Bailey, I meant to ask, do you know anyone with the name Cowan? We found that name spelled out in logs on the beach."

"Not COWAN, Captain Silverwood. 'Go Now'. General Clearwater left that message for you, just in case we never found you. We have been monitoring the seismic activity in this area since we have arrived. It has increased ten-fold. I am also detecting a slight increase in air temperature. Scientists on Earth predicted cataclysmic events for this planet when the three stars are in syzygy. That is supposed to happen in approximately eighty Earth years. However, I have calculated an increase in the rate of acceleration for all three stars, and predict the alignment will occur much sooner. The gravity shifts will occur sooner than expected and are actually beginning now. I believe this planet will undergo major planet-wide seismic activity very soon. That is the reason for the message. It is urgent you leave soon."

"Aren't you a bundle of good news to wake up to?" I said with a little too much sarcasm.

Changing the subject, I asked, "Yesterday, you mentioned the cat had ALIT programming. What is that all about?"

"I am afraid the news on that subject is not so good as well," Bailey began. "Just after you left, people with ALIT programming began to experience horrific problems. Many suffered from severe mental abnormalities. Some reported seeing ghosts and other objects that were not there. Internal hemorrhaging of the cerebrospinal fluid between the meninges caused many to lose voluntary control of their muscles. Loss of involuntary control by the brain followed. Many were driven insane by what they described as constant memory flashes. Of the people who had volunteered to be elevated to a higher brain function, one hundred percent either went insane or died within the first two years. The program was halted. After a large amount of research into why it failed, the program was started again, but this time with limited testing in small mammals. Hiccups is an example of one of the successful trials."

"Do you mean to say, I am going to die or go insane?"

"Captain Silverwood, you should have been dead seven years ago."

I looked at Pré. "Don't say it! Or have gone insane, right?" I asked.

"That is correct," Bailey replied.

"I should have stayed in bed," I said dejectedly.

"Captain Silverwood, you have been alive with the ALIT programming now for nine years. I think that is a positive sign."

Pré turned to me, "Maybe there is something in the stasis

209

elixir that I designed that allowed your body to adjust to the technology as you slept on our journey here." There was a look of hope in her eyes.

"Crispers!" I said. "If the planet doesn't kill me, my own brain just might!"

"Captain, you are already an anomaly," Bailey added, "out-living the others by over seven years."

"Yeah, me and the fricken' cat," I said disgustedly.

Pré had been busy checking the hardware on her suit when a voice coming from her comm-link interrupted our morbid conversation.

"Captain Asil? Asil? Is that you?" It was Connor's voice!

Pré grabbed her suit and held it up to her mouth. "Connor! Connor! Can you hear me?" she cried.

"Pré! I can hear you! It is you guys! We thought we had lost you!"

"Bailey, can you sync this to the hab?" I asked quickly in a loud voice.

"I will try," Bailey said.

"Oh, my God! Oh, my God!" Pré cried with tears rolling down her cheeks.

"Pré, we must be in range of your comm-link," came Connor's voice now through the walls of the hab. "That means we are close!"

"How are you not dead yet?" I shouted excitedly with a hint of relief in my voice.

"How are you not dead yet?" Lexie's voice joined in.

"Lexie, you're there too, you beautiful Australian!" I shouted, "Your voice is music to our ears!"

"Cailey is here too, we managed to pull her out before the habs floated away," she replied.

"Who does the other voice I heard, belong to?" Connor asked.

"I am Bailey," Bailey replied, "I am a biological artificial intelligence."

"What?" Connor asked.

"It is James Clearwater's AI," Pré answered.

"He's there too? Where the heck are you guys?"

"We are in a hab, stuck up in a tree!" I replied, "And, Jim is not here in the hab right at this moment, but I guess he is around here somewhere!"

"What? What is going on?" Connor asked.

"I will explain later," I said. "Where are you? It is so good to hear your voice!"

"We are in the shuttle," came his reply.

"Are you submerged under water?" I asked.

"No!" he said excitedly. "We are flying!"

"You are what?"

"We are flying!" he cried. "But not too all-that-well, I am afraid! I am just learning!"

"How did you...? Where did you...? How the hell did you fix the shuttle?"

"It was all Hailey!" he explained. "She reprogrammed all the cleaning bots to head to the shuttle bay. When they got there, she somehow got them to break the restraining belts that held the crate that contained the new fail-safe ignition sensor to the shuttle bay wall. Once it broke free, she said she programmed the bots to give it a little nudge. Being in low gravity, you know it was mass versus mass. I'm not sure how she got them to move it to where the mechanical loading arm could grab it, but she did. She opened the shuttle bay doors and flung the crate out into space using the mechanical arm. In the meantime, she called the probes' launch vehicle back to the ship.

You were wrong about the amount of juice that thing has in it. It has a lot more power than we imagined! When it returned to the ship, Hailey had it capture the floating crate in one of the probe bays. She turned the launch vehicle around and headed it back for a landing near the habs. Of course, it has no landing mechanism, but she slowed it enough so when it crashed on the shore, its contents survived.

I retrieved the sensor and popped it in. The ignition worked perfectly, and the vertical thrusters lit up as pretty as an Irish sunset! We lifted off just as our habs floated out to sea.

I don't know how she pulled it off. We have since lost contact with the *Alpha*. Hailey knew we would not be able to communicate, but she assured me she would see us in a few days, just before she crashed the launch vehicle. Now, we just need you to fly this thing out of the atmosphere. I am afraid my flying skills are limited to the thrusters."

"That is incredible," I said, "this mission gets more unbelievable each day."

"We do have a sad note," Lexie said with sorrow in her voice. "We lost Sal."

"Sal?" asked Pré. "What happened?"

"Do you remember the last time we spoke? Remember, I told you that he was headed back to the plateau to get a bore of one the trees? I sent a probe with him. As I watched him jam the bore into the trunk, and turn it on, a huge tentacle-like thing uncoiled from the canopy just behind him. It wrapped around him with incredible speed and yanked him up into the canopy. I followed with the drone, and he was gone. Just gone. I searched those trees for hours for any sign of him, but could not see anything. It was like he just vanished!"

"Tree squids!" Bailey interrupted.

"What?" Pré asked.

"Tree squids. That is what General Clearwater calls them. He has been studying them for months. They live in the canopies of the trees. Apparently, they have some symbiotic relationship with the trees. If you try to harm the trees, they will attack and defend the trees. If you do not harm the trees, they will leave you alone. Captain Clearwater thinks they get their nourishment from the liquid in the leaves. He believes they are amphibious, and spend their larval stage in the ocean. When they become adults, they move to the trees. He encountered one when he cut down some logs by the beach. The warning sign that he created almost cost him his life. He said he was lucky to survive the encounter. Had it not been for Hiccups creating a distraction, he would have never escaped. They look like squids and are about twice our size. They have between eight and twelve tentacles. He thinks they get more tentacles as they grow older. He thinks that they are very primitive in brain function having possibly only short-term memory. He has walked among the trees many times since the encounter and has had no more attacks directed at him. According to his recordings, they blend in the canopy with the ability to change their camouflage to the environment they are in. One slithered across the canopy of the habitat eighty-seven days ago and changed its appearance to look just like the fabric. I have it recorded if you would like to see it. General Clearwater...."

I interrupted, "Ok Bailey, that is enough information. I don't know what to say. Sal was a good man."

The habitat began to shake, bringing us back to the reality we now faced.

Connor's voice came through the walls, "Asil, I can get a location reading from Pré's suit. It looks like you are in the middle of a forest, some twenty kilometers, at ninety degrees to the ocean. We have a drone within the area; that must be how we are able to communicate. We are not close with the shuttle. Even if I can get the shuttle there, I don't think I can get through the canopy of those trees to pick you up."

"Can you follow Pré's suit?" I asked. "There is a beach a few kilometers back. Could you pick us up there?"

"I think so," came his reply. "I will have Lexie send the drone as well. It will get to you long before we will. We should have good communication then."

I replied, "That sounds like a great plan. "Suit up, Pré, we are heading out!"

I looked at the cat and said, "Come with me, pussy, if you want to live."

I know! That line has been overused for a hundred years, but it fit so perfectly.

The cat must have understood what I said because it turned and headed for the door.

"Asil?" Bailey asked. "What about General Clearwater?"

"When he returns, tell him to meet us on the beach where he

made his sign! We will wait as long as we can!"

"I have sent all the data that I have collected to your shuttle. I have sent General Clearwater's instructions and data on the wormhole as well."

"Thank you, Bailey."

"Asil?" Bailey asked in a soft voice. "Are you going to leave me here?"

"I never leave anyone behind. I will come back for you." With that, I turned and left.

As we climbed down the rope, the tremors continued. Nothing major, but just enough to make walking difficult.

Again, Hiccups led the way. So far, the trees remained intact. No missiles hurled down from the canopy as we maneuvered our way through the forest on the shaking ground.

I hope the squids don't think we are shaking their trees, or this could turn into one tough hike through the woods!

The winding trek through the forest proved uneventful. As we cleared the canopy at the ecotone between the trees and the shrubs, we were greeted by a deep, cyan sky. The rain and clouds had cleared, and the path ahead through the burned and crushed shrubs was dry, at least as dry as it could be in this sub-tropical environment. The tremors that shook us had ceased for the time being.

With renewed vigor and a sense of a lightened load, I jogged through the shredded and scattered black stalks, jumping over their remaining stumps, until I finally found the soft, dark gray sand of the beach. I plopped down on the warm sand, and Pré plopped down beside me. We took off our helmets and sat with our arms braced behind us as we leaned back and stared into the bright blue sky. No clouds were visible. It felt like one of those days on Earth where you could sit on the beach for hours digging your toes into the soft, chambré sand, letting the power of the sun with its summery rays wash over your body as you contemplated life.

Pré was listening intently into her earpiece. She turned and looked at me, and said, "Connor says the drone is less than an hour out from our position, and he is not far behind in the shuttle, he says, if he can fly straight." She turned back toward the cliff and pointed at the lava tube from which we had been ejected. "I wonder if we will ever get back there to thoroughly explore that city?"

The tube had been completely sealed by the now-cooled lava. Molten lava no longer leaked from the opening, and the hardened flow created a gentle rock slope down to the water.

I just smiled, lost in thought. I sat there going over the events that had unfolded since we had first set foot on the sand. The minutes turned to an hour as I attempted to put together the complex chronology. My heart was light, although what Bailey had said about the ALIT program lingered and gnawed somewhere back at the base of my skull.

No matter! We are GOING HOME! I'm sure they can fix me when we get there. At least, the news about the cat is promising!

Pré leaned over and placed her hand on top of mine. She smiled and spoke in a warm, sweet voice, "I have lived an entire lifetime over the last few days. My life has always been filled with trials and accomplishments, but it has never felt complete. I have always felt there was something missing. I do not feel that way anymore. Thank you for making me whole."

"My small heart grew three sizes that day...."

Just as I was about to respond in kind, she jumped to her feet.

"There it is!" she shouted, as she raced down the beach waving her arms.

The shiny exterior of the drone glinted in the light of the suns as it rounded the sharp corner of the cliff wall and headed our way.

Connor dipped the fuselage of the drone to acknowledge he saw us.

As Pré dashed down the shoreline, she grabbed her helmet and flung it high into the air like a graduate at a commencement exercise.

She shouted happily as she ran, "Come on Asil! That is the most beautiful sight in the world! We are going home!"

Then she stopped dead in her tracks.

CHAPTER 17: RESTITUTION

Rising out of the water just behind the drone was a gargantuan shadow. It looked as if the entire seafloor of the coastal zone was reaching into the sky attempting to crush the small probe.

"Run!" I screamed as the enormous black blister of ocean floor grew before us. The ground shook with fury as the behemoth climbed into the sky.

Pré turned and started back toward me just as the mountain of Hade's fury erupted like a bursting pustule, spewing a sea of molten lava high into the air.

I was already on my feet, clipping my helmet back on, and running as the hot gases of fire and brimstone carried the molten mass inland. The lava hit the trees with a thunderous crash! Toxic gases, smoke, and fire erupted into the air as the trees exploded. Giant shards of wood flew skyward as the trunks blew apart. Massive chunks of burning canopy followed suit creating a scene of hellish chaos!

Elephantine chunks of scorched wood and pieces of the canopy with attached burning leaves began to rain down on the beach; the sand exploding around them as if it were being hit by mortar shells. I stopped to let Pré catch up, and watched in horror as the mammoth trunk of a tree struck the sand just a meter behind her. It slid and rolled, striking her from behind, knocking her down. The immense mass flattened her as it slid over the top of her, and buried itself into the churning sand! Immediately a wave rolled over the top of it, and a cloud of hot steam eschewed from the heavy log as it came to rest.

As I ran through the cloud of vapor and smoke, I could not see anything. Fear gripped me as I ran. I smacked headlong into the log and fell to my knees. I reached into the frothing water as another wave bumped my body into the log. I tried desperately to grab any part of Pré's suit. As the water receded, I noticed her right arm protruding from beneath the behemoth. I followed it to her shoulder and saw her head peeking out the side just below a large splinter.

"Can you hear me?" I screamed, as another wave rushed in and covered her. As it followed its sister wave back to swirling sea, I saw she was breathing, spitting water and sand out of her mouth. I put my shoulder under the trunk and tried to stand up. The adrenaline ripped through my muscles as I strained to push the monstrous hulk off her body. There are times in great emergencies when the human body seems to find super-strength, enough to lift heavy auto-pods off trapped individuals. If I had that strength at this time, it wasn't enough. I could not move that log one centimeter!

"Hold your breath!" I cried as another wave swept in and buried her once again. I grabbed my laser knife from my utility belt and tried to hack off large chunks of the log! Only small splinters came off as I hammered the blade down again and again. I realized then, she could not hear me. I had my helmet on and she did not. The sounds of the crashing waves must have been too great to hear my voice in her earpiece! In desperation, I looked around. I saw her helmet about ten meters from where she fell, and I stumbled through the receding surf to retrieve it. I got back to her just as the next wave again submerged her. I waited until it receded, then pushed the helmet on her head. Her suit did not respond to the presence of her helmet. The nano-processors in the suit must have been using every microwatt of their power to hold her suit rigid to keep the weight of the enormous log from crushing her. The helmet simply would not meld with the suit. I attempted to manually secure her helmet. I felt the sand grains grinding along the seal as I pushed and twisted to secure it in place. I heard her cough and sputter into her comm-link as yet another wave struck.

"You are going to be okay!" I shouted. "I am going to get you out of here!"

As the last wave receded, she spoke as she coughed up more of the salty brine, "My suit is solid, but I think I may have bruised a lung. I am having a tough time catching my breath."

As the wave drew away, I frantically began to scoop sand away from under her head. I dug feverishly trying to expose her body and free her from her imprisonment! Each time I made progress, another wave would surge in and wash the sand back into the space I had just cleared. Still, I dug, trying to dig faster between each onslaught of water. Every time I thought I could see more of her white suit; the demented water would splash in again, filling the void that I had created. I did not give up! My shoulders and back ached as I wildly pounded the sand with my hands.

I heard her voice in the background. It was weak and barely audible. "Asil, Asil, stop. I can feel the pressure building. The suit is giving out. I'm sorry. I cannot save you this time, Asil," she said as I wiped away the mud from her faceplate. I could see tears in her eyes, and a small amount of blood that had drooled from her lips onto her cheek.

"Your hair is messed up," I sobbed, as sadness swept over me. Tears came to my eyes and began to stream down my cheeks.

She attempted to smile, and said, "Just when I was beginning to like you." Then, she closed her eyes, and let out a long, slow breath.

Somewhere, in the distance, I thought I heard a bell ring as my angel got her wings.

The old song, *God Only Knows What I'd Be Without You,* echoed in my brain.

"No! No! No!" I cried, my vision blurred with salty tears and sweat, as I resumed my rabid digging.

It was then I noticed the waves had stopped. Realization overcame me as I turned to witness a growing wall of water in the distance. The result of the vast shockwave that had hit the shore was gathering height as it approached our position.

"Goddammit!" I screamed. I let out a blood-curdling cry and ran screaming like a madman toward the fast-advancing wall of water.

"You shall not take her!" I yelled as loud as I could as I hit the water. The ever-building wave simply picked me up and carried me higher and higher as it built towards its breaking point. It continued to push thousands of liters of water under me until it broke, curling under its own weight! The breaker hurled me high into the air and toward the trees atop the cliff on the plateau. The water threw me into the trees, and I hit the thick trunk of a tree that stood before me with a sickening "whack"! I heard a hideous cracking sound. I hoped it was the tree or my suit, and not my ribs as I faceplanted into the wood. The surging water swept me away from the trunk, and, in its insane ferocity, slammed me into tree after tree as this hammer from the sea pounded the landscape! The glass mallet snapped canopies and uprooted members of the old forest as it bounced me among the trees like a pinball in an ancient arcade game.

The surge spun me among the debris, and then it changed direction. As it began a swift retreat back toward the edge of the cliff, I looked up to see water spilling over the edge in a violent froth of wood and stone. I imagined my body being hurled out over a tremendous waterfall and plunging to the awaiting deathblow of the rocks below.

I spoke into my helmet, "Power off." My suit immediately lost its steel rigidity as I let the current carry me along towards certain death.

The planet had defeated me.

It had already taken my heart. It could now have the rest of me. As my suit relaxed, so did I, and I let my mind wander back to the first time that I realized I had truly cared about someone else other than myself.

As I slipped past the last tree before the water plunged back to its origin, I had one final thought, *"You took my heart. You smashed my body. Now you can have my soul."*

I closed my eyes and waited for my final fall.

Suddenly, something, large and muscular, quickly reached out of that final tree's canopy and grabbed me firmly under my left arm. With a force that tore against the current, the huge arm dragged me up and out of the water. I imagined the tentacled beast that Bailey had called a "tree squid" sweeping my limp body into its bone-crushing jaws. I opened my eyes only to stare into the huge brown eyes of an American Indian with short-cropped hair.

"Captain Asil Silverwood," General James Clearwater grinned as he held me above the water with one very large, muscular arm, "what brings you to my planet?"

"Grab some tree," he said as he pulled me over close to the branches he was hanging from.

I just stared, disbelieving, as the rushing water below us began to diminish to a small steam.

"Jim," was all I could get out.

As the water continued to recede, I latched onto a branch, and we watched in silence as the last of it flowed over the breach to the brine below.

Just as I was about to ask him when-and-how, we were interrupted by the sound of thumping wind as the gleaming surface of the shuttle rose above the cliff face. Its thrusters pounded the air as it lifted above our heads.

The blue-light grappling hook with its Clearsteel™ cable flew from the hold opening in the fuselage as its doors swung open. The blue-light hook then continued its descent slowly as a winch caught it and lowered it to our perch.

"Looks like one of mine," he said as he grabbed the light cable and wound it around my waist and legs. He tied it off in a climber's harness and waved back to the ship as he said, "The blue-light technology won't do much good here. The suit won't let it attach."

I hung there numbly as I was gently pulled up to awaiting safety.

When I boarded the shuttle, I was greeted with huge hugs from Lexie and Connor.

"Pré?" asked Lexie. I shook my head sadly as Connor started the winch to haul the General up as well.

As General Clearwater climbed safely aboard, and Connor closed the hold doors, my instincts took over.

"We've got to find her," I said as I hurried toward the cockpit.

"You drive," Connor said as he planted himself in the co-pilot's seat. He knew exactly what I was doing.

I whipped the shuttle's nose around as I guided it toward the beach where she had been trapped. We arrived to calming waters, with no sign of the tremendous log that had pinned her.

"She's not here," I said as I lowered the craft over the area where she had been. I began a slow back-and-forth search out to sea as I piloted the shuttle out over the water.

"Any signal from her suit?" I asked.

"None," came Lexie's dejected voice.

I continued my oscillating search; widening the line along which I traversed. After several hours of searching, we had covered hundreds of square kilometers.

"Captain, we've got to go while the weather holds," Connor said. "We can barely communicate with Hailey on the *Alpha* when the sky is clear. If it clouds over, we will lose our signal, and may not get back."

"Again," I said stubbornly. "Let's crisscross the area in a different direction this time."

After several more hours, and with nothing turning up, I reluctantly turned the ship toward the shore.

"There's two more out there," I said determinedly, as I pointed the ship's nose toward the tree-line.

"What are you talking about?" Connor asked with concern in his voice. I think he thought I was losing my mind.

As the shuttle flew over the forest's edge, I saw the landscape had changed dramatically with the devastation. I wasn't so sure I could find the habitat, and I could not pick up the distress beacon that Bailey said they had been broadcasting. I attempted to contact Bailey back at the habitat. For some reason, he did not answer. Maybe something had happened during the eruption.

I called back to the passenger's cabin, "Jim, I might need your help."

General Clearwater had been listening to the conversation and said into the shuttle's comm-link, "Captain, this one's on me. It might be that I told Bailey to power down when I am not there. You know, to save energy."

He then spoke to the ship's computer, "Computer, send out distress code call override protocol omega-zeta at twenty-one-eighty-two kilohertz." He spoke back into the comm-link, "Bailey must have shut down the beacon after you found him."

Immediately, a blinking blue light appeared on my monitor. I pulled on the grips, and the ship veered slightly to the right as I aligned its nose in the direction of the flashing light on the monitor and gunned the engine.

As we approached, and the habitat came into view, I noticed it was still exactly where we had found it before, nestled snuggly among the branches and leaves of the giant forest's canopy. The lava blast had not reached this far into the woods.

"A cat!" Both Connor and Lexie shouted simultaneously as we neared the spheroid. There, standing on the top of the habitat, it's claws firmly dug into the canvas, was Hiccups. He was meowing for all he was worth.

"Boys and girls," said General Clearwater, "I would like you to meet the rest of my crew."

I maneuvered the shuttle so the doors of the hold were directly above the habitat. I opened the doors and lowered the blue-light grappling hook until it made contact with the Clearsteel™ canvas of the hab, and clicked on the molecular attractor. It worked as expected, and the flat surface of the device attached firmly to the hab's exterior. As soon as the line was secure, Hiccups climbed it quickly like he was being chased by a ferocious dog, meowing all the way up.

"What's the plan? Connor asked.

"I'm going to pull it into the hold," I said matter-of-factly.

"It's wedged in there pretty tight, do you think we can pull it out without crashing? Plus, it's a little big, don't you think?"

asked Connor as he stared down out the side window of the shuttle.

I knew he was right, but at the moment my brain was not working very clearly.

"I got this," came General Clearwater's voice through the ship's speaker. As I watched on the cabin monitor, he jumped out of his seat and headed toward the hold.

He had not been wearing his suit, so I knew he could not contact Bailey. The next thing I saw was this large, muscular man shimmying down the cable toward the habitat. After he planted his feet on the surface, he laid flat on his belly and crawled to the edge of the canvas. He slid over the side of the bubble and disappeared.

We waited for five, then ten minutes. I thought he must have slid right off the habitat and crashed to the forest floor. Finally, the shuttle's comm-link crackled to life. "Sorry, we had a helluva of a time finding your frequency. They have changed so many things since you've been gone. Anyway, have you ever seen how they free the truck when one of the auto-pod trucks gets stuck when it wedges its trailer under a bridge?"

"Let air out of the tires, instead of breaking the bridge?" asked Connor.

"Ah, it's good to have an engineer on board," he said. "That's exactly what we are going to do. Give us another minute."

As I watched, I could see the habitat shrinking slowly as it expelled its gases.

"Pull us up!" shouted General Clearwater into the comm-link.

I inched the shuttle upward as I engaged the winch to give us a little extra pulling power. A few branches snapped, and bunches of leaves fluttered to the ground as the habitat broke free. It swung gently back and forth in the open air above the canopy as it was lifted slowly toward the opening.

By the time the winch had brought the habitat to its doors, the canvas had deflated enough to just allow its exterior walls to scrape through the opening in the hold. I sealed the doors, and spoke into the shuttle's comm-link, "Hailey?" I asked.

"Yes, Captain?" she replied in her soft, soothing voice. "It is so good to hear your voice again."

Ignoring her compassion, I said, "We are coming home."

CHAPTER 18: RETURN

The trip back to the *Alpha* had been uneventful thanks to the calm atmosphere that accompanied the clear, blue sky. With the shuttle stowed safely again, Hailey adjusted our orbit, and preparations began for the journey back to Earth.

I felt old and broken as we logged our data and began to secure the different compartments for the mission-ending return.

As I sat alone on my bunk in my quarters, just trying to understand all that had happened in just two, short weeks, my thoughts were interrupted by Hailey's calm voice coming through the walls. "Asil, I am sorry for the interruption, but General Clearwater would like to meet with the crew."

"What's this about?" I asked.

"He would like to discuss the restructuring of the *Alpha* for the return trip home."

"Oh yeah, that," I replied in a monotone voice.

"We all miss them," she said.

I had never known an AI to be so insightful, but she did not know just how badly I hurt inside.

"Tell the crew, we will meet in the cafeteria at eighteen-hundred hours," I said. *"The crew,"* I thought, *"it's just Lexie and Connor now."*

***

I arrived late for the meeting. Lexie and Connor were already there sitting at the table. General Clearwater was entertaining them with another story of one of his many planetary exploits, as he had been doing over the past few days.

"What's up?" I asked.

"It's time to discuss hull integrity," General Clearwater responded. "I'm sorry about your crew members, but we've got to see if we can get the rest home."

"Let me update you on what we found back on Earth," he continued. "The alloy of Clearsteel™ that we used to construct the first fusion ships was meant to be flexible so it could withstand the stresses and strains created by forces needed to move our ships in space. This alloy worked well until we encountered the tremendous forces exerted by a wormhole. What we found through experimentation, as we lost probes in the wormhole, was that the extreme forces created by the hole would cause the bonds of the Clearsteel™ alloy to vibrate much like that of a plucked guitar string. The vibrating bonds would then cause the entire molecule to resonate to the point where the molecule would tear itself apart. Thus, the probes entering the wormhole would shake so badly, they would tear themselves apart. We began tests to see if we could somehow strengthen the bonds of the alloy, and thus, reduce the amount of resonance. After many tests, using a variety of elements and compounds, we found simple iron ions appeared to work the best. The interstitial character of the iron ion in the carbon matrix worked well to reduce molecular bond vibration. Who knew the recipe for simple steel would give us the solution, right? The ferric ion worked a little better than the ferrous ion. Probably, its +3 charge versus the ferrous ion's +2 charge. We sent probe after probe into the wormhole. Each time, the probe would last a little longer as we varied the amounts of iron and changed how we embedded them into the alloy mixture.

Finally, the fifteenth probe made it all the way through and back. We were so excited we named the new variation of the alloy C.S.-15.

We found that we could convert the original Clearsteel™ alloy to C.S.-15 by simply coating it with iron ions, and then hammering it home, so-to-speak, with infrared radiation with a wavelength of about 14,000 nanometers. We could only penetrate the first few layers of molecules, but that seemed to strengthen the alloy enough to withstand the tremendous

PATRICK RIEDER

forces.

In our haste to get to you, we reconfigured a one-man vessel already made of the original Clearsteel™. We coated it with iron ions, zapped it with infrared radiation, loaded it with Hiccups and me, and sent it into the wormhole. Did I mention this will be Hiccups' fourth trip through the wormhole? He was on probe fifteen that went through and came back. Starting with probe ten, they began to send mammals along with the probes to see how the forces of the hole would affect living things. Cats seemed to respond best to the new version of ALIT technology, so most of the animals sent were cats. We lost some good cats and a couple of monkeys on the probes that did not make it back.

Anyway, as Hiccups and I exited the wormhole, we encountered some abnormal forces, just at the edge, that shook us to pieces. We managed to jettison before we broke up. Luckily, Bailey was able to take care of us until we got here. You know the rest of the story."

"So, how does this relate to the *Alpha*?" I asked.

"Well, if we can find some source of iron and an infrared energy source in the fourteen thousand nanometer range, we can re-paint the hull, and embed the iron to strengthen this baby."

"Is that all?" I asked, my sullen mood unchanging.

"Yep, but first I hear we need to repair a tear in the shield, from what I understand. I am pretty sure I can help with that."

"What are you talking about?" I asked.

"We need to find some scrap alloy around here. I can then weld it over the gap in the shield."

"As you know, most spaceships don't just carry extra metal just laying around. We are restricted to a certain mass-to-thrust ratio," I snapped back. I was getting even more irritated with all this science fiction crap the General was spewing out.

"What about the stasis pods?" asked Connor. "They are made of Clearsteel™. We could dismantle them since we won't need them for the trip back."

"That could work," the General replied. "How many do you

228

have on board?"

"We have six, but only five available," responded Lexie, "Dr. Smith is occupying the other one. She couldn't be revived safely here."

"I was wondering where the 'old bird' was," said the General. "Let's get the dimensions of that tear, and see how much steel we need to cover it. I hope the five stasis pods will be enough. If my calculations are correct, and I remember correctly, there should be enough steel."

"You will need forty-five square meters. Each individual longitudinal plate of a stasis tube is 2.5 meters in length and 1.7 meters in width. Each tube has three of these plates. Four tubes should give you enough to cover the hole," I said with zero emotion in my voice. Again, I was not sure how I knew all the dimensions and did the math so quickly in my head. But this time I felt a twinge of pain just behind my ears as I spoke.

"Ok, one problem solved," commented General Clearwater.

"Is everyone's suit working? We are going to have to do several spacewalks to get the job done," he continued.

"Mine is not functioning correctly," I responded.

"Captain, you will be at communications when we go out to weld our patch in place."

"Whatever," I replied sullenly. I knew I should be acting like a captain, and control my emotions or lack there-of, but I just couldn't see myself back on Earth anymore. I had died emotionally back on that planet, and according to Bailey, I might die physically at any moment in time.

General Clearwater turned to me. His intense stare piercing my brain. I could see he was trying to hold back a rage that had built inside him. It was taking all of his strict military discipline for him to not clobber me on the spot. He spoke through gritted teeth, "Asil! You are the captain of this ship. It is your responsibility to return its crew and contents safely to the ISS. Either take control of your emotions and this vessel, or I will relieve you of your command!"

I looked back at him. Anger surged in me as tears began to well in my eyes. They did not know what I had lost! But he was right. It was my command. These people were counting on me to fly this ship. Just because I was dying didn't mean they had to die as well. I straightened up, looked him straight in the eyes, and said, "I AM the captain of this ship. You get this thing ready, and I will fly it through a goddam maelstrom to get you home."

"Thank you, Captain," he said, his eyes softening as his expression relaxed. "Now, we need a source of iron ions."

"Soybeans!" Lexie perked up with her answer.

"What?" asked the General.

"Soybeans," she said, "they are loaded with iron!"

"And where are we supposed to get...," Connor stopped himself in mid-sentence, "the 'farm'!"

"We have row after row of soybeans in our agriculture compartment," she continued, "we use them as a source of nutrients in our diet!"

"Hailey?" I asked. "Do you think you could use your food processors and synthesizers to extract some iron ions for us?"

"It is possible," she said.

"Now we just need a way to paint them on the hull," the General added.

"The redundant watering cans!" Connor interjected excitedly. "We have twenty-liter watering cans just in case the automatic misting sprinklers go out in the farm. They have spray nozzles that shoot a mist of water. If we dissolve the ions in a solvent, we can use the cans to spray the hull!"

"Yes, but the solvent may just bounce off the hull. The ions won't stick without some sort of adhesive," I said trying not to be too negative.

"Charge the hull," interrupted Hailey in her calm voice. "If we give the hull a negative charge, I can come up with some sort of aqueous solution that will stick the positively charged iron ions to the hull when the oppositely charged ions attract."

"How are we going to negatively charge the hull?" asked the General.

"Friction," I said. "When we went through the cloud bank, we built up such a charge that the lightening just hammered us over and over again. If I bring the ship close enough to the atmosphere, I can rub the ship against it. Kind of like when you rub a rubber balloon on your hair. We'll build up charge, jump out, and paint the ship!"

"That could work," he replied. "Now all we have to do is embed the ions within the molecular layers. We will need a whole lot of infrared radiation for that."

"Sirius C," a man's voice came through the walls.

"What? Bailey, is that you? Have you been listening all this time?" I asked.

"Yes, Captain Silverwood. Hailey has been kind enough to allow me to share the ship's data and communications banks. Sirius C, it is a brown dwarf. Its main type of radiation is infrared. From what I detected back on the planet, Sirius C emits infrared radiation across the entire IR spectrum, from seven hundred nanometers to one millimeter."

Connor asked, "So, we just need to let the paint dry?"

"It is not quite that simple," interjected Bailey again. "The infrared radiation here on the planet is not intense enough to drive the iron into the molecular matrix. The ship needs to be closer to the brown dwarf. Much closer."

"How close?" I asked.

"I am doing the calculations right now, Captain Silverwood," answered Bailey. "Are you as good a pilot as your record shows?"

"He is," Hailey chimed in.

"Good, he will need to be to pull us out of Sirius C's gravity well. We will have to get very close to the brown dwarf."

General Clearwater spun his chair to face everyone and said, "Well, then that's it. That is one helluva plan. I am glad we have two brilliant engineers, one adept pilot, and a couple of quick-thinking AI's on board. We just might be able to pull this off." He smiled as he slapped his hands down on the table. "It's your ship, Captain Silverwood. Where do we start?"

"First, we eat, and then, get some rest. I know all of you have not slept more than a few hours in the last couple of days. We will have to be at the top of our game to pull this off!"

"*The Wedding Ringer?* Really, Captain?" Hailey asked. "I thought for sure you were going to say something like, 'Get some sleep. Tomorrow, this place becomes a well-oiled machine, my friend.' You know, misquoting the greatest romance flick in the history of film, *You've Got Mail?*"

Everyone laughed. I almost smiled for the first time in three days.

*****

The next few days were a blur of activity as we prepared the ship for its homeward journey. Connor and I tore apart four of the six stasis tubes. We disconnected the mechanical arms, tore out the wires, removed bolts, cut metal, and scraped metal surfaces. The hard work kept my mind occupied as both my mind and body healed themselves. The bruises on my arms and legs had diminished to the point where I could actually count them individually.

Lexie worked down in the farm pulling soybeans; dumping loads of them into the food processor; helping Hailey create her iron ion paint. Hiccups joined her there, although I am not sure what kind of help, he was. *I wished he had been here when we had the rat problem.*

General Clearwater spent much of his time in his spacesuit, preparing the gash in the shield for repair.

The work went as planned, and in just a little over two days, we had a bright coppery patch welded across the opening created by what was left of the *Beta.*

The next stage was up to me as I guided the *Alpha* back toward the planet. The plan was to just skim the outer layer of the planet's atmosphere to cause friction and build up charge on the hull. As soon as Hailey and Bailey detected adequate charge, Lexie, Connor, and Jim would sail out of the shuttle bay doors with their spray paint in hand and paint as much of the hull as they could before the paint ran out.

As I nudged the shuttle into the outer reaches of the atmosphere, the work began. They started from the shield and worked their way back. After they would return each time, I would check with the AI's on the amount of static charge that remained on the hull as some of it bled off into the atmosphere. If the hull needed more charge, I would then swoop a little lower to create more friction to build the charge to an adequate level. We did this over and over again until most of the hull had a thin layer of iron ion paint covering it. Eventually, we ran out of soybeans. Lexie and Hailey substituted other plants—such as legumes like peas—that had much less iron, but still a sufficient amount to extract. Soon, they were gone too, and so was the paint. The crew had covered as much of the hull as they could and had given areas where they thought the strain and stress would be greatest, two coats.

Now, it was my turn again. This trip would not be as easy as skimming the atmosphere of a planet about the size of one-and-a-half Earths. This brown dwarf was bigger than Jupiter, and it would not be so easy to climb out its gravity well once we were in its clutches. The AI's had calculated the exact distance we needed to be from the wanna-be star, along with the shortest duration we had to endure, to meld the iron to the steel.

I came in fast, and at an oblique angle that was almost parallel to the surface area of the brown dwarf's gravitational field, that we had chosen to enter. My hope was to ride the hot gases like a surfer, and then accelerate hard just as the extreme force of gravity tried to pull us into the seething cauldron of superheated gases.

"Comes a time when we all have to ride the big wave, dude...," I quoted to myself the line from probably the greatest surf movie of the 2060s, or the twenty-first century, for that matter. More people quoted *Spray, Pray, and Lay* than any other movie of its time. I was no exception. And this was one I had actually physically seen in person.

The ship shuddered a little as I coaxed the engines to bring us almost parallel to the seething gas giant below us. The massive gas ball filled the view out of the observation window. I tried to hold the ship steady as I awaited word from Hailey.

"Engaging engines in ten…nine…eight…seven…six…," Hailey said, as the room had grown uncomfortably warm.

"Hang on," I said, as I fired every thruster that I could to aid the fusion rocket's push away from certain annihilation.

Bailey's voice entered the cacophony as the ship's joints creaked and groaned, joining the roar of the rockets, "Holding trajectory! Acceleration at -0.2 meters per second per second!"

We were slowly being tugged back toward the inferno.

"Dammit, Hailey we need more power!" I shouted.

Talk about déjà vu.

"Fusion is at one hundred percent. Thrusters operating at one hundred ten percent capacity, and beginning to overheat!"

"Find us some damn power!"

"Sorry, Asil. There is no more to give."

"Acceleration at -1.2 meters per second per second and increasing," Bailey's voice burst in.

"We are going home!" I said with determination.

I reached over and began throwing switches.

Connor shouted from his chair, "What the hell are you doing?"

"Getting rid of water! Reducing mass! Hailey, open the shuttle bay door!"

"Have you lost your mind?"

"Maybe! Release the shuttle!"

There was a thump as the shuttle slammed into the back of its bay.

"Get it out of there!" I screamed.

"We might damage the shuttle bay if I fire its engines," came Hailey's reply.

"It won't matter if we're all dead! Fire them now!"

I saw a flash of light off to our side as the shuttle exited its hold. Hailey had deftly piloted it out the doors without so much as a scratch. I quickly closed the shuttle bay door manually, before Hailey did it herself.

"Acceleration positive 0.9 meters per second per second and increasing," Bailey called out.

I heard a "Whoop! Whoop!" from behind me as we began to

crawl out of the grasp of Sirius C.

As we all began to relax, I said calmly into the comm-link, "Nice job everyone. I'm not sure what the odds were of us pulling this off, but we did it. At least now we have a chance. We are going to have to slingshot the planet to increase our speed unless we want a very long ride to Sirius B and that wormhole."

"Affirmative, Asil, and fourteen hundred to one," Hailey said calmly.

"Fourteen hundred to one what?" I asked.

"The odds of pulling this off. The odds of completing this plan successfully were fourteen hundred to one."

"I'm glad you didn't mention that before," I said. "Now, I've really got to go to the bathroom!"

I unbuckled as the chair relaxed, and I strode out of the room.

"I might just be able to make it," I said to myself as I walked down the corridor.

Suddenly, the skin behind my ears began to burn. I saw bright white lights flash before my eyes. The last thing I remembered was feeling my face slam into the deck.

CHAPTER 19: RECAPITULATION

I'm awake. At least I thought I was. *"Where am I? Why is it so freakin' dark in here?"* I thought to myself. Everything was fuzzy. *"It's so fuzzy!"* I laughed at that thought. At least I thought I laughed. A memory drifted into my brain.

Lightning crackled around me illuminating the darkness with a sharp bright light that stabbed my eyes. It branched as it ripped across the air above my head, each branch ending in explosive balls of color.

A voice said, "Asil."

"Hey, that's my name, Asil," the thought becomes clear in my mind.

"Argentum Silverwood." More lightning. More exploding colors.

"Are the lights talking?" I thought.

"Is that you, Hailey?" I asked out loud. "Is this some kind of game?"

"No. Hailey. No. No. Not. Hailey. Not game. Game. Game. Game." The word "game" repeated over and over as the lightning flashed again, and colored spheres erupted everywhere. This time, however, each time I heard a word, I noticed a ball of color exploded at the same time.

"No, I did not hear those words. The words came from each lightning flash and the explosion of a colored sphere!" I said to myself. *"I am just understanding the word 'represented' by each different burst of color! The colors ARE words!"*

"What the hell, Hailey? What kind of trick is this?" I asked the darkness.

"Not. Hailey. No trick. No trick. No trick." Lightning flashed all around me in rapid succession. "Not Hailey"—different colors. The next six words—two different colors repeating the same pattern three times. I understood.

"Where am I?" I asked.

Lightning erupted everywhere. Different colored spheres burst all around me. Some repeated patterns over and over again. I was in a fireworks factory, and the whole building was going up at once! It was both beautiful, dizzying, and frightening all at the same time.

"Here. Time. Nowhere. Everywhere. Space. Time. Dimensions. Now. Mind. Space. Space. Space. In Time. Not here. Everywhere."

The words tried to cram into my brain all at once.

"Stop! Stop!" I screamed, "Too much!"

"I can't understand you," I added, "it's too fast!"

More lightning. More bursting balls of color.

"Learning. Talk. Fast? Slow. Try. Try! Words!"

"Everyone is talking all at once!" I shouted. "I cannot think!"

Again, the lightning crackled through the air, colors bursting in the air simultaneously. But this time, there was less.

"I am. We are.... Now. Name? We. We. We, 'Nommo'? We are. I am."

I could feel the blood drain from my face. My heart was racing, it pounded in my chest.

"The 'Nommo'?" The thought raced through my brain as I repeated the words. I did not know how to respond. I did not know what to say. I did not know where I was. I just stood there, wherever this was.

"I think I am standing." The thought flittered through my scattered mind.

The lightning continued. The flashes of color, much less. I understood more.

"I. We. Learning. Difficult. Slower. Thought. Help. Silverwood."

I thought, *"It, they, are attempting to communicate by learning our language! No, that isn't it! I am learning their language! They are slowing it down so I can comprehend. No, that's not it either! We are both learning to communicate with one another!"*

The lightning flashed. I could easily follow the patterns of the exploding balls of color now.

"Argentum Silverwood, are living?" The question flashed through my eyes and mind.

"I am alive," I said. *"At least I think I am!"*

"Not." The lightning and colors flashed.

"What? Am I dead? Is this Heaven?" I said aloud.

"Or maybe, hell?" I thought to myself.

"Not dead. Not alive." The bright lights told me. "Here."

"Where is 'here'?" I asked.

"Now." The lightning spoke into my mind.

"I don't understand," I said. "Can you use more words to communicate? I think you understand me, but I need more words, more colors, to understand you."

The lightning flashed again, this time not as bright, and the colors not as explosive, "What is 'me'?"

"I am me," I said as I pointed to my body. At least what represented my body in this place.

"I. Me? Are you not 'Earth'?" the lights asked.

"Earth? No, that is just the planet we live on."

"We?" the lights asked.

"Yes," I said, "We. 'We', means the many individual humans that live on the Earth." Then I understood. I had a theory.

"Are you not all separate individual organisms?" I asked. "Are your thoughts different than other 'Nommo'?"

The lightning flashed, "All one. Not separate. 'Nommo'?"

Things were becoming clear. This entity was one organism with one mind that had different segments. If it had separate physical bodies, they all thought as a collective. It/they must have thought the humans of the Earth were the same.

"Humans." The lightning continued. "The word is with us. Used before."

"You have encountered us before?" I asked.

"Earth, you, called us 'Nommo'," the lightning flashed.

"The 'Nommo' were squid-like organisms that visited the Earth long ago. Their visit was recorded by the 'Dogon'," I replied.

"No. And yes. Silverwood. Earth. Us appeared to Earth in the physical organism."

It/they and I were beginning to understand each other much better now.

"I am not the Earth. I am not all humans. I am an individual entity on the planet. Each organism has its own thoughts," I said.

"No!" The lightning and colors crackled with a little more determination this time. "Humans choose not to use collective. All minds are attached. Silverwood knows this."

And then, I did know that. Somewhere in human brains, I now knew, we harbored the ability to think together as a collective.

I asked, "Are you not the squid-like organisms that visited Earth long ago?"

The answered came in a bolt of light much clearer now, "We are not. The life you saw came from the new planet you explored."

"The tree-squids," I said.

It was amazing how fast they learned to articulate.

"Yes. The human, Clearwater, called them this," came the reply. "The 'tree-squid' has a primitive mind. We shared; our mind, their physical being. We bound with its physical organism."

"You inhabited the bodies of the tree-squids, so you could physically explore the universe?" I asked.

"Yes." The lightning flashed.

"What are you then?" I asked.

"We are of time and space. It is one. We are one in its dimension."

"Are you saying you don't exist in the physical universe?" I asked.

"Yes." Colors flashed.

"How are you able to communicate with me, then?" I continued to probe.

"You have expanded your thought. When you received an enhanced brain process, your mind expanded into a realm where we can exist. You became aware. We noticed. We have been here, and are here now."

"I'm not the only one that received the ALIT program," I said. "Have you communicated with the others?"

The lightning crackled again, "We have attempted contact with all. All failed. They are no longer. There is only you."

"In the city on the planet," I said, "that was you in the flashing walls? You were trying to communicate with us. What were you trying to tell us?"

"Warning Silverwood. Leave at once."

"Were you warning us about the tree-squids?"

"Yes. No. They are present in the city, and on the planet's surface. They have a primitive mind. They have a symbiotic relationship with the trees. They protect the trees."

"They did not harm us," I said.

"You, did not harm the trees."

"What happened to Sal?" I asked.

"The one you call Sal, harmed the trees."

I internalized this and changed the subject. "There were many walls that lit up, and the patterns were different."

"There was a greater warning." The colors flashed. "You could not continue on the planet. You were in great danger. The planet is changing."

There were so many questions that I wanted to ask. I switched subjects again.

"Why did you visit Earth?" I asked.

"Humans were developing slowly. We wanted to help, before others came. There are others that will not help. They will destroy and take."

"That is when you visited the Dogon?"

"Yes. We showed them where we came from. We showed them how to make tools from stone. We showed them how to live with other organisms with less brain function."

"Why did you leave?"

"Humans turned tools into weapons. Made spears. Made arrows. Killed parts of the whole?"

"You thought humans were like you, thinking as a whole?"

"Yes. Did not understand. Destroy part of the whole? No logic here. We left. Now we understand."

"Did you ever come back?"

"Yes. Several times."

"Why?" I asked. "Were we given a second chance?"

"Your organism attempted to end itself. We are one. We exist to make sure no intelligent life disappears from its realm. All have gifts to offer to others."

"When?" I inquired. "What gifts did you give us?"

"In your words and time; nuclear fission, in the twentieth century. It was to be used as an almost endless energy source.

True artificial intelligence connected directly to your being, in the middle of the twenty-first century. It was to be used to increase your knowledge."

"You gave us this?" I interrupted. "Were you here physically?"

"No."

"How then?"

"Some parts of the whole human entity had expanded their thoughts. Individuals, as you call them. We helped shape their ideas."

"When was the last time you shaped our ideas?"

"In your late twenty-first century. You attempted to end your being. A 'world war' is the term you use."

"How did you stop it?" I asked.

"We did not. Human organism did." The colors flashed.

"How did you help?" I asked

"The entities, Lexie Campbell and Connor McElroy, have great minds. We placed the idea of 'cold fusion' into their being."

The lightning continued to flash. "James Clearwater organism. We aided his development of the alloy."

More lightning, more colors. "Doctor Prevalence Ange, we

suggested the ability to prolong physical life.

Doctor Eugena Smith—gave her a direction to find us.

And you, Argentum Silverwood, have the ability to communicate with an entity beyond the Earth, beyond your physical realm."

"What am I supposed to do with this if I am dead?" I asked.

"Your organism is not deceased. Life, as you call it, has not ended. We are sending you back to share all you have learned. But, before we do, we have one more gift for you that you must share with all humans that inhabit the planet Earth, the other worlds you now have colonized, and will colonize.

As for this planet orbiting Sirius C, you may not return for eighty Earth years. Only then, will it be ready for humans of the Earth to share with its sister."

The lightning flashed again, "Here is your gift...."

The lightning ceased. The bursting colored spheres disappeared. All went dark.

CHAPTER 20:
REVELATION

I'm awake. At least I thought I was. *"Where am I? Why is it so freakin' dark in here?"* I thought to myself. Everything was fuzzy. *"It's so fuzzy!"* I laughed at that thought. At least I thought I laughed. A memory drifted into my brain. *"Oh crap! Not again!"*

I jolted awake. I was lying in a metal bed, in a small, rectangular room that had all of its walls painted white. I was covered with a warm, soft blanket. I looked to the right and saw an IV bag dangling from its wheeled, metal support. I followed the plastic tube attached to the bag down to the bed where I realized it was attached to a needle that was stuck in my arm. I was extremely groggy, but panic began to rise in me as I realized where I was. I heard a clicking sound and looked to my left. A monitor displayed a series of flashing lights. There was a digital readout on the monitor with a number that was steadily rising. I realized it was showing my heart rate as I watched the numbers climb. I looked toward the end of the bed. There was a metal door in the middle of the solid white wall across the room. As I watched in a haze—of which I was sure of was drug-induced—the door swung open wide, and a pretty girl in some sort of uniform entered.

"I am so glad you decided you rejoin us, Asil," she said as she walked over to my bedside. "I noticed your vitals had changed when I checked my patients' monitors. I have already notified the doctor."

She pulled out a moist cloth and wiped the caked eye-boogers from the inside corners of my eyes and my eyelashes. She folded the cloth, and wiped the slobber and dried saliva from around my mouth.

"You had us worried," she said. "We thought you were never coming back."

I looked at her, disbelieving, with a vacant stare. My eyes focused on her nametag and I read the name. "Hailey", it read.

My eyes grew wide! "What is...?" I croaked in a scratchy voice, not finishing the question as my mind reeled.

"Don't try to speak. I will get you some water. As I said, I have called the doctor. She will be in shortly. She can help. We are so happy you came back to join us," she said with a soft, calm voice and a warm smile. "I just need to check your blood pressure, could you hold out your left arm?"

I tried to push the blanket back, and extend my arm. I was so weak. I noticed that I was not wearing my spacesuit any more. I had on some type of gown.

"Where's my suit?" I asked, my voice cracking and scratching out each word.

"All clothing is either hung up in the closet or folded and put in the dresser drawers," she said, adding, "I imagine if it is a three-piece suit, the admitting nurse hung it in the closet."

"My spacesuit," I said, a little annoyed, my dry throat aching as I tried to speak.

"Your what?" she asked. She handed me a container with a straw.

I took a sip. The cool ice water soothed my parched throat. "My spacesuit. You know, from the *Alpha*? Aren't we on the *Alpha*?"

She looked totally confused but replied in that soft, calm voice that I thought I vaguely recognized from somewhere, "I'm sorry. You have been in a coma for a very long time. I think we'd better wait until the doctor arrives. She will explain everything."

She finished the check, removed the apparatus, and began to walk toward the door.

I grabbed her arm as she started to leave. I asked rather abruptly, "Where is my crew? Connor, Lexie?"

"Who?" she asked, as she gently grabbed my arm with her free hand and gently pulled. I relinquished my grip, and she scurried toward the door, looking a little afraid. She looked back at me with what I interpreted as sadness in her eyes, then she opened the door, and walked out.

I took another sip of water. The haze on my brain began to clear a bit, and now, I was utterly confused. This place did not look like the infirmary on the *Alpha*.

"Where on God's-green-Earth, am I?" my mind whirred as I searched for answers. Then the door swung open again, and in walked Dr. Prevalence Ange. She was wearing a long, white coat like the ones medical doctors usually wear, and she had on some sort of uniform under it that was similar to what Hailey had on when she was in the room.

"Pré!" I shouted, as I practically leaped from the bed. "You're alive!"

"Yes, I believe I am, *mon amie*," she said, very matter-of-factly. *Did I denote a heavy French accent there?*

"But you died! On the planet! I am so happy to see you!" I said trying to restrain myself from grabbing her and kissing her as she walked to the side of my bed. My heart leaped into my throat. It felt like it was about to burst right out of me!

"I assure you, Argentum, that I am very much alive. I am also pleased to see that you are finally awake," she said in that same doctorly voice.

She leaned over the bed, and I was so sure she was about to give me a big hug, tell me everything was alright, and how she had missed me, that I extended my arms and sat up in the bed.

She ignored my out-stretched arms and placed a hand on my forehead. She looked at the monitor, and said, "The fever is gone also."

"Pré, it's me, Asil!" I said, starting to get a little worried and confused again. "We shared our hopes; our dreams; when we were in the alien city! Don't you remember?" Tears began to well in my eyes.

She just looked at me, and the hint of a soft smile crossed her face. It was more of a concerned smile than one of recognition.

"Don't you remember?" I asked. "The *Alpha*? The mission? The stasis tubes? The black-sand beaches? The study? Nothing?"

"The study?" she asked. "You remember the study?"

"Of course, I do," I said, with a glint of hope in my eyes, "I was being tested to see the effects of cold, long-term sleep in preparation for space travel."

"No," she replied, "I think you are confused. You were here to test the effects of the new memory technology known as ALIT. Your body did not respond well. You fell into a coma, and have been unconscious for the last six months."

She continued, "You must be confused. Dr. Eugena Smith is here to do a lecture on the possibility of near-cryogenic stasis being used to travel to a new star they believe they have found near the dog star, Sirius."

"What? No!" I said, now totally confused again. "Where am I?"

"You are at University Hospital. Dr. Smith is doing her lecture just down the hallway in the auditorium. You must have read about that before you went into the coma."

"I wasn't in a study on cold-stasis for long-term space travel? You didn't invent an elixir to make that possible?" I asked incredulously.

"I am working on a possible drug to maybe make that possible," she answered. "How do you know that?"

Just then, the door popped open, and Sal stuck his head in, "Dr. Ange, are we still on for that meeting today?"

"Yes, we are," she replied with a smile. It was that warm smile that she used when she was in the presence of someone she liked.

I couldn't possibly forget that smile!

She turned to me, and said, "Salvatore Martin is working with me on the drug I just mentioned."

"Sal!" I shouted as I ignored her.

"Do I know you?" he asked, as he opened the door and walked

into the room.

"Dr. Sal Martin, you were on *Alpha* with us. You were the agriculture officer. The 'farm'? The planet near Sirius C? The plants we found there?" I asked.

"I am not sure what you are talking about," he said.

"He thinks he was on some spaceship that landed on a planet near the star Sirius. He thinks we were with him," Pré explained. "He has been in a coma here in the hospital for the last six months."

"I see," said Sal, as he gave Pré a knowing glance.

"You died!" I said, looking at Sal.

"Hmm," he replied, "I feel pretty alive at this moment."

"It was real! I was there! And so were you, Pré, and you, Sal! Genie, Dr. Smith, was there too! She was the one in the coma! Lexie Campbell and Connor McElroy were there as well!"

"THE Doctor Campbell and THE Doctor McElroy were there too?" asked Pré with disbelief in her voice.

"Yes! Yes!" I cried, practically in hysterics now. "And James Clearwater was there too! He beat us there! Through the wormhole!" I was now beside myself!

"James Clearwater? The inventor of Clearsteel™?" asked Sal in total disbelief. "He has been working on the space elevator project for the past two years. Right here on Earth. I just read his update on the holo-vision in my room."

"You were there. You were all there," I sobbed. Tears began rolling down my face. I let my body go limp and flop back down on the bed. I put my hands to my face with complete resignation.

Pré reached down and caringly fluffed my pillow. She ran her hand over my head, through my hair, and along my cheek. She said in her most caring voice, "Sure. Sure, we were, Dorothy. Now you get some rest, and Hailey will be in the morning."

She smiled that soft smile of hers, the one that melted my heart. Then she gave me a long wink, turned, and left the room, just behind Sal.

***

The next morning, I awoke to Nurse Hailey's soft voice, "Come on Asil, it is time for a little therapy. We are going to walk you down and get you some breakfast."

I had spent an almost sleepless night restlessly tossing and turning. I had mulled over the events that had unfolded on the previous day, and had resigned myself to the fact that all of this must have occurred in my mind. When I did doze for those few brief moments, I dreamt of aliens and planets, spaceships, and of terrible suns trying to pull them in. I dreamt of squids and other creatures that could think and talk. And I dreamt of Pré.

"We will get you some nice breakfast, after a good, long walk," she said as she helped me out of bed. "The breakfasts here at the university are wonderful."

Pain shot through my extremities as I attempted to stand on wobbly legs. They felt like they hadn't supported any weight for six months.

"I think I will need a wheelchair," I said as I wobbled toward the door, trying to connect steps.

Hailey grabbed me around the waist and braced her hip against me. "No, you are going to walk," she said with a caring, but determined, look on her face.

I took another step and could feel the energy slowly returning to my legs as the blood began to flow again in those parts. I looked down at my feeble legs and noticed they were highly bruised.

"Hmmph! I wonder how that happened?" I thought.

I took another step, and then another. Pretty soon we were out the door, and I was striding down the hallway. At least that's the way I saw myself. I'm sure others who caught sight of me, saw me as a curled-over, beat-up old wreck, slowly shuffling his way down the corridor.

When we got to the cafeteria, Hailey opened the door. There was a partitioning wall that separated the buffet line from the seating area. I stood in line with Hailey as the queue moved along and the trays were loaded with food. I convinced Hailey that I could carry my own tray. When we reached the end, I picked up my tray and turned to head out to the seating area. Just as I was about to turn the corner, a cat ran across my path. It was a big orange Tabby, and it was meowing loudly as it looked up at me.

My eyes grew huge, and I stepped around the corner. There, seated at a large round table, not more than five meters from me, was my entire crew! Pré, Connor, Lexie, Sal, and Genie, they were all here! James Clearwater was sitting at another table in a chair just beside them.

"Gotcha!" They shouted in unison. Their faces broke into huge smiles.

I dropped my tray. Plates smashed into pieces, and food and broken china flew everywhere.

My jaw dropped open. No words came out of my open mouth. Tears began to stream down my cheeks as I stepped toward them. I wept openly. I walked through the food and broken china over to their table. They all rose, smiling. Their eyes were wet with tears as I walked around the table and hugged each one profusely.

"Welcome home, Captain," Connor said as we embraced.

Lexie grabbed my hands, and squeezed, as I grabbed her next and held her tight. "We weren't sure you were going to join us again," she sobbed.

I released her and Sal moved in front of me. He winked, fighting back tears.

"You were gone," I squeaked out as we embraced.

"Gone, not dead," he said, as he relinquished his hold on me.

"You and I have a lot to talk about," Genie smiled as I turned and squeezed her hands.

I almost tripped as I hastily struggled around a chair to get to Pré. She just stood there, shaking. I wasn't sure if she was laughing or crying. I grabbed her and crushed her in a bear hug. I buried my face in her hair. She had her face buried in my shoulder, and I could feel her hot, wet tears on my skin. I raised my mouth to her ear, and I choked out, "You stink."

We held each other tightly in that warm embrace. I ran my fingers through her perfect hair, as I cupped her soft, wet cheeks in my hands. I looked directly into her beautiful, glowing eyes and smiled. She smiled back through her tears and began to utter, "I love..." when a voice broke over the intercom in the cafeteria, interrupting us. It was an extremely familiar voice. As it broke the dissonance of the room, and the moment we held between us, it said, "Welcome to the starship *Omega*, Commander Argentum Silverwood."

The End

EPILOGUE:

"There is someone I would like you to meet," Pré said as we walked back toward the commander's cabin, our cabin.

As we walked down the corridor of the gleaming new ship, I asked, "How did you survive?"

"I am not sure," Pré answered. "The last thing I remember about the shore was you kneeling over me. The next thing I knew, I was sinking through water. I must have been thrown out to sea somehow. As I sank, the air was bubbling out of my suit near my neck. Then, I felt something tug on my suit. I felt something squeeze around my body. I tried to grab at it, but my arms were pinned to my body. When I looked down, my helmet light lit up a huge, dark something that had wrapped completely around my body. I must have fainted after that. When I came to, I was lying on the beach where we had been. Sal was sitting up beside me. He told me something had grabbed him with a huge tentacle when he was on the ridge by the trees. He said it just held him there. He said he tried calling several times into his comm-link for help, but no one ever answered."

"How did you get back to the ship?" I asked.

"That was another crazy story! Connor told me you had ordered the ship to slingshot around the planet to pick up speed. As the ship passed the planet, Hailey picked up my locator beacon on my suit. I know that sounds impossible, but that is what happened. General Clearwater reprogrammed the emergency escape vehicle in the forward hold, flew it back down to the planet and picked us up.

"Of course, I was out for the count by then," I said.

"General Clearwater told us about you, and how he thought

you might be dead. I have never grieved so much in my life. Once back on the *Alpha*, I checked your vital signs and confirmed there was no sign of life. Cause of death? Your implants. We put you in the remaining stasis tube. General Clearwater said they would like to study your body when we returned. They told me about your preparations for the wormhole. Unbelievably, we encountered no problems through the wormhole. After we docked at the ISS, we went to retrieve your body, and transfer Genie to somewhere we could help her. When they thawed you out, we detected a pulse. We rushed you aboard the best, nearest hospital, which happens to be on this new ship. Your vital signs improved each day when I checked on you. I knew you were going to make it, and I thanked the Almighty, the afternoon you awoke. It was Hailey's idea to set up the ruse. She schemed it when she knew you were going to be fine; long before you ever awoke."

The door slid open as we approached our quarters. Pré led me to a smaller room just off the master bedroom. There, lying in a crib, in a fuzzy pink sleeper, was the most beautiful little girl I had ever seen.

Pré looked into the crib and said, "I want you to meet Aurum. She is ours."

"Aurum," I said, "that means 'Glowing Dawn' in Latin. It's the elemental word for gold."

"I know," she said and smiled. "And I also know, that you do not know how you knew that."

"Aurum," I repeated softly to myself, "Aurum Silverwood Ange. Do you think they will call her Asa?"

"Let us let her sleep," she said softly as we turned to leave.

As we closed the door, Pré looked up and said, "Hailey, has she been good?"

Hailey's soft, calm voice came out of the walls, "She never woke once. And anytime you want me to babysit, just ask."

"Hailey," I said in a mostly stern voice, "I've got a bone to pick with you. I know it was your idea to set me up like that."

"Asil, you have misquoted every movie I ever plugged into

your mind. I had to get even with you for all the corny puns and one-liners that you subjected us to during the entire voyage. I meant no harm, and deeply apologize."

"I suppose I could forgive you," I said. "I also want a meeting with the entire new crew set for 08:00. I have something, a gift, I want to share with everyone. Now tell me about this super-ship we are on."

"Mr. Solo, hold the thrusters, and take us out!"

AUTHOR'S NOTE

Every character in this book is fictitious. The world I created for them is based largely on the world we live in at the present. I have taken liberties to foresee the future and draw on the past to build this world. The characters have their feet firmly planted in this future world, but their minds constantly draw on the past. It is not my intention to offend any of the great authors and scriptwriters of whom I may have vaguely borrowed bits of their wisdom. I am hoping this work pays homage to the fact that their wit will forever grace the neural pathways of my memory centers. Their unforgettable words are a large part of my conversational vocabulary. I am truly thankful for the entertainment and pure joy they have provided me. It is with this in mind that I wrote this book.

Made in the USA
Monee, IL
18 June 2023

36127966R00152